Who Are You,
Trudy Herman?

Who Are You, Trudy Herman?

A Novel

~

B. E. BECK

SHE WRITES PRESS

Published 2018
Printed in the United States of America
ISBN: 9781631523779 pbk
ISBN: 978-1-63152-378-6 ebk
Library of Congress Control Number: 2017957934

Book design by Stacey Aaronson

For information, address:
She Writes Press
1563 Solano Ave #546
Berkeley, CA 94707

She Writes Press is a division of SparkPoint Studio, LLC.

For Ron, Stephanie, and Teresa

Chapter One

The bond we feel to those names in our family tree can be powerful—family names and faded photographs, stirring tears and a sense of history, a sense of loss. Yet, if we trace back far enough, aren't we all related—all deserving of equal justice?

*M*ost of my family's history on my mother's side—their pleasures and struggles, their successes and failures—I learned from Granddad Weber. I never questioned how much was true, because he told the stories as truth, isolated from the grief, pain, and misery that can reach deep enough to form layers around our hearts.

In 1909, when Mom was three, a letter arrived from an old friend of Granddad's encouraging him to leave Germany and come to America where jobs were plentiful. After careful consideration, Granddad said, he and Grandma Rose sold their belongings and bought passage on the ship *SS Rhein*, bidding farewell to family and friends. With two young daughters and Grandma Rose's brother, Werner, they sailed to a new home.

After seven days at sea, the ship arrived in New York

waters. The sun, low over the horizon, painted the sky beautiful shades of pink. Catching sight of Lady Liberty for the first time, Granddad and Grandma Rose believed the torch she held high beckoned them to the shores of America like a lighthouse guiding ships safely into its harbor. Relieved the journey was over and they would soon walk the land of their new country, Grandma Rose cuddled my eight-month-old Aunt Hilda to her heart and cried.

From the ships, immigrants were ferried to Ellis Island for medical evaluations. Werner was diagnosed with weak lungs and a hernia and was not permitted to land in New York. At nineteen, he sailed on to South America to join a community in Argentina as many of their German shipmates did. "That just about broke poor Rosie's heart," Granddad said. Still, he and Grandma Rose loved being in America with the hope of employment and a good life.

Those years marched along well until during a cold, harsh winter in Virginia, Grandma Rose and Aunt Hilda died of influenza leaving Granddad with Mom to raise on his own. She was thirteen at the time.

Granddad spoke often of Grandma Rose and Aunt Hilda. For him, they were here only yesterday. He talked to Grandma every day, especially when he didn't know which way to turn. "Your grandma always knew exactly what to do," he said with a look of longing as though the past was moving before his eyes.

Today, we—Angel, the small wooden angel Granddad whittled for me when I was four, and I—sat on Granddad's lap. I'd crawled onto his lap when I was two and Mom, smiling, insisted I had been there ever since. Resting in Granddad's easy chair, we listened to the storm's wind beat against the walls and windows and heavy rain pound the roof of the old farmhouse.

Granddad was quiet. Having no reason to talk, we simply relaxed in silence and listened to the workings of nature. With one arm wrapped around Angel and me, Granddad held his pipe away from my face with the other hand, his long, crooked fingers gripping the stem. White streamers curled upward, leaving a scent of cherry in the room, up and up until the circles of smoke spread out and disappeared.

I leaned my head on Granddad's chest, his worn brown sweater smelling of tobacco and soap, of safety and comfort. When I woke, the smoke, the cherry scent, and the storm's darkness had disappeared.

The sun peeked through the clouds, its yellow face laughing and shining in the windows while it warmed the earth drawing moisture into the air.

"Storm's over. Let's go." Granddad scooted me from his lap to my feet.

We'd started to pick beans earlier, then without warning, dark clouds blew toward us like a flock of black crows soaring across the sky and forced us indoors.

"I still feel like having fresh beans for supper."

Water plowed furrows into the land as it flowed downhill to the creek. We held hands and stepped over the narrow ditches on our way to the vegetable garden at the back of the house. Granddad stopped, pushed his hat back on his head, lifted his face, and squinted at the yellow sun. "I believe the heavens is going to give us another drink tonight, Trudy."

I watched the clouds encircle the sun wishing I could

read the signs like Granddad did. What I saw were white clouds bunched together in clusters like cotton balls, the dark ones all blown away.

"Clouds deliver sustenance and disaster," Granddad explained, his German accent still evident after all his years in America.

He walked slowly and stopped frequently for no reason, his tall body erect, and his face shaded by his hat. He never rushed, but always took time to enjoy the roses bordering the path and comment on the size and color of the blooms. He usually remarked the flowers were not as fragrant since Grandma Rose went to heaven.

Often, Angel and I chased gray squirrels from the garden. We'd run after them until they'd climb up the acorn tree and hide among the branches and leaves.

"Clouds bring storms with wind, rain, sleet, and snow." Granddad tightened his hold on my hand. "Winds either cool us or destroy us, water nourishes the soil or floods our homes, and snow blankets the earth for protection from the cold and provides moisture or buries us." He hesitated and glanced downward. "Are you listening, Trudy?"

Thunder rolled in the distance. I nodded and scooted closer to Granddad's side, clutching Angel tighter.

"Yes, indeed. Storms can shake our very foundation."

"How do you know what they're going to bring?" I asked leaning against his legs.

Granddad's deep-set hazel eyes, the exact color of mine, studied me from beneath his thick gray brows. "It takes a little living first, young lady."

He let go of my hand and placed his on top of my head, a

familiar gesture. His fingers slid down and brushed my hair from my face.

"Remember, clouds are signs of what's to come."

"How much living, Granddad?"

His lean, bent fingers lowered to my shoulder and squeezed gently. "You have foresight, Trudy. Give yourself some time."

☙

I LOVED GRANDDAD Weber and his easygoing ways. He was my favorite person in the whole world. Granddad's thick gray hair, like his eyebrows and long, leathery face, did not change. He rarely smiled, but he was a kind man. A quiet man. He didn't speak unless he had something to say. He once said I rattled on enough for the both of us.

Granddad never spoke to me like some adults speak to children. He never asked about my toys or books. Granddad never asked about school. He calmly related life's lessons.

Granddad said our lives were best remembered through stories and recounted many details of Mom's childhood. Hearing about Mom as a little girl gave me a sense of belonging.

"It would take forever to get through all of them," he said one afternoon.

Sunlight and shadows traveled slowly across the porch. Flies as drowsy as Granddad and me crawled around on the crumbs we'd left on our plates from lunch. Angel and I sat on Granddad's lap in his favorite rocker, the chair Grandma Rose once used, rocking leisurely, setting the pulse for a story.

"Well now," he began.

Angel and I slid back into his left arm, my head against his chest and Angel, in my hand, alongside me. Granddad's right arm, weak from an injury suffered as a young man, lay across his belly.

"When your mom was ten, she snuck off with a friend and went wading in Milton Creek in spite of my warnings. You see, that's a wide, deep stream that runs into the James River and at that time was filled with trash and nails from the construction of those homes up in the highlands. She and Alice, a friend from school, were often gone for hours. They roamed that stream for days always wishing for a canoe they could paddle out into the river. It being a hot day, they decided to cool off."

Granddad batted a fly away from Angel and me with his hand.

"That was about the time your mom was learning to swim." He hesitated as if gathering his thoughts. "And that day, she stepped on a piece of broken glass and hopped home with a smile on her face and blood dripping from her foot."

Angel slipped from my hand. Granddad caught her before she hit the porch—my wooden angel practically disappearing into his right hand. He stood her on his knee, holding her with two fingers.

I could see she was safe, and the musical squeaks from the rocker lulled me further into a sleepy trance.

"What did you learn from your mom's misfortune?"

I yawned, ready for a nap. "She should have worn her shoes."

The rocking stopped, and I felt his body shake with

laughter. "Well, that's one way to think of it, I suppose." He ran his hand lightly over my hair.

I was five when Granddad shared that story. Later, when we'd put on our shoes, he'd chuckled. "You think like your daddy, that's for sure."

⁓

"THE HEAVENS IS glorious," Granddad declared one morning.

I thought it strange he didn't use the word *sky*. It was always "the heavens." And I was awed by his knowledge and foresight. He was the one who sat with Angel and me on an oak stump. He had a story about cutting down the oak, but we sat on the stump together, me half asleep.

"Look there, Trudy." He gestured eastward. "The heavens is awakening."

At night, we sat on the same stump while Granddad pointed out individual stars and constellations.

"Learn to read the stars, Trudy," his voice close to my ear. "They offer us a guide just like they did the Ancient Egyptians. Those Egyptians studied the heavens to predict Nile floods. They called Sirius the Nile Star, and the priests, who attended to the calendar, kept watch for its annual appearance right before dawn on the summer solstice."

Granddad taught me how to locate the North Star, the Big Dipper, and the star cluster that fascinated him most, the Seven Sisters.

I stared hypnotized by sparkling lights.

"Time provides wisdom," he promised. "And it's important

to locate the brightest stars in the heavens and share them with others."

His hand gently squeezed my shoulder.

"Be brave, Trudy. Do what's right—for there's a unique light in each of us."

⸛

GRANDDAD DIED WHEN I was nine and a half. Mom said he died in his easy chair with the newspaper in his hand, but I knew differently. He'd come to tell me he was leaving. That sounds crazy, I know, but it's true. Angel and I were buried deep into the bedding with my eyes closed listening to sleet drum on the window beside my bed when I sensed a movement near me. I opened my eyes and rose up on my elbows.

There he was wearing his hat.

"Granddad," I whispered and wiggled into a sitting position. "You've got your hat on indoors." Granddad's habit was to remove his hat upon entering a building, except for the chicken house. He claimed the chickens, unlike Grandma, didn't care what he wore.

Grandma had insisted he take off his hat inside, because, she'd admitted, she liked to see his thick, wavy hair. After Grandma went to heaven, Granddad felt her watching him and took it off to please her.

He stood there, at the side of my bed, and with his slim, twisted fingers adjusted the hat on his head.

"Well, Trudy, the heavens is calling me." His voice was strong and steady.

I swung my legs over the side of the bed. "No, Granddad!"

I felt his large hand on my head, then he faded, a shadow nudged away by the light.

Granddad was never one to say goodbye. "The heavens is calling me." That was it. By the time I ran to my parents' room to tell them Granddad was gone, he was walking on the clouds.

Chapter 2

(1943)

*W*aiting for spring to arrive, I'd jumped out of bed, pulled back the white ruffled curtains, and rolled up the paper shade covering my bedroom window. At first, frost had been etched on the glass like delicate handmade lace. Later, raindrops collected at the top of the window, forming perfectly round clear pearls, their weight pulling them down the glass, leaving bits of themselves behind until they vanished. Finally, the sun's smile on the glass warmed my hand.

With a sigh, I considered Dad's words.

"Memories are linear, with a beginning and an end," he'd said out of the blue when teaching me linear equations a few months back. Dad always said things like that.

Maggie, my best friend who was almost a whole year older than me, thought it was because Dad taught at the college and teachers there were supposed to repeat smart quotes to confuse others.

But I didn't exactly remember the beginning of the cold, snowy winter when Maggie and I built snowmen until our hands froze, longing to be at the pool in the new swimsuits our mothers had picked up on sale at JC Penney's. Those freezing days had gone on and on.

Today, the sun was playing hide-and-seek behind white fluffy clouds when Maggie, who lived across the street, knocked on the door before I'd had an after-school snack. We grabbed our bikes and rode like the wind to Woodlawn Park to spy on her seventeen-year-old sister Patricia and her red-headed, clown-faced boyfriend Gordon.

We'd caught them kissing last week and hoped to catch them again. We were curious how it was done.

We snuck up behind a large oak beginning to leaf, and hid.

We waited. And waited.

"I wish he'd kiss her," Maggie whispered.

"I bet I'll never get a boyfriend," I complained and sank back against the trunk, the bark rough on my back. Without a big sister to offer me advice, I was sure I'd never even get a date.

"Shh, kissing takes time. He works up to it."

"He's slow."

"He's holding her hand."

We leaned forward straining to overhear their conversation.

Patricia and Gordon sat cross-legged, face to face on the grass, in the position to play patty-cake.

He leaned over and whispered in her ear.

She smiled and stroked his jaw with her fingertips.

I was sure he'd kiss her then, but instead, he covered her hand with his. So far, Patricia and Gordon had held hands and stared into each other's face. I couldn't see the fun in that.

"I'm hungry." I was bored, too.

"Shh."

Being older than me, Maggie seemed more anxious to figure out this kissing stuff. "You're always hungry," she said. "Let's go."

We ran back to where we'd parked our bikes.

Maggie grabbed a Red Delicious apple from the white, round basket covered with fake plastic daisies hooked over the handlebars of her bike.

"We'll share." She bit into the apple. Juice ran down her chin.

We dropped down onto our backs, the earth and grass cool through my sweater. I shivered. The pale sun overhead made me long for the end of the school year. Six more weeks.

"Here," Maggie mumbled, her mouth stuffed and puffy like a small balloon.

I took the half-eaten apple and rotated it with my fingers to find a perfect bite. I heard her chewing next to me. "Do you think being a big sister is hard?" I'd been begging for a sister, and Mom and Dad announced last week we would be getting a new baby.

I dreamed of being a big sister like Patricia. She was nice, the most popular girl in high school, and always had a boyfriend to take her to the latest movies. I felt Maggie's movements next to me.

She bent her legs and checked out her new Keds.

"All you have to do is boss the younger sister around. How hard can that be? Patricia is always ordering me to do things."

Maggie's words were still hard to understand. She chewed louder.

"But you're lucky. You get to try her makeup and lipstick. Mom says I have no business thinking about those things." Mom also says I'm still her baby girl. I didn't want Maggie to know Mom called me her "baby."

"I just can't wait three more years." Maggie snapped off a blade of grass, rolling it between her fingers. "Mom insists I can't look at a boy until I'm fifteen."

I ignored Maggie and watched the leaves sway gently in the spring breeze.

Mentally I counted the days until our first trip to the pool. Maggie and I loved to swim. We spent much of our summers at the pool pretending to be great swimmers like Esther Williams and Gloria Callen. Sometimes on hot days, our mothers took us to the seashore to collect shells and swim in the ocean.

What I really wanted to do this summer was go to Washington, D.C. I'd been begging Dad for a trip to see the White House ever since Mr. Anderson, our teacher last year, showed the class pictures of his trip. He'd insisted everyone should visit our nation's capital to see the people's house where our presidents lived.

"Darrell seemed happy for you today," Maggie mumbled.

I was pulled from my daydreaming. "What?"

"Darrell was friendly to you."

Maggie and I both liked Darrell, a boy in our class. After I'd won the blue ribbon for Best Speller, I had been proud listening to Miss Pruitt's comments about my good study habits. But, I became embarrassed as her voice droned on and on and hunched my shoulders to shorten my five-seven frame. Only Eddie Gutschmidt—bucked-tooth, four-eyed Eddie, the smartest boy in school—was taller than me. Uncomfortable, I'd stared out the window until I noticed Darrell's smile, then I'd blushed. He was the best-looking boy in sixth grade. "He was being nice," I said, hoping to make Maggie feel better.

Maggie rolled onto her side. Her ear disappeared into short, green grass that cradled her cheek. "How did you know all those words?"

Homework was something Maggie hated to do, and she rarely completed assignments. She despised math, said it didn't make sense and copied my answers when we got to school. "Dad and I practiced the list of words Miss Pruitt gave us," I told her. Dad was always willing to help me with homework.

"I'm glad my dad isn't a teacher." Maggie flopped over onto her back for the second time. "How'd you do on the English paper?"

I disliked punctuation. I couldn't understand comma placement. When I did put one in my writing, I was wrong. And semicolons were an unsolved mystery. Why not use a comma instead? I understood math. Numbers were logical. Five was always five. "I got a C plus. You?"

Maggie lifted her shoulders off the grass and glared down at me. "You got a C? What happened?" She fell back.

I shrugged, wanting to change the subject. "Do you think he kissed her today?" I examined the tiny, green leaves overhead. The question of Patricia and Gordon's relationship had made its way around the neighborhood, with no one wanting to be last to hear the latest gossip. "Do you think they'll get married?" Mom said she thought they were too young for marriage. I didn't tell Maggie.

"Daddy told her 'absolutely not.'" Maggie straightened her legs and crossed her ankles. "Daddy said she has to graduate first. And if Gordon goes into the army, he may have to go overseas. Being separated like that is no way to begin a marriage."

"I'm going to be like her someday. I hope I get a sister." I'd overheard Mom tell Dad she would like a boy this time.

I relaxed, letting my eyes roam the sky. Yawning and stretching from a winter's nap, the sun floated over the branches, the light as crisp as the air. Leaves created patterns on our bodies. I lifted an arm, waving it back and forth from light to shadow, checking the blonde hairs on my forearm—were they getting darker? I wanted to be more like Maggie and Patricia with their dark hair and eyes. Instead, I was tall and skinny, with long legs, big feet, blonde hair, freckles, and hazel eyes like Granddad's. At school, some of the boys called me Beanpole. By sixth grade, I'd gotten used to the nickname.

A shadow inched across us. My body stiffened. A band of dark, threatening clouds formed in a corner of the sky. I studied them as they changed shape and galloped toward us. As I watched the sky blacken, I recalled Granddad's words: *Clouds are signs of what's to come.* A shiver ran through me. "Look at those clouds. What do they look like?"

"A stallion?" Maggie guessed.

I hunched my shoulders, letting her know I wasn't sure.

"Your granddad would know, wouldn't he?"

Maggie had gone with me several times to visit Granddad the year before he died. She even spent a night with Granddad and me on one of those special nights Mom allowed me to stay with him. At first, Maggie didn't like him because he was old. But after Granddad saved us from a neighbor's dog that chased us home from the creek and made us hot cocoa with marshmallows, she'd changed her mind.

I continued to study the clouds as they twisted into a giant, four-legged creature, its legs pumping forward, its body laboring. My eyes strained to make out a rider, but I saw none. *What drove the beast forward?* A stream of air swept across my face, but the leaves did not stir. I briefly closed my eyes, making it all disappear.

"I wish I had a horse." Maggie sat upright and crossed her legs like Patricia and Gordon had been sitting earlier. "I rode one last year when I visited my cousin. It was fun."

Maggie wanted a horse and two kids when she was older. She got all dreamy-eyed when she talked about living on a large ranch in Colorado. Most likely she'd change her mind the next time she read a book she liked better than *The Lost Ranch*.

I tried to ignore the clouds and listen to Maggie complain of the unfairness of her cousin, who was three years younger, having a horse. But the park was different now.

The clouds hid the sun, and the air chilled.

I was still hungry and wanted to leave. Dad often teased I had a hollow leg because I was always ready to eat. Plus, I wanted to check my homework before supper. "Let's go."

In the summer, Maggie and I rode our bikes around the neighborhood when we weren't at the pool. Our favorite places to visit were the community park at the end of our street and Dressler's Market down on Twelfth. Dressler's had double-grape Popsicles for a nickel. Sometimes, with only one nickel, we shared. At the park, we lay in the shade and read or imagined our future with boyfriends more like Darrell rather than Gordon, and flipped through pages of glamour magazines Maggie snuck out of Patricia's room. Once, she brought scissors and let me cut her hair. The style didn't look exactly like the girl's in the magazine, but Maggie liked it.

As we rode home past the Perry house, Michael Perry stepped out the door dressed in his army uniform. Michael graduated last year and joined the army straightaway. Patricia had liked him, but he hadn't dated any of the girls at Somerville High School.

To Maggie and me, the war was a world away. It only affected our lives when we heard the long, tiresome conversations between our fathers and their friends in the neighborhood about the war and American politics. They'd talk for hours explaining the decisions they'd make if they were in charge of the country. Dad loved President Roosevelt and agreed with his unpopular decision to ration gasoline.

At school every morning, Miss Pruitt spoke of the war in Europe and the Pacific. She frequently asked about the parents serving in the military and read aloud articles about Germany's march through Europe and the Japanese bombing of Pearl Harbor.

As we reached our street, I pushed my long hair behind my ears with one hand, holding the handlebars to steady the bike with the other. I was disappointed Patricia and Gordon hadn't kissed but had only talked and held hands. Maggie and

I could hardly wait to be teenagers and that was two more years for me. But it felt like forever. Maggie prayed her pimples would disappear, and I prayed I'd grow breasts. I checked often and saw no change. Not even tiny changes, and here Maggie was nearly ready for a bra.

I was taller than Maggie, even though she was older. And with Dad being six-foot-two, I had little doubt that I would add a few more inches to my current height. I hoped Maggie did, too.

"I'll help you be a big sister since I know what they're supposed to do," Maggie said. We waved goodbye and rode into our respective driveways.

I pushed my bike to the garage at the side of the house, rested it against the inside wall of the detached building, and entered the back door. "Mom," I called.

As I came into the room, I saw Mom's last music student of the day standing by the piano, thanking her for his lesson.

Mom had three students each afternoon, and all attended the private school that dismissed earlier than my school. A car honked, and the student left.

Without a comment, Mom hurried across the room to the radio that sat on a table in the corner by the fireplace. There was a time when she tuned the radio to a music station, but today, a man's voice boomed, "War Reports from London."

Blonde strands of hair fell from the twisted braid around Mom's head. Her hazel eyes were much like Granddad's too, and her smooth skin, with a row of freckles marching across her nose, glowed from the warmth of the oven as she checked on dinner.

The aroma of meatloaf filled the room. My stomach rumbled.

Mom grabbed her red apron, shaped like an apple, and tied it over the tiny bump in her stomach and around her waist. "Don't yell when you get home. That's not a way I like my lessons to end." She opened the refrigerator and leaned inside twisting around with a head of lettuce in her hand. "Make sure your homework is finished before supper. And, you could use a little more time at the piano."

My parents were sticklers about homework. I tried to finish my assignments at school, but when I had questions, Dad helped me after supper. And no matter how much I practiced, I could not play the piano as well as most of Mom's students.

I took a tumbler from the cupboard, filled it with water, and drank until the glass was empty.

Mom reached over and pushed hair away from my face. "Stand tall, honey." She smiled and wiped her hands on the apron. "How was your ride to the park?"

"Good, Mom."

After grabbing a piece of raisin bread from the plate on the counter, I went to my room, plopped down at my desk, and opened my notebook. The shiny blue ribbon was there tucked into the side of the frayed, faded-blue fabric notebook I'd gotten last fall.

I pulled out my math homework and checked each calculation making sure the answers were correct and the numbers neat and legible. A raisin dropped on a nine. I quickly picked it up, stuck it in my mouth, and wiped the paper with the edge of my shirt. Miss Pruitt was a believer in neatness, but the small, round smudge wasn't very noticeable. I reviewed my geography assignment, all counties in Virginia labeled neatly in ink on the state map. Done.

⚬⚬

AS WE SAT down to supper, I placed the blue ribbon next to my plate, waiting until we were settled to hold it up for Dad to admire. Mom rarely acknowledged my academic accomplishments. She left that to Dad. Mom said a good education was reward enough.

"Did one of your students award you with a ribbon?" Dad grinned at Mom, purposely ignoring me.

"It's mine, Dad. I won it today in spelling."

"Spelling? Your studying paid off. Congratulations, Trudy. And, I have a surprise for you and your mother." Dad winked and slowly spooned mashed potatoes onto his plate.

Then he reached for the gravy in such a relaxed manner I squirmed in my seat.

He cleared his throat and paused, smiling at my anticipation. "We're visiting the nation's capital this summer." Dad stuffed his mouth with meatloaf and mashed potatoes.

"Washington, D.C.? When, Dad?" Suddenly, I was too excited to eat.

He shifted the food in his mouth and glanced to Mom for approval. "July?"

Mom's jaws tightened and her lips thinned. "Karl, I'm not sure this is the time to be spending that kind of money or even to be going on a trip." She placed her fork on her plate and her hands on her lap.

Dad wiped his mouth with the white napkin. "Veenie, Trudy's been wanting to go for a whole year. And wouldn't you like to get away?"

I stared down at my food and listened. I'd learned as much about my parents from their disagreements as from what they told me about themselves.

"But I'm not sure this summer is a good time. The baby . . ."

"This will be the last trip for the three of us. And we've saved for years for this baby."

I sensed, rather than saw, Dad reach for Mom's hand. "Educators get a discount on hotels. One week?"

I took a bite of meatloaf, but my hunger was gone. The list of sights to see in Washington, D.C. that Mr. Anderson gave us was taped to the side of my bookcase: The White House, the Capitol, the Smithsonian, the Washington Monument, the Lincoln Memorial.

I continued to listen to Mom and Dad's conversation. Last year, I'd overheard Miss Pruitt tell Mr. Anderson that life was about balance. Miss Pruitt didn't believe Mr. Anderson spent enough time on his lessons. After that, I searched for the balance between my parents, remembering how Granddad often said they were well suited.

Before last year, I had simply thought of them as my parents. Though I knew Dad, an established professor, had been raised in a well-to-do family in Freiburg, Germany. He was older than Mom, with an affable outlook on the world, and he believed life was a journey to be enjoyed. Dad's brother, Uncle Kurt, was a renowned scientist, and both parents were educators. Dad left for America because he'd disagreed with the direction of the German government at the time.

In contrast, Mom grew up quickly. She turned thirteen three days after Grandma Rose and Aunt Hilda died. At ten, she had a mother and younger sister, and three years later she and Granddad were alone. She changed from the little girl who snuck out to wade in Milton Creek and dreamed of canoeing downstream to the James River with her best friend, into a premature adult who shared housekeeping responsibilities with her father.

Dad also teased and laughed easily, usually with a twinkle in his blue eyes, and I hoped he'd soon have my kind, caring mother as excited as I was to see Washington, D.C.

I looked from Mom to Dad, trying to read the signs. *Would I get to see the White House?*

"Pete said he would lead the men's Bible study for a couple of Sundays if I couldn't make it." Dad explained, proving he'd given quite a bit of thought to this trip. "And Loretta could cover for you like last time."

Mom played the church organ at Sunday services.

"And your service group can certainly spare you. You always do so much."

My parents were serious when it came to personal responsibility. Last year when I signed Mom's name to a note allowing me to leave school early to join Maggie and Janice at Peggy's house, both Mom and Dad made it clear that I alone was responsible for my actions—not Mr. Anderson for accepting the note and allowing me to leave, nor Peggy's mother for picking us up. And I've received similar talks since.

Once the meal was over, leftovers stored, and the dishes washed, I was left to sweep the kitchen. I swung the broom back and forth across the green linoleum, eager to tell Maggie about our upcoming trip.

I stopped sweeping when I heard a loud knock on the door.

Chapter 3

*T*hree men positioned themselves in the doorway, dark forms blocking the waning sun, each holding a hat, wearing a black suit, a white shirt, and a dark tie. The scowls on their faces caused me to stop sweeping and listen to their conversation. I heard the words *Germany* and *war*.

Did something happen to my grandparents in Germany? Or Uncle Kurt? Dad spoke frequently of his concern for them.

The war was often the topic of conversation in the neighborhood and at church. Pastor Daniels asked everyone to pray for our troops and to pray that evil would be defeated. But I rarely thought about the war unless someone else brought it up. The battles were so far away, I never considered the evil could reach our doorstep.

The aggressive manners and harsh voices of the men warned me something was wrong. The tallest of the three, who wore black-framed glasses, held papers in his right hand and kept glancing down at them as he spoke. When he lowered his head, I saw the last of the day's light, a gray misty glare, sinking behind the clouds. I knew something bad was about to happen, and my hands tightened on the broom handle.

I stepped closer to the doorway. The other two men, younger, shuffled their feet back and forth like bulls ready to charge.

I heard the taller man say something about a search and saw Dad's body slump against the door frame, a look of disbelief on his face.

"What did you say?" Dad glanced over his shoulder. "Edvina, come here!"

The tone of his voice brought Mom rushing from their bedroom with a hairbrush in her hand. "Yes, Karl?"

Dad noticed me standing in the doorway. "Go to your room, Trudy."

I hesitated, not wanting to leave.

"Now!" Dad ordered.

I sat on my bed and wished those men away. I wanted to convince myself they would soon be gone and all would be well, but both my mind and body told me that would not happen. My stomach tossed, and I was filled with fear. Without thinking, I rose, moved to my dresser, picked up Angel, and hugged her to me like I had done when I was five.

The hum of conversation, like a radio broadcast, could be heard, but the voices were muffled. I reached for the door, my hand on the knob, but I was afraid to open it and instead, moved back across the room to my bed. I sat straight, tense, the mahogany headboard that once belonged to Granddad rigid against my back, and listened to the constant murmur.

Storm's coming, Trudy, Granddad whispered in my ear.

I rose and walked to the window where I stood until Mom opened my bedroom door, her eyes and nose red from crying. "What's wrong, Mom?" I ran to her.

Without speaking, she gently took my hand as she'd done when I was a small child and led Angel and me to the living room. We sat on the sofa with Dad while two men searched our home and the tallest man, the one with the black-framed glasses seated across from us, remained in the room. *Was he guarding us in our own home? What was he guarding us from?* I looked first to Mom and then Dad for answers. They had none.

The room, full of tension, became narrower. The air was being sucked out, and the walls were closing in on me. My chest tightened, and I huddled against Dad. Our house felt foreign. A strange place, not the home I once knew. Fear consumed me and my lungs craved air. I took deep breaths.

In front of my eyes, Dad's favorite chair transformed into a chariot pulled by the rider-less cloud creature Maggie and I had seen earlier in the park. The small fire in the fireplace burst into a blaze, flaming higher and higher to destroy what lay in its path, and the radio in the corner shouted strange warnings. I felt the fear and anxiety emanating from my parents.

"What are they looking for?" I whispered, but still, my voice crashed loudly into the room. No one moved, no one answered, or even turned in my direction for several moments.

Dad took my hand. "I'm not sure, Trudy," his voice stiff.

I sat confused as one of the men entered my bedroom.

When I started to stand, Dad's firm grasp held me to the sofa, disbelief flashing across his face. The drawers in my room were opened and slammed shut, one after the other. *Would they take my blue ribbon? The friendship necklace I bought for Maggie's birthday next week? The cat-eye marble I'd found in the creek by Granddad's garden that now lay on the window sill to catch the light?* Again, I made a motion to get up and go to my room, but Dad's grip tightened and kept me in place.

Closets were searched, boxes opened, and baskets rummaged through. I imagined my possessions calling to me, disapproving of the touch of strangers. But I could not go to them; instead, I sat on the sofa between my parents, and wondered why these men invaded our home. *Who are they? What are they looking for?*

The search continued for what seemed like hours as the two men went from room to room. I tightened my hold on Angel, and Dad put an arm around me. The thud of drawers closing and the scraping of closet doors sliding over the rails echoed through the otherwise silent house. Dishes clinked in the kitchen.

I stole a look at Mom, her muscles tensed, her face became rigid.

A pot fell to the kitchen floor. The sound startled me. I straightened.

Mom pushed herself up, paused, and then sank back onto the sofa.

Our guard flashed us a look of regret. Another crash. This time our sentinel muttered something under his breath and leaned forward, his forearms resting on his thighs, eyes down. He shifted his feet as if inspecting the shine on his black shoes.

After the search was completed, the men had found a box of letters, with family photographs, written in German from Uncle Kurt in Freiburg.

Dad had to go with them.

"Where are you going?" I cried and clung to Dad's arm.

The three men remained at the door. Waiting.

"Should I pack a bag?" Dad asked.

Our guard pushed back his glasses. "Not now. Your wife can bring what you need later."

"Where are you going?" I asked again and tightened my grip.

Dad bent down and wrapped his arms around me.

I pressed my nose into his neck and sniffed his after-shave. He smelled like the ocean, cool and fresh.

"I have to go with these men. Mind your studies and help your mother." He leaned back and kissed my forehead. A tear tracked down his cheek.

The cloud creature I spotted earlier at the park now ruled the sky and spewed rain down on us as the three men marched Dad down our walkway to the black car parked at the curb. Mom and I stayed side by side on the porch as Dad slid into the back seat.

Neighbors, too, stood on their porches or peeked from behind shades as the car drove away. No one spoke or waved.

I glanced toward Maggie's house. She, her parents, and Patricia turned and went inside.

"Where did Dad go?"

"We don't know," Mom answered. "We'll have to wait to hear."

The coldness of Mom's voice frightened me even more. At that moment, I suspected we were captives. Of whom or what, I was not sure.

Chapter 4

*P*ursuant to the Alien Enemies Act (presidential proclamation 2526), Dad was interned.

What did internment mean? I was stunned and frightened. I missed my dad.

I hadn't given much thought to my German heritage. I was born in Virginia, just north of Richmond. I knew Dad and Mom were originally from Germany, but they had permission to be here. Besides, that was before I was born. At age eleven, I didn't care about any of that. I simply wanted everything to be the way it was before Dad was taken away. I wanted our lives back.

Our neighbors refused to look our way. If they were in their yards while we were outside, they turned their backs to us and whispered when we got near. Everyone knew a German family who had *not* been detained. What had Karl Herman done? He must be a threat, otherwise the US government would not have come to his house. America was the land of freedom. Innocent people didn't get taken away in our country.

I heard bits of gossip as I passed neighbors.

"Karl Herman?" They questioned. "Who would have

guessed? He seemed like such a good man. A family man with a young daughter. Why, my child was in her class at school last year. She seemed normal. Who knew what her father was hiding, even if he was a teacher at the university? These university people were in all sorts of organizations. And that wife of his, with the unusual name, my cousin's nephew took piano lessons from her in their home. He liked her, enjoyed piano, but that was before. Well, you know. Before . . ."

Most of the German families we knew also stayed away. The fear of association showed on their faces. Many of them sympathized with us and wanted to help, but they said they thought it was best not to appear too close to our family.

Dad's colleagues wanted to write letters of support, but no one had heard of the Alien Enemies Act of 1798, and no one understood exactly what criteria the US government used to intern Germans. We heard the Japanese on the West Coast were interned because Japan had attacked the United States. But why were *some* Germans taken away while others remained free? And what was the Alien Enemies Act? No one had an answer. However, any contact with someone detained could be cause for investigation. Therefore, the colleagues remained silent and quietly distanced themselves from us.

When no music students arrived at our door after the second week, Mom took a job at Lester's Five and Dime on Twelfth. It lasted three weeks.

We heard a neighbor had complained to the manager. "Hiring the wife of a German who was taken away by the government was downright un-American. Haven't you heard all the terrible news about the war? It's awful."

The following week Mom rode the bus to Ashland up by

Milton Center, a neighboring community, where no one knew us. She was hired to work mornings in Peterson's Florist next to the Sears building.

⌒♾⌒

EVERYTHING CHANGED AT school, too. Classmates pretended they didn't see me and whispered when I walked past. A few called my father names. Darrell made ugly gestures at me, and Maggie wouldn't talk to me. She went to school early to avoid going with me. "Why?" I asked her one morning. Maggie and I had walked to school together since the first day of first grade when we'd held hands and cried to be placed in the same classroom.

"I don't know. Daddy told me not to be seen with you," my best friend said.

"But *why?*"

Maggie shrugged and ran away.

I made my way to school alone not understanding how my best friend could have changed.

I was so lonely I cried into my pillow at night. My world had flipped upside down and out of control. I didn't know how to set it right. At times, my mind was numb and even though I completed my assignments, neither my head nor heart went into my work.

Often, I switched off the bedside lamp and sat by the window, Angel on my lap, watching the heavens and wishing I could read the stars as Granddad had. Was our future written there, and I simply could not read it? I searched for guidance among the stars and planets. Finding none, I sought out the brightest stars, but I had no one to share them with. I'd never missed Granddad more.

I was still the best speller in sixth grade. I was still the girl with good study habits. I was still the "beanpole." I was still me. I wanted to yell those assertions to everyone, but I knew my words would fall on deaf ears. No one would hear me. No one would listen.

After a week of rejection, I was relieved when Eddie Gutschmidt came up to me at lunch. Fear marked his features. His buck-toothed smile was gone and his eyes were large behind thick lenses.

"They took my dad away, too," he whispered.

"Why? What did he do?" The questions tumbled out. The same questions others asked Mom and me.

Americans struggled to understand why their government would arrest and detain an innocent person.

"My mom said Dad didn't do anything. It has to be a mistake. She cries a lot now, though." Eddie stepped closer to me.

We both shared a secret. A secret that became important to keep to ourselves. Meeting someone who did not know about our dads' internment was a relief, but we were always careful what we said. That silence also weighed on us.

Eddie and I became friends. Even though we never spoke of how we felt, having him by my side was somehow easier. He and I walked the halls together, and because he was the tallest and smartest kid in school, nobody called us names.

On Saturdays, Mom allowed Eddie and me to ride the bus to Ashland to meet her for a sandwich at lunchtime. She said we could use a break from the whispers and gossip. Pleasant salesclerks at Sears and friendly waitresses at the tiny Vine

Street Café next door served as reminders of what had been lost in Somerville.

One Saturday, Eddie and I saw Maggie as we waited for the bus. When she saw us, she ran away from the bus stop.

Three days later, Mom lost her job.

Mr. Miller, her supervisor, said he was informed he employed a family member of an enemy of America.

Mom tried to explain that Dad was a respected educator and would be coming home soon once the government realized its mistake. After all, Dad's internment had been appealed and once that appeal was processed, Dad would be released.

Mr. Miller said he couldn't take the chance. If customers found out, he'd lose business.

Sick with the bitter truth my best friend must have told on us, I was miserable. Maggie and I had shared many secrets. I knew her father broke her sister's arm. I knew she copied answers on a math test because her father told her he expected her to bring home an *A*. I knew that when her parents fought, she sometimes wet the bed. I'd kept Maggie's secrets, never telling anyone.

By the last two weeks of school, the taunting ceased. I'd become invisible. No one cared about me. My friends and classmates had forgotten I existed. They no longer saw me. Miss Pruitt didn't call on me even with my hand raised. She returned my homework unmarked. *Was I truly disappearing?* I checked the mirrors often and sometimes sat in the sun staring at my shadow.

After hearing two boys blocked my way home from school, knocked the books from my arms, and called me a kraut, Mom would not allow me to walk alone. Each afternoon, she waited for me outside the school.

My dreams used to be simple and pleasant: Maggie and I spending day after hot summer day at the beach hunting for special seashells. Mom and Dad presenting me with a new pink bicycle that I could ride to stores beyond Dressler's Market. I was a big sister, like Patricia, with a boyfriend who didn't have freckles. But those dreams were gone. Dark faceless figures controlled my nights. I woke in tears and wanted to go to Mom's room until I heard her cry out from her own ghosts.

The sun disappeared and a cool gentle rain cleaned the air. I wished it would wash away the hurt and fear. I continued to check the mirror each evening before bed to make sure I was still visible. *What if I disappeared and didn't know?* I asked myself over and over.

⁓

WATER AND WIND raged at me when I left the building. I scanned the street for Mom. She wasn't there. I scooted backward to stand under the eaves, waiting. The school emptied and no one looked my way. Everyone left. I went unnoticed.

Tears streamed down my face. Water dripped from the roof onto my head. Drip, drip, drip. Was I disappearing with each drop like the Wicked Witch? I didn't know what to do. Should I wait as I'd promised or walk home alone? I searched the sidewalks. Nobody. Imaginary shadows and strange sounds surrounded me. I slid down the wall and sat on my heels, my head down and my elbows pressed against my ears. Water dripped from my nose.

"Trudy," a voice said.

I lifted my head.

Eddie stood above me. He pushed back his glasses. "Your mom called mine. Come on." He bent, took my hand, and pulled me to my feet.

Eddie and his mother, Helen, walked me home. Eddie shared his umbrella. No one spoke. I knew I should ask about Mom, but the truth was, I was fighting my own sorrow.

"Get on some dry clothes," Eddie's mom said when we stepped inside.

I glanced around; my stomach tumbled. "Where's Mom?" The question popped out.

Helen was a tiny woman with a face full of freckles, and her light auburn hair was tied back at the nape of her neck. She was slim and willowy in her homemade dress, and I wondered how she could have such a tall son. "Edvina's going to be fine, hon," she said, patting my arm.

"Where is she?" I asked loudly, my body stiff with fear.

Hesitating, she finally said, "Well." Her gaze rested on the picture of Mom, Dad, and me in the wooden frame on the piano before moving toward the darkened fireplace for several seconds. "Your mom is at the hospital. But don't worry, she'll be fine. Matt will bring her home tomorrow. Meanwhile, Eddie and I will stay here with you."

Matt Muller was Helen's younger brother. He and his family lived in Ashland. Why wasn't he taken away by the government, too? After all, he came to this country just eight years ago.

Later, Eddie and I sat at the table with untouched glasses of milk and a plate of banana bread in front of us when the door opened. "Mom." I jumped to my feet.

Matt stepped inside. Hat in hand, he shifted his weight from foot to foot but stayed close to the door. His features were similar to his sister's. He nodded to Helen, then without speaking, he quietly left.

Helen placed her hands on my shoulders and gently guided me to the sofa. "Have a seat, honey."

Eddie moved across the room and sat beside me.

"I'm sorry, Trudy, your mom lost the baby." Helen's words were weak and shaky. "She will be home tomorrow, and she will be fine, just fine," she repeated, uncertainty filling her voice.

The air rushed out of me like a deflating balloon. A sadness took root inside. *Why was life so unfair?* This was not the first baby Mom had lost. She had difficulty carrying a child, a doctor told us a few years back. Tears spilled over onto my cheeks. "I will never be a big sister."

Helen put her arm around me and pulled me to her thin chest. "Now, Trudy, we don't know that for sure."

Her words offered no hope.

I felt Eddie's hand on my forearm.

"You all right, Trudy?" he asked.

I'd asked God to please let Dad come home and to bring me a baby sister. *Had I lost my voice? Was it possible that even God could not hear me?*

Chapter 5

We missed Dad, and by July of '43, Mom was a stranger. She didn't want to leave the house. When we were forced to go to the market, she searched the crowds, afraid we were being watched. Her voice was barely above a whisper, her body shrunken. At home, she spent much of her time in front of the piano filling the house with music that spoke of her battered spirit.

After our bank accounts were frozen, Mom sold her jewelry, including the necklace Dad had given her for her birthday, and the fur coat that once belonged to Grandma Rose to pay the bills and buy food.

One evening I passed her bedroom and saw her sitting at her dresser. I watched as she pulled a brush through her hair, gleaming golden in the artificial light. She stopped mid-stroke and reached for the antique brush that lay front and center on the dresser top. The one she never used. The one that belonged to the set her grandmother had given my Grandma Rose before Grandma left Germany. A silver set, including a comb and hand mirror. On the handle of each piece a vine twisted around and around supporting a rose. A bud decorated the comb and large opened roses were formed on the back of the brush and mirror. At the base of each rose was a small crest. The crest belonged to her family, our family.

As a small child, I'd run my fingers over the cast flowers and make-believe the mirror was magical like the one in the fairytale *Beauty and the Beast*. I wished now the mirror was enchanted and instead of seeing inside the Beast's castle, we could see our future.

Mom held the brush in one hand and with the other reached for the mirror. Admiring them for a moment, she ran her fingers lightly over the small crests, before hugging both to her chest and lowering her head.

"No, Mom." I went to her. "We can't sell those. That's all we have of Grandma."

She lifted her head and blinked several times as a tear dripped down her cheek.

The pain reflecting in her eyes frightened me. A look of raw misery. Unable to handle her sorrow, I left her alone.

From our front window, I watched Maggie, now a year older, pull into her driveway. With one hand she maneuvered her bike while the other hand held a Popsicle. She'd ridden down to Dressler's. Her long, dark hair hung over her shoulders, and in the late afternoon sun, streaks of red flashed on her head. She had been spending time at the pool, a place I was no longer welcome, and the chlorine and sun had lightened her hair. Without once glancing in my direction, she went inside.

Tears burnt my eyes, and something was growing inside me—anger and rage at the unfairness.

Behind me, Mom entered and picked up the phone. Every day she called for information about Dad. I listened to her conversations. Dad was being moved out of state, and she had been trying to find out where.

"That far away?" she said loudly.

She set the receiver firmly into place. A long silence hung between us. Finally, she said, "We are going to Texas to be with your father."

"Is Dad in Texas now?" My chest ached. Texas was a long way from Virginia.

"Not yet. But he will be." She rose and picked up the picture of the three of us from the top of the piano. "At least we will be together. Maybe this terrible war will be over soon."

"Do we have to go? Can't Dad come home?" My stomach cramped, and tears coursed down my face. I wanted our lives back. If we left our home, I was afraid I'd be forgotten by everyone I knew.

Shortly afterward, I found Mom back in her bedroom. "Go get a few things you want to take and bring them here." She placed a dress into the brown suitcase lying open on her bed.

I stood in the center of my room. My life was in this room, and now, everything I knew was being left behind. *How could I choose what to take? What to leave?* I was still standing there holding Angel when Mom came in and gathered clothes from my closet and drawers.

Feeling lost and isolated, I sluggishly followed her back to her room and watched as she carefully folded dresses, sweaters, underwear, and socks, and pressed them into the large suitcase, so full now I didn't think the case would close. For a moment, I imagined she was packing for our trip to Washington, D.C., and tears burned my eyes. *Would I ever get to see the White House?*

She smiled as she asked me to sit on the case so she could get it closed. "Life will be better with your dad," she said.

The afternoon before we left our home, Matt returned. Mom and I helped him load his car with five boxes of our clothes, a box of Dad's books, and a box of what Mom said were important papers. She also removed the portrait of a younger Dad she'd painted that hung above the fireplace, examined his face for several minutes, and then, with tears in her eyes, passed it to Matt without a single word.

He gently took the painting from her hands and carried it to his car. He would store our possessions until we returned.

Mom gave him the key to our house. "Thank you, Matt. You've been a lifesaver."

"If you need me to sell more . . . If you lose the ho . . ."

I heard Matt's voice but marched away. I didn't want to hear the details.

The next morning, Mom said we needed as much cash as she could accumulate and selected several items to sell. Matt came and drove her to a pawnshop to see the owner, Andy Browne. He agreed to purchase whatever Mom brought him.

In a phone conversation, I'd heard Mom tell Dad the rumor was we would lose everything. I realized Mom didn't believe we would ever come back to Somerville. I was sick with fear.

Later, Mom sat at the kitchen table with her head in her hands and three thin stacks of cash in front of her. After a moment, she picked up a needle and thread and sewed one stack into the lining of her jacket. The smooth, blue silk hid its secret. Another stack was rolled, tucked into a pair of socks to be hidden in a shoe in the suitcase, and the last stack was put into a small, black-cloth jewelry bag that she pinned to her bra. Satisfied, she spoke softly, "Trudy, this is a secret. You shouldn't tell anyone."

Another secret. *How could I keep so much inside?*

That night, Angel and I sat by my bedroom window staring at the sky. As my eyes roamed the heavens, I searched for Pleiades, the misty dipper of stars said to be the dancing sisters being chased by the hunter Orion, or by Kiowa legend, bears from the Devil's Tower. The sisters were safe, neither the hunter nor bears would ever catch them. They would continue to dance, night after night.

I wasn't so sure about us.

Chapter 6

*E*arly morning light streaked the sky bringing back fond memories of the finger painting Granddad and I created one summer. "Add light to the world," he'd said, and I'd dipped my fingers into the round, yellow paint can and swiped them across our paper canvas. I wondered what happened to our picture. Had it been discarded?

In the thin daylight, Mom and I waited in the unnerving silence on the crowded platform—the brown suitcase at our feet. Mothers held on to their children, clinging to them, believing this was the one way to keep them safe. The women were dressed in their Sunday best, a stark contrast to the apprehension etched on their faces. No one spoke or moved, but we waited, our movements already confined. I searched the crowd for Eddie and his family.

Suddenly, I heard a piercing whistle and the screech of metal on metal, faint at first and then growing louder and louder as the train pulled into the station, the engine like a puffing dragon, hissing smoke and fire. I leaned closer to Mom. "Where's Eddie?"

"Matt is forever late. He'll get them here, though," Mom said.

I didn't want to go to Texas, and the anxious looks from the people around me said they didn't want to go, either.

A black cloud wheezed from the top of an engine followed by rail cars—a wild, untamed beast that could devour whole villages. Still, no one moved. Before leaving our home, we had become detainees, not allowed to perform the ordinary act of boarding a train without permission.

With clipboards in their hands, two men in black suits and hats, like the men who had searched our home, stepped down from a railcar. Heads together, they spoke in low voices before calling names.

We moved to form a line, the first of many that were in our future, as they guided us toward the four railcars reserved for internees.

Once our names were checked off and we boarded, Mom guided me to a window seat and scooted in next to me. Mothers and older siblings ushered smaller children along the aisle. The clipboard-carrying men strolled behind checking family names. Standing at one end of the railcar, the two men huddled close, as if confirming the list of names on their clipboards. They moved through the aisle a second time, asking names, and counting to see if all family members were present.

I leaned forward and saw that at the rear of the car stood a woman wearing a black hat and black-and-white dress, her face full of panic, and a small girl clinging tightly to her leg.

Somewhere, a child screamed, and the woman spun around as the two men opened the door and left, returning moments later with a crying boy. When he saw his mother, he cried louder and ran to her.

Eddie and his family boarded last.

I was happy to see them.

B . E .   B e c k

〜

FINALLY, THE TRAIN rolled forward and the endless
rhythm of wheels spinning over the tracks became our reality. We shifted our luggage to new positions and settled in
for a long journey. A journey that Eddie and I, guessing the
route, had drawn on a map. For the next three days, we
would travel west through the woods of Virginia, into the
steep hills of West Virginia and Kentucky, and south through
Arkansas, as though we were tourists joyfully traveling across
the country rather than detainees on our way to internment
in Texas.

Exhausted from lack of sleep, I fell under the spell of the
swaying rhythm of the rocking train. When I woke, the
noonday sun was beaming down through the dirty window.
My blouse was fused to damp skin and my hair clung to my
neck. I slid closer to Mom to get out of the hot sun.

"Here." Mom said as she placed a cup of water in my
hand. She opened the cloth bag she'd carried over her shoulder and pulled out a homemade bun stuffed with ham and
cheese. "Let's eat a little now," she said. "Tomorrow, we will
be escorted to the dining car for our meals."

The food stuck in my throat even though I chewed
slowly, the sandwich reminding me of home. A memory of
what I'd left behind. Mom had made ham-and-cheese sandwiches for Maggie and me to take to the pool.

"Feel better?" she asked after I'd taken several bites.

I nodded. I didn't trust myself to tell Mom what was on
my mind. I didn't want to think about home. I dug into my
bag for my book, *On the Banks of Plum Creek*, but didn't feel

like reading. "Can I go see if Eddie wants to play match?" Match was a card game with the goal of having more matching pairs face down than your opponent.

Eddie was seated in the last row at one end of the railcar.

"Sure, honey. Ask Helen if she'd like to come visit me. I think she'd appreciate a quieter seat for a while."

The young child seated across from Helen was screaming.

Eddie and his sisters, Lise and Freda, were squished on one bench. Eddie smiled when he saw me. I turned to Helen. "Mom asked if you'd like to come sit with her for a while."

Helen sat facing her three children, a suitcase beside her. She grinned. "That would be nice. These kids have been bickering all morning." She rose and shook her head, giving her children an unhappy stare.

I took Helen's seat across from Lise.

Eddie hopped over to join me.

Lise was older than Freda by a year, but they were nothing alike. Lise had long blonde hair, blue eyes surrounded by dark lashes, smooth milky skin without a single freckle, and a nice smile. I sighed and wished I looked like her. Freda, on the other hand, had brown eyes and hair, and her face was covered with freckles like her mother's, but she was very smart and always at the top of her classes. I also wished I was like her.

"Hi, Trudy." Lise smiled. "I like your blouse."

Lise was nice, too. This was my favorite blouse with its stylish, oversized white buttons. "Thanks." I blushed.

Freda scooted closer to the window, moving farther from Lise. "Did you and your mom get a row to yourselves?" She flashed an annoyed glance at her sister, and they both glared at Eddie.

"Let's go see if we can find a place to play match," Eddie said as he pulled the cards from his sack and set off toward the other end of the car.

"Bye," I said to Lise and Freda.

"Bye," Lise said.

Freda continued to stare at the landscape speeding by the window, not paying any attention to me.

Eddie and I stopped at the last double-seat at the other end of the railcar next to an old woman who was wearing a red hat and traveling alone—a large, black bag lay on the seat next to her.

"You two looking for a place to rest?" Her English was difficult to understand, but she gave us a kind smile before opening the black bag. "Please, sit with me. Tell me about yourselves." She retrieved a small sack, her wrinkled hands loosening the drawstring and pulling out small pieces of hard peppermint candy.

We each took a piece, stuck the candy into our mouths, and dropped down onto the empty bench across from her.

"Thank you," Eddie said, his cheek rounded with the candy.

I nodded my thanks.

The woman smiled again. "You're not brother and sister, are you? You don't look like you have the same family. Features are too different. But, since you're both together, you must be friends."

Her insight reminded me of Granddad's.

"We went to the same school. I'm going into seventh grade. Eddie is a year ahead of me."

"So, you're Eddie, are you? Well, I'm Ruth Schuler. And what's your name, young lady?"

"Trudy."

"Trudy. Please tell me about yourself."

I don't know if I responded because of Ruth's soft, encouraging voice or because of the comforting motion of the train. Or because I'd had no one to talk to for so long.

As the train flew west across the land, traveling closer and closer to the internment camp, I sorted my memories of the last weeks. Memories that were jumbled like the dots in a picture I'd seen at Maggie's house. One glance and an image appeared, a second look and a different figure leaped out. Reflections flashed from memory to memory until one came clearly into focus—its pain exploding in an outpouring of emotions.

I shifted the hard candy to my jaw and spoke of my life. Of how happy we were with a baby on the way and a trip planned to Washington, D.C. Of Maggie and my plans to spend the summer at the pool learning to swim like the champions, Esther Williams and Gloria Callen, and the secrets we shared. Of our dreams of being like her seventeen-year-old sister, Patricia, who was beautiful and always had a boyfriend to take her to the movies. I spoke of winning the blue ribbon for being the best speller in my class. I took a deep breath, recalling when the war came to our door and described the three men arriving, searching our home, making us feel like captives, and taking Dad away. Everything changed, I said, and explained how our friends and neighbors ignored us, how it seemed I became invisible to Maggie and the other students at school, even to my teacher, and finally, the heartbreaking loss of my baby sister or brother.

Tears rolled down my face. I wiped my forearm across my eyes.

Eddie slid closer.

"I'm sorry, Trudy." Ruth handed me a white handkerchief with a tiny, pink flower embroidered on a corner. "Can you tell me about your parents?"

"Dad came to America when he was twenty-nine, fourteen years ago. He's a professor of mathematics at Richmond University."

Ruth nodded. "And your mother?"

"Mom is a piano teacher." I gestured toward the seat where Mom sat with Helen. For some reason, I thought of the portrait Matt was keeping safe for us. "And, she's a painter."

Next, I told of Granddad and his talk of the heavens. How he taught me to find the Big Dipper, the North Star, and the Seven Sisters. How we watched the sun rise in the east. How I used to make-believe Granddad was a pirate in his sailing ship with the night sky to guide him. I was good at make-believe, I admitted. I still dreamed of Granddad, and missed him, but I didn't speak of his visit to my room the night he left. That night, I kept to myself.

I wiped my nose on Ruth's handkerchief.

Then, with the lull of the railcar's steady rocking and Eddie by my side, my words continued to flow. I spoke of the recesses I'd spent hiding in the girls' restroom crying from the heartache I suffered at the hands of my classmates and teacher.

I described the scornful looks of the two boys who stopped me on the street and called me a kraut, a term I didn't even understand. And my terror from the loathing on their faces as they taunted me.

At last, I explained the resentment I felt that out of millions of German immigrants in America, my dad was designated as an enemy, when I knew he was not.

After that, I was drained and again, wiped my face on the handkerchief.

Eddie touched my arm for support. He had not pushed to play cards.

I gave him a smile.

"You're a strong, brave girl, Trudy. And to see what's happening to you two young people breaks my heart. However, rest assured, this experience will change the young girl and boy who dreamed childhood dreams into adults who demand justice. We might have true Paladins in the making here." Ruth said.

"Paladins?" Eddie asked.

"Don't you know the legend of Paladins?"

Eddie and I shook our heads.

"Here." Ruth gave us another piece of candy.

"Paladins," she began softly.

I scooted forward on the bench, not wanting to miss any of her story.

"The original Paladins were twelve brave knights, also known as twelve peers, who were great warriors of the Emperor Charlemagne. A Paladin used magic gifted to him by the high heavens to uphold the causes of virtue and truth, to help all. Today, a Paladin is an advocate or defender of truth and justice. I believe we still have Paladins in our world, though with what's going on, I wonder where they are."

Ruth's voice was strong, but once the legend was told, she settled back in her seat. Her face sad, her eyes closed. Eddie and I stood to leave.

As we rose, her eyes snapped open. "What do you know about Texas? It's a big state from what I hear."

We settled back in our seats. "Austin is the capital, and it's the largest state of all the forty-eight with lots of cattle and cowboys. It's called the Lone Star state, but I don't know why," Eddie said.

"Texas has lots of ranches, right, Eddie?" I asked.

"I've never been there. I don't know much else about it." Eddie shrugged.

Ruth grinned. "I hear it's pretty hot."

"Why are you going to Texas? Surely you aren't an enemy of America," I blurted.

"I've been visiting my son who's now an American citizen and my little grandson, Harry, in Virginia. And with the war escalating, I was unable to return to Darmstadt. I'm going to Cedar Camp along with everyone else in the railcar. Frederick, my son, is employed by the US government and is working to have me released. He's already appealed my internment. When I'm released, I will stay with him." Ruth sat with her back straight and her chin up.

She was the one person on the train who appeared confident and composed. Uncertainty and doubt were written on the faces of the other adults as clearly as if they'd spoken their worries aloud.

"What do you think the camp will be like?" Eddie asked.

I'd never heard anyone talk about what was ahead. *Were we afraid to know, or even speak about it?*

Ruth's gaze scanned the railcar—the mothers and children. "I think we'll be all right."

The afternoon was gone, light shifted and leaped around

the car when we said goodbye to Ruth and returned to our seats. We liked her, and she invited us to visit again when we felt like a talk or a treat.

꩜

EDDIE'S QUESTION ABOUT the camp cast a gray mood over me. Worried what lay ahead, I slid closer to Mom, and when the train jerked forward increasing its speed, she grabbed my hand. I felt safer.

Mom soon fell asleep, her purse pressed tightly to her side. Not wanting to wake her, I held my body still, my mind frozen. I didn't want to think about what life would be like in Texas or what I was leaving behind.

Shadows crisscrossed the car, and the compartment smelled from the odors of sweat, vomit, and poop. Sounds of tired children crying and bickering filled the hours.

I became hypnotized by the train's silhouette floating across the land as I stared out the window. No clouds were visible. The late afternoon sky was a soft blue. I felt Granddad's presence and relaxed against the seat.

The empty land lay endless for miles, then out of the blue, we were surrounded by trees and the train slowed as we entered a tunnel. The temperature cooled and windows were slid open, allowing fresh air to blow away the horrid smells.

Emerging from the tunnel, I saw a cluster of buildings. After that, building after building came into view along the tracks, and painted names appeared on water towers. These wooden buildings standing in the middle of nowhere looked the same and, after a short time, offered nothing to distract me from the boredom.

Sitting motionless in the rocking car, hour after hour, was wearing. We welcomed each stop, even though we were told we couldn't get off. And no one boarded.

Some time later, we stopped again. The stationary train and the silence of clacking rails made me even more restless, and I fidgeted in my seat, waking Mom. She opened the window next to us. With my knees on the seat, I leaned out the opened window, hoping to see something, anything, that would relieve the monotony of the long hours.

After a brief stop, the train rolled forward. More wooden houses drifted by, most in need of paint, some with porch swings and rockers. Occasionally, a woman was hanging out her wash—everyday living still taking place while I journeyed to an uncertain future.

As the train crossed the plateaus and valleys carrying us farther from our homes, the atmosphere in the railcar changed. The adults became more nervous and the children more restless.

When the sunlight dimmed, Mom stood to stretch. "Are you hungry, honey?" She pulled the bag toward her.

I nodded and accepted the other half of my sandwich. As I took a bite, I saw Lise coming toward us with a handful of cookies. I had moved to the seat across from Mom when she was sleeping, and Lise sat next to me.

"I baked these last Tuesday." Lise gave each of us two flat, star-shaped cinnamon cookies decorated with vanilla icing.

Mom put a cookie to her mouth and paused. "Do you like

to bake?" She bit off a point and her eyes lit up. "These are very good."

Lise smiled at Mom's reaction.

"I want to be a baker. I love baking. It relaxes me." She pushed her hair behind her ears and slid back on the bench. "I would like to own a small bakery someday."

"These are delicious, Lise," Mom assured her and put the last of the cookie in her mouth.

"Mom thinks I inherited Grandma Schultz's talent. She was a baker in Regensburg."

After eating my cookies, while Mom and Lise talked of Lise's future as a baker, I fell asleep, my head against the window. When I woke, Lise was gone. Outside the window, limitless black covered the land and in the vast darkness was a pale light from a crescent moon.

Mom was asleep across from me, her breathing even and comforting. I rested my head back against the window and studied the moon. It reminded me of my pink tooth-fairy pillow, with the tiny pocket for a tooth, that swung from the inside knob of my bedroom door—a baby gift from a woman who worked with Dad at the college and a happy keepsake from my childhood.

☙

OVER THE FOLLOWING hours and days, Eddie and I visited Ruth often. We sat with her, speaking our thoughts and fears freely, and she listened without judgment or condemnation. The time with her consoled us and helped us survive the visible tension and uncertainty that surrounded us.

Sucking on peppermint candy, Eddie told us about his father, Dave, a watchmaker. Dave learned his skills from Eddie's grandfather, who was still living in Germany. Dave and his brother, Ray, came to America together. Dave was hired at Watch Works, his dream job, he'd often said, and Ray became a butcher and moved to Chicago. When Watch Works' owner refused to give Eddie's mother her husband's last paycheck, Ray offered to send Helen a little money, but she declined the gift. Her brother-in-law had a wife and five daughters and didn't have the money to spare. Ray also invited his brother's family to live with them, but with their small house already full, there was no room. Helen had pretended her husband wouldn't be interned long, but with their money gone and no hope for employment, they were forced to join Eddie's dad in Texas.

Eddie's sisters, especially Lise, didn't want to leave Somerville. She was a high school senior and had made plans for graduation. But when she'd learned a boy in Freda's class accused their father of being a German spy, she accepted their mother's decision without further argument.

Eddie was angry at his father for getting the family in this mess, but inside, he said he knew, his father was a watchmaker, not a spy or traitor.

Chapter 7

*W*e stepped off the train in the small Texas town of Traybold, spotting the name painted on a wooden sign nailed to the side of the dilapidated train station. As far as I could see, dry scrubland covered the landscape, not a tree or hill in sight. *This was Texas?* I'm not exactly sure what I expected, in fact, I'd tried not to think about what waited once we left the train. But, when a vision slipped through, I saw cattle roaming large ranches like the one Maggie dreamed of owning in Colorado.

A huge expanse of blue sky overwhelmed me, and the glaring sun forced me to lower my head and raise an arm to shield my eyes. I dashed toward the narrow strip of shade along the edge of the building.

Mom and I were given food and a jug of water and sat on a bench with our luggage at our feet—waiting. Surrounded by the wide blue heavens, I could almost smell Granddad's cherry pipe tobacco. My arm scraped the rough wood of the building and droplets of blood oozed from my broken skin. My eyes filled with tears, and I wished I were five again with my head against Granddad's chest, rocking away the afternoon.

After we'd waited in the heat for more than an hour, which felt like an eternity, the two men from the train called our names, and we lined up and boarded buses to take us the last miles to the internment camp. From the window, I saw Eddie, standing in line with his mother and sisters, searching for me. I waved, and he smiled and waved back. The bus pulled forward. I watched until Eddie became smaller and smaller and disappeared.

We arrived at the camp and passed through a wide gate. I turned in my seat and saw several more buses following us through. My chest tightened, and my mouth felt as dry as cotton.

The compound was surrounded by a barbed-wire fence, guard towers, and searchlights. *This was our new world?* Fear filled my body until I could hardly breathe.

We internees huddled together like cattle in a storm as we stepped off the buses dragging our luggage. Mothers clung tightly to younger children who were tired and crying while the adults surveyed the grounds, wondering where to go.

The camp was a colorless world: brown earth, brown dying grass, and brown buildings. The barbed wire seemed to extend forever. Guards appeared to be watching our every move. A large carved sign read WELCOME, but this enclosure was far from a summer camp we might have chosen to visit. I was so scared I wanted to cry.

"Form lines." A booming voice from a loudspeaker ordered.

I checked the towers searching for the commanding voice and saw two guards staring down at us. *I was an animal inside a zoo.*

"Why, Mom? Why are we here? Did Dad do something wrong?"

"Absolutely not," she answered. "But your dad was still in touch with family in Germany."

I looked around. "Where's Dad?"

"I was told your father would be here very soon."

I stood in line, not knowing what lay ahead. My eyes combed the camp for a spot of green or a sign of hope. I caught sight of a tiny yellow flower along the outside perimeter of the fence and it made me feel as if Granddad had journeyed with us. I reached for Mom's hand.

Inside the barbed wire, unpainted buildings crowded together, row after row along one side of the compound and the other side was lined with tiny cabins. But I was stronger now that I felt Granddad's strength.

We stood, hanging on to each other, not wanting to move out of line. As our names were called, we stepped forward to receive our housing information. A man with a clipboard called it our living assignment. *Living?* Not a sign of life was visible inside the grounds except the weary internees shuffling about, waiting for a place to reside.

We trailed behind a guard as he led us to the front of one of the long wooden buildings. He stopped at the steps, moved aside, and motioned for us to enter.

In front of us, a small boy began crying and hopping around on one foot. Evidently, he'd taken off his shoes and a splinter was stuck in his big toe. His mother pulled him out of the way.

We left the sun outside, but inside, the building was hot and stifling. With no breeze coming through the opened windows, the stagnant air, odors, and heat were worse than on the train. As I moved farther from a window, the odor of disinfecting bleach was thick and heavy.

Several families were assigned to our building and no hope of privacy was evident. Lining both walls were narrow wooden beds covered with thin mattresses and thinner blankets.

Mom and I sat side by side on our beds. Between us was a shelf for our clothes.

Looking uncertain, Mom rubbed her neck and twisted around to face the opened window near us.

Was this to be our home? Two beds and a shelf painted gray like the walls?

For a building filled with people, this one remained quiet. The only sounds I heard were those from the guards outside issuing orders.

When one of the guards stepped inside and called names, families rose and were escorted out.

I fidgeted on my bed. "Where do you think Eddie is?"

Mom leaned back, sticking a pillow under her head. "His family must be in another building. I'm sure we'll see him later. Lie down and try to rest."

～

I WOKE TO the sounds of small children chasing each other inside the building, and Joey, the boy with the splinter, crying as his mother rebandaged his toe. I sat up and rubbed my eyes. I was thirsty.

Ruth stood in the doorway.

"Ruth." I waved to the tiny woman who was shorter than I'd first thought.

She removed her hat. Her short hair was styled neatly around her face, her blue eyes full of spirit.

"Trudy." She waved back and came to join us. She introduced herself to Mom. "I enjoyed visiting with Trudy and her friend on the train. I think we established quite a friendship." She laughed. "I expect to be here for only a short time. My son is a US citizen and has filed an appeal for my release." She repeated what she'd told Eddie and me on the train.

Women nearby stared at this smiling woman and then seemed to relax. Hers was the first laughter we'd heard since the gate closed behind us. After all, how bad could this place be if this woman could remain hopeful?

Ruth's hope slowly spread and filled the building. Once processed, everything would get better, or so everyone believed. The mood changed, and when the husbands and fathers would join us became everyone's main concern.

Ruth, having been processed, claimed the bunk across from ours. She and Mom chatted as Ruth pulled out a skein of blue yarn and a pair of knitting needles.

"Do you sew, too?" Mom asked.

"I do. My husband is a tailor. I do the small work, the work done by hand." Ruth wrapped the yarn around her fingers. The needles clicked in rhythm. "Do you knit, Edvina?"

"Yes. I learned when I was very young. At home, my church group knits mittens and hats for underprivileged children."

"It's a good skill to have. Many young women are abandoning homemade clothes and sweaters for poorly made store-bought ones," Ruth said.

"What are you making?" I asked as the needles darted in and out of the yarn.

Ruth held up the piece. "A blanket for little Harry."

Mom sucked in her breath and pain flickered across her face. "How old is he?"

Ruth laughed, the sound again attracting the attention of the women around us, and shoulders relaxed even more. "He's almost two and a handful, that's for sure," she said.

The needles continued their work.

⚬◦๛◦⚬

A GUARD EVENTUALLY called our names to report to the processing center. As we were directed, we followed the gravel path toward a two-story building, the only such building inside the compound.

Mom stopped just feet from the entrance to focus on the fence and guard tower. Time passed, but she did not move.

"Mom?" I was concerned by the frightened look on her face.

She closed her eyes and lifted her face to the sky, the sun caressing her skin.

I wondered if she was saying a silent prayer.

Then, without a word, she walked up the steps.

Double doors opened into a wide corridor. A man sat behind a desk holding the phone handset. When he saw us, he stood, the black receiver still to his ear. He leaned forward and motioned to an opened door. "Down the hallway, fifth door on the left."

Several doors lined both sides of the long corridor. No picture or sign hung anywhere, but a drinking fountain was mounted midway down on the right. I went over for a drink, and the water, though warm, refreshed my dry mouth.

A man rose from behind a gray metal desk when we stepped into the office. He introduced himself as Paul Ridge. Paul Ridge had brown hair, blue eyes, and a small nose. When he smiled, his front teeth, too big for his small jaw, reminded me of the Big Bad Wolf. He waited behind his desk for Mom and me to be seated, then picked up a pair of wire-framed glasses and placed them on his face—his nose nearly disappearing beneath.

"I'm here to welcome you to Texas." He said.

Then he asked Mom to verify our names, dates of birth, places of birth, religion, address in Somerville, and Dad's occupation.

Once Mom verified the information, he asked, "Do you have any skills we might utilize here, Mrs. Herman?"

"I'm a fairly good cook," Mom answered.

I became restless as he continued to question Mom. Outside the window, the side of another building blocked any view Mr. Ridge might have had, so my attention returned to his office. Against one wall were six, five-drawer metal file cabinets and two more cabinets rested against the adjacent wall. White labels were stuck to the front of each drawer with letters A–C, D–F, and continued throught the alphabet. *Lives on paper and filed in folders.* The cabinets were a dull gray, and to pass the time, I tried to see the difference from cabinet to cabinet— darker, grayer, taller. A dented drawer caught my eye, and I wondered if this cabinet was used more than the others.

My attention turned to a painted landscape hung slightly off-center on the wall behind Mr. Ridge's desk. The brush strokes were visible and uneven. In the picture, a wide river snaked through a canyon below red and brown rocky cliffs. The Grand Canyon. I examined it and thought Mom could have painted a more colorful scene.

Three wooden chairs were placed in a line in front of Mr. Ridge's desk. Two were occupied by Mom and me, and the third chair, where Dad should have been sitting, sat empty. My mood matched the room's gray, and I felt lonely.

On the desk beside a stack of manila folders was a photograph in a metal frame of a woman and two small boys sitting on a park bench. My gaze lifted to Mr. Ridge's face, and I saw he was watching me.

He picked up the framed photograph and held it out to give me a better view. "My wife and sons, Joe and Eddie."

"I have a friend, Eddie."

"Is he in Somerville?" Mr. Ridge asked with a kind smile.

"No, he's here," I answered. "But we did go to the same school there."

Mr. Ridge's smile faded. "Having a friend is good."

"Will we be able to go to school?"

He leaned back. "Yes, the classes should be starting soon. Do you like school"—he scanned the papers inside the open folder in front of him until he found my name—"Trudy?"

I had been reduced to a name inside a folder. "Yes." My voice sounded thin in the large office.

"Good. I'm sure we have some good teachers."

I nodded, thinking of the last weeks of school at home. "Is that the Grand Canyon?" I pointed to the painting. The cliffs reminded me of the picture in my geography textbook last year.

You are nothing more than a name in a folder repeated in my head.

Mr. Ridge scooted back his chair and turned to the painting. "Yes. Isn't it magnificent?" He rose to straighten it, then pointed to the light and dark pigments. "The light tones create a sense of life and movement as though clouds were crossing over the canyon."

I felt Mom straighten next to me. "Why the barbed wire?"

Mr. Ridge's mouth opened and he stared at Mom. "Ma'am?"

"Why the barbed-wire fence? Surely you don't think we'd run away in this desert."

He cleared his throat. "Well, Mrs. Herman, it's for your protection, too. We wouldn't want a child to wander away and get lost. The heat gets mighty intense here, and we're a long way from everything."

"And you need a barbed-wire fence for that?"

Mr. Ridge took his seat and glanced down at his hands folded neatly on top of the desk. "I understand how you feel, Mrs. Herman. Sometimes that fence gets to me, too."

"You can leave whenever you wish."

Startled, I felt frightened. Mom's voice was that of the angry stranger she'd changed into since the night the men searched our home and took Dad away.

I was not used to this mother. The mother I knew spoke softly. But at that moment, only hours inside the barbed wire, I was afraid the loving soul of my mother would not survive our stay. By the time we left this place, when the war was over, I would be leaving with a different parent.

Bands of white wispy clouds gathered closer as we left Mr. Ridge's office, and as hard as I tried, I could not tell if they brought signs of nourishment or disaster. I hoped for Granddad's reassuring strength as we walked back to our barracks.

Chapter 8

*W*e were to stay in the crowded building until Dad joined us, then we would be moved into one of the small cabins set up for families. The buildings, including the cabins, had large black numbers painted on both sides and over the doorways.

That first night, the oppressive heat, sounds of mothers quietening their crying babies, and complaints from small children made sleep impossible. I lay on the bed next to Mom recalling our walk back to the building from Mr. Ridge's office. Mom had left the gravel path to go to the fence.

"I'm afraid this fence will suffocate me." She'd said and wrapped her hand around the wire.

I had seen her tears, and my fear deepened. My world had been ripped away, and now, I was afraid of losing my mother.

I was miserable that first week. The beds were hard, the heat was suffocating, and human stench permeated the stagnant air. Bathrooms were basic, and we had to wait in line for a turn. Everyone whispered instead of using normal voices, and no one smiled.

Except Ruth.

She believed she would soon be released.

The other women kept their heads lowered, not looking at one another. Humiliation was apparent in their posture and walk, but worst of all, resignation reflected in their eyes. We were internees moving from place to place, every action forced.

A blaring siren woke us each morning. I rolled from my bed and straightened my blanket over threadbare sheets, then rushed outside to stand in line for headcount. After the count was taken, I waited in line for the lavatory. Side-by-side showers covered the walls in one room, another room held two rows of sinks, and a third, toilets. Mom and I hastened through our morning routine and hurried back to our building to place our bathroom articles on our shelf.

Minutes later, a bell rang. We walked to the mess hall to join another line. Unpleasant smells drifted from the large kitchen behind the service counter. The rationed portions of powdered eggs and fried potatoes were filling, but bland. Along with our meals, everyone under the age of ten received a cup of milk and, for some reason, so did I. Mom held my cup in her hand, not allowing it to set on the table for fear one of the younger kids would knock it over. She wouldn't pick up her fork to eat until I drank all my milk.

The first full day in the camp, I searched the mess hall for Eddie and his sisters. Once I spotted them, I relaxed. As soon as my plate was empty, I went to their table, leaving Mom and Ruth to finish their meal.

Lise scooted toward her mother, and I slid onto the bench beside her.

"Mom and I are in building six. What building are you in?"

"Four," Eddie said with a shrug. "Did you hear we'll have a school?" He pushed back his glasses. Eddie loved school.

"Yes. Mr. Ridge told us. When do we start?"

Eddie stood. "Let's go find out."

"Will you let my mom know I'm with Eddie?" I asked Helen.

"Tell her yourself, Trudy. I wouldn't want her to worry."

I wondered if the loss of Mom's baby was still fresh in Helen's mind.

Mom seemed hesitant about my leaving the building.

Ruth encouraged her. "Edvina, we should be safe inside this," she waved her hands, "compound. What could happen to them?"

Reluctantly, Mom finally agreed.

But as we got to the door, a guard held up his hand to stop us. "Chow isn't over."

"We want to find out about school," said Eddie.

After considering the women and children still eating, the guard let us pass.

Eddie and I rushed out.

Mr. Ridge was also in charge of camp education, and during our arrival interview, he'd said to come to his office with any questions we might have.

The man in uniform who sat behind a desk inside the entrance to the two-story administrative building asked, "Shouldn't you be at chow?" He stood.

We stepped back, unsure if it was all right to be here.

Eddie pushed back his glasses again. "We want to ask Mr. Ridge about school."

The man checked a clipboard. "He's not here right now. Classes will take place, but no start date has been set. The decision will be made by Friday and posted on the bulletin board outside the cafeteria."

⌒⌒

EVERY MORNING THE weather and the routine were the same. The sun rose early and by mid-morning the heat and dry winds were almost unbearable. Mom and I moved slowly in line until our turn came to use the facilities. Afterward, we sat on our beds, waiting to be called to breakfast. After breakfast, Helen and Eddie joined us in our building. While Helen, Ruth, and Mom knitted or sewed and chatted, waiting for the daily list of workers needed, Eddie and I read the books we'd brought, played cards, and talked about school.

One afternoon Eddie said, "Let's ask Mr. Ridge for an area to play baseball."

We ran across the grounds to his office.

Mr. Ridge wasn't in, but the man at the entrance agreed an area could be found.

Eddie and I went from building to building looking for players. We signed up nine, but then, our mothers decided we should wait until after the weather cooled to play outside.

To fill our days until school started, Eddie and I visited the newly opened camp center and put together puzzles of landscapes, some so worn the pieces were ripped and bent at the corners. We played Match, along with checkers and Chinese checkers. Granddad had told me the history of Chinese checkers after I found Mom's old set in a closet. He said the game was invented in Germany in 1892 and was based on an older American one by the name of Halma.

Helen asked Sergeant Benson, who was in charge of the center, if he might section off an area for a library. He agreed and sent out a call for donated books. I gave two I'd already read, and Eddie, who hated to part with his books, gave one. Sergeant Benson drove into Traybold and returned with a box of books donated by the town's library board. After that, Eddie and I, along with several others, spent much of our time in the reading room furnished with three square tables and metal chairs, or in the activity room. It was too hot to do much else.

Many afternoons, Mom, along with other women, could be found by the barbed-wire fence a short distance from the row of buildings.

They stood motionless, as though trying to keep their world steady, as if a small movement from them would cause the Earth to spin out of control like a globe on a pedestal. Often, I'd find Mom, skin red from the sun and damp curls tight around her neck. Sometimes I'd go to her and wrap my arm around her waist. At first, she seemed not to feel my touch.

Then, she'd gradually lift a hand and place it on my arm.

"Let's go, Mom." I spoke softly.

She'd look up as if marking her place on the blue sky, then we'd walk away. Some afternoons, we did nothing more than stand close and stare at the dirt road beyond the fence, willing Dad to appear.

At night, I lay confused about what was happening, my thoughts playing slowly through my mind like a discordant musical scale performed by one of Mom's students. One note and I thought of Granddad and all I'd lost. I remembered the account of his journey to America. Of the Grandma I'd never met, who was happy to be in this country, and of Mom's younger sister, who never had a chance to grow up. The second note was played and I relived my trips with Maggie

down to Dressler's for Popsicles. I saw my room, my favorite
games and books, my blue ribbon, and the unopened birthday
gift. With a sour third note, I was back listening to the men
in suits search our home and take Dad away. My life was not
making sense. I had been torn away from everything I'd
known and confined in this strange place. I had no idea why.

Two days later, Ruth gave Mom thick, rough paper,
paintbrushes, and jars of paint her son, Frederick, had sent.

I wondered if Ruth had sensed Mom's aimlessness and
drifting.

Eddie and I helped Mom set up her new art supplies, and
she began painting. She created many beautiful scenes. Even
the dark ones, where the land lay beneath thick black clouds,
were gorgeous. But in every picture, the barbed wire stood
visible and threatening.

Chapter 9

*A*s the earth traveled in its orbit, summer passed, days shortened, and temperatures cooled.

In October, following the autumn equinox, after other schools across America had begun, children from the camp filed up creaky steps into a wooden building much like all the others around us and started school. I was assigned to one of four classrooms, Mrs. Bachman's class. Three grades of fourteen students sat in wooden, straight-back chairs around three tables.

Mrs. Bachman was from North Carolina and had come to Texas to be with her husband. She was young and kind and had a bubbly personality. The students loved her right away. She began each day with what she called "the news." It wasn't world, national, or even Texas news unless, of course, she obtained a newspaper from Mr. Ridge. Sometimes, he'd pass on the local newspapers, always three days to a week old.

I listened intently, wondering what was happening outside the camp when Mrs. Bachman read from those newspapers. Otherwise, the news was of camp events, her way of telling us ordinary life was taking place here. Mrs. Strutzman gave birth to her first son, William. Baseball sign-up, practice dates, and times would be posted Monday on the bulletin board. Books had been ordered for the school library, and she'd placed a hold on several for our class. She said she was looking forward to getting her hands on the *Last of the Mohicans* by James Fenimore Cooper and would read it aloud. "A chapter a day," she promised.

My younger classmates lit up, not because of the book itself—it was obviously unknown to them—but in response to Mrs. Bachman's enthusiasm.

The best news of the week was that four students would receive their high-school diplomas at the end of the school term.

I was happy for Lise.

Since the classwork was easy and undemanding, I often found myself daydreaming. The drawing of a large, round pumpkin Mrs. Bachman taped behind her desk reminded me of my last October with Granddad. We had driven several hours north to a roadside stand to buy a quart of maple syrup from a toothless old woman who didn't speak but merely handed us the jar.

"Hello, Mariam," Granddad had said.

The woman had leaned her head to one side to get a better look at Granddad before a wide smile spread across her crinkly face.

Once home, I had waited impatiently at the small wooden table for a plate of thick, fluffy pancakes covered with butter and Mariam's syrup. I loved Granddad's pancakes.

Movement at the chalkboard drew my attention back to the classroom. A shortage of paper and pencils kept classwork to a minimum. However, Mrs. Bachman used the blackboard a great deal. Her handwriting crammed the board when we arrived each morning and was full of numbers or artwork when we left. She spoke with her hands waving about and used the blackboard for lists, diagrams, or to demonstrate how to solve a math problem. Mrs. Bachman was a firm believer in examples and provided an endless stream as she taught math and history.

Three days after school began, I convinced Mom that I was capable of getting myself up and ready for the day. Eddie, Lise, and Freda came to our building and walked with me to class, leaving Mom free to work with Helen and Ruth on the morning shift in the kitchen making the day's supply of bread.

We settled into a routine. When I thought about where we were and how easily we'd accepted the guards running our lives, I was bothered by how swiftly we'd given up our independence.

༄

A MONTH LATER, the long-awaited announcement was posted on the bulletin board—husbands and fathers would be arriving the following week.

On a bright afternoon, we crowded together, anticipating the appearance of loved ones as a faded blue bus maneuvered through the gates into the compound and halted in front of the administration building. Sounds of joy sprang from the group.

As each man disembarked, squinting into the glaring sun searching for family, the families waited with eagerness.

Finally, Dad stepped from the bus. I couldn't believe how much he'd changed over the five months. His hair was grayer, and his clothes hung loosely on his frame. The Dad I'd known looked like a stranger to me. His gaze moved from Mom to me. *Was he seeing the changes in us?* We were brown from the Texas sun, and our clothes were different on us, too; mine were smaller while Mom's were larger. Dad pulled us to him and his arms closed around me, familiar and comforting.

"I missed my girls." He leaned back and kissed my forehead.

After the men arrived, families moved into the tiny two-room cabins of simple wooden construction with no plumbing or cooking facilities. These small houses were furnished with only beds, dressers, and a round mirror. Small square windows had been installed on each side of the rooms for a cross-breeze.

Eddie's family was assigned the cabin next to ours. Single men, or men whose families stayed behind with relatives, were housed in the barracks.

Mom said she was glad to have our own place with some privacy. But I missed Ruth, Little Joey, who was learning to read, and Paula, with two front teeth missing and thick glasses, who sat on my bed looking at pictures in my books.

Mom was more relaxed now that Dad was with us. She borrowed a Sears & Roebuck catalog and placed an order for her own art supplies.

When the box of paints, brushes, and canvases arrived, she smiled as she opened it, one of the few smiles I'd seen. At sunset, she went to the fence and painted.

Dad praised her paintings and encouraged her to continue.

Sometimes, in late evening when the temperature cooled, she and Dad walked around the compound.

I believe during this private time they spoke of their circumstances these past months.

Dad and Dave Gutschmidt were assigned to the construction detail. Wharton, a cattle town to the west, needed rail service and the internees cleared the land for tracks. The work was hard, especially for Dad who'd spent his life in front of a classroom. But as he grew stronger from the physical work, he said he enjoyed working out in the fresh air.

Those who held jobs were paid twelve dollars a month, and my parents kept that money in a pickle jar tucked under their bed, dipping into it to place orders for clothing and shoes for me, personal items, art supplies, and books. Sears & Roebuck and JC Penney's catalogs became popular.

⌒⌒

WITH DAD BESIDE us, our lives took on a normalcy, but that troubled me even more. How could being kept inside a barbed-wire fence like cattle feel normal? I did a lot of reading to escape.

Books from the camp center now filled the shelves of the small school library. Access to the library was available until curfew. Book checkout was on the honor system. A small table by the door held paper and a pencil, and we were asked to write down the book title and our name next to it. Outside the door was a cardboard box for book returns, and each morning a teacher arrived early and shelved the books before classes.

Eddie waited for me after class each day, and we went to the library to either read or work on our research projects. Each student, in fourth grade and above, was assigned a history topic to research.

One afternoon, after we'd completed an assignment and were placing the books we'd used in the return box, I asked Eddie if he knew when we could sign up for baseball practice. I longed to be on a team like Mom had been when she was twelve.

Eddie closed his folder. "Let's go to the office and put our names on the list. Come on," he said, and with long strides headed for the door.

AFTER DUSK, MOM didn't allow me to go anywhere alone because of the many people she did not know, plus the many guards. I wanted a book to read the following morning in class and since I'd rushed to baseball sign-up, I hadn't checked out a new one. I asked Mom to walk with me to the library.

"Come on, Trudy, I'll go with you." Dad laid down the *San Antonio News* he'd found in the mess hall.

I grabbed my green sweater and forced my arms into the sleeves. I'd grown and the sweater no longer buttoned around me, but it was my favorite of the two Mom had brought along.

The flat, open land radiated heat from the sun during the day but lost that heat quickly when the sun sank below the horizon. And tonight, a light desert breeze stirred.

Dad reached for my hand, and it disappeared inside his.

I felt the calluses and roughness of his skin. So unlike the way it used to feel. Still, his touch gave me a sense of well-being as we strolled from the glaring light over the front of our building into the darkness of the grounds.

"I'll say one thing about Texas, Trudy." Dad stopped and lifted his face skyward. "It has gorgeous nights."

The black sky was covered with bright glittering stars. "Like magic." I said and moved closer to Dad.

Granddad would love a night like this.

Dad let go of my hand, placed his on my shoulder, and bent down. "There." He pointed to the sky. "The North Star, Polaris. See?"

A dazzling star stood out among the others. I didn't tell Dad I could find the North Star on my own. Granddad had taught me how when he'd said to share the beauty of the heavens with others.

"This is one of the good things you can remember about this place," Dad said, his voice soft and glum.

Dad's face had grown thin, and sometimes he looked really sad. He lived with the painful knowledge he was the reason we were here—away from our home and friends. We were hidden from society as if we carried a contagious disease and living inside an encampment with good people whose only fault was sharing a common ancestry. I could see the pain in his eyes, so I took his hand again.

He straightened and cleared his throat. "The weather is changing."

In his voice, I heard a hint of foreboding, and a shudder ran through my body.

We continued across the grounds and entered the long building. A guard was behind a desk to the right of the entrance.

"Good evening, Sergeant Peters," Dad greeted him. "Another nice day."

The sergeant looked up from a magazine. "How are you, Mr. Herman?" He glanced at the book in my hand. "You here for another one?" He checked his watch. "It's less than thirty minutes till curfew."

"She can't live without a book." Dad grinned.

I rushed ahead, while Dad remained with Sergeant Peters, down the long corridor then into another building that housed the library, which was connected to the school. At the library's open door was the box for returns. As I walked toward it, I heard a noise. I stopped. The hallway was empty. I stepped forward and heard the noise again. I walked quietly into a darkened alcove once used for storage and peeked around the corner.

Lise stood with her back against the wall.

Her large eyes, full of panic, caused me to move back and hold my breath. Giving a second look, I saw tears streaming down her cheeks and blood forming on her bottom lip. The tears and blood dripped down onto the arm of the man in uniform pressing her against the wall.

Lise's arms were bent at the elbows, her palms flat on the man's chest. Arm muscles strained as she tried to push him away.

The man placed one forearm across her upper chest, holding her in place.

She continued to push, determination on her face.

My eyes followed the movement of the man's other hand.

He leaned, reached lower, and ran the hand up Lise's leg, lifting both her dress and cotton slip.

Her legs were white and thin next to his wide dark trousers.

She brought her legs together, but he pushed her feet apart and placed his inside hers, forcing her stance to widen. A shoe slipped from her foot as he lifted her off the floor.

"Stop!" Her voice quivered.

One of his hands continued up her thigh and then, in one quick motion, he leaned back and twisted her around, her cheek touching the dingy wall, her fingers clawing, searching for something to grip, to hold onto. She opened her mouth, and he clamped a hairy hand over it while the other hand struggled with her clothing. The hand moved quickly over her, pulling at the dress.

"Dad!" I yelled. The sound was only a whimper. My heart hammered in my chest. I tried to run, but my legs were frozen. Tears blurred my vision. I wiped my eyes and willed myself to move. The book slipped from my hand and fell to the floor with a loud thud.

The man's head whipped around and his dark eyes focused on me.

His eyes brimmed with hate, unlike anything I'd seen before, and his face was a mask of disgust and contempt.

"Damn, stupid krauts," he muttered. Without another word, he stomped over, grabbed my book from the floor, tossed it into the book box, and stormed down the hallway toward the back exit.

Lise slid down the wall to the floor, her shoulders shaking. She covered her face with her hands and sobbed.

His footsteps faded.

Moving to Lise, I squatted in front of her, put her foot back into her shoe, and then dropped down beside her. I didn't know what to do. Ruth was wrong. A Paladin I wasn't. I wasn't able to help. I placed my hand on her arm. "Are you all right?" A silly question but I could think of none other.

She lifted the hem of her dress, dried her face, and then pressed her head back to the wall and closed her eyes. Her pretty face was a blotchy red, her lips swollen. A single drop of blood fell from her bottom lip and ran down her chin. "Trudy, you can't tell anyone what you saw."

I felt a hard squeeze on my hand.

"Promise?"

"Why not! What he did was wrong. Why not tell Captain Nelson? He said to let him know if we had trouble with anyone."

She wiped her nose on the back of her hand. "Nobody would believe us."

Her voice was low and harsh, her face flooded with emotion.

I wondered if hate was growing inside her, too.

"You heard what he called us. I'm sure others feel that way."

I whispered my agreement. *No one would believe us.* We were German-American detainees. I now understood why Mom and Dad were changing. I also suspected not one of us would leave here without scars.

Lise braced her hand against the wall to get up. Her wet hand slipped. She lowered her head. "It's almost curfew," she mumbled. A moment later she tried again, tears streaming down her face dripping onto her dress.

I took her hand and helped her to her feet.

"You promised," she said, her voice nothing but a whisper, and limped away.

I waited until I heard the back door close behind her, then took a deep breath and headed back to Dad.

When I got to the main entrance, Dad and Sergeant Peters stood by the door talking about Milwaukee, Sergeant Peters's hometown.

"You have a good night, Sergeant," Dad said when I reached them.

"Couldn't find another book?" Sergeant Peters asked.

I shrugged.

"She can take a while to make up her mind," Dad said as we turned to leave.

We went out into the darkness. I was trembling.

Dad reached for me. "Your hand's cold. Are you all right?" He stopped to gaze at the stars.

I refused to look up. The sky had lost its beauty, and I certainly couldn't find directions in the stars. Granddad had been wrong. I would never learn to read the heavens. I thought about telling Dad what I'd seen, but I'd promised not to, and besides, he could do nothing. *Who would believe us?* While my mind relived the details of Lise's struggle, my body felt exhausted.

Later, lying on my bed with Angel next to me, what happened to Lise lingered in my thoughts. I'd collected another secret, Lise's secret, to squeeze inside the box hidden in a corner of my mind.

I felt different. The child in me was gone. I'd been in the presence of evil. More of the ugliness of the war had made its way inside the camp—slithered in without me knowing.

When I was in first grade, my teacher spoke of America being a "melting pot." I'd conjured up the image of people blending inside a large black cauldron. *Were we put into the melting pot?*

Dark shadows filled my night, taking me back into that hallway. The scene repeating over and over—the terror on Lise's face, the blood on her lip. The eyes filled with hate. The muttered accusation. I fought the terrible visions, hurled them from me wanting to forget, to deny what I'd seen. But they returned again and again not ending with the morning light.

Chapter 10

Parents, teachers, and ministers shape our world, guiding us through childhood as we form our attitudes and beliefs. But there are times when circumstances, unforeseen events, and the unpredictable intervene, and we change.

*L*ise changed.

She did not show up to breakfast the next morning, and Freda said she was having her monthly and stayed in bed with cramps.

Later, when I saw Lise at school, she was different. Instead of the shiny curls floating on her shoulders, her hair was braided and twisted around her head, her beautiful, bronzed skin was now pale, and her shoulders drooped. She kept her eyes lowered and didn't look my way.

Images of what happened to her plagued me with guilt and shame. I could not get the terror in her eyes out of my head. I could not concentrate on anything else. When Mrs. Bachman asked me the date of the American Revolution, I could not even answer this simple question even though I had studied the assignment the night before.

After school, on our way to the library, Eddie noticed my behavior and pulled me aside. The sun shining through the window crowned his head exposing streaks of auburn in his hair. His keen gaze roamed my face. *Could he read my thoughts?*

"What's wrong?" he demanded.

I knew he would not let the question go unanswered. "I'm worried about Mom," I lied, hoping he'd believe me.

He gave me a compassionate, lopsided grin. "She'll be fine now that your dad's here. What are you reading?" He rushed ahead, then called back. "I'll grab a book for you. What do you want?"

"I've been waiting for *The Secret Garden*," I answered.

⤳❦⤳

DURING THE REST of the afternoon, I held the open book in my hands without seeing the words. *Could I do anything to help Lise? I'd promised to say nothing. Should I keep that promise, or should I tell someone?*

When we got back to the cabin, Mom wasn't there. She usually rested in the afternoons. Not wanting to be alone, I dropped my books on my bed and called to Eddie as he left. "Let's go see if Mom's with Ruth."

We rushed up the steps of Building Six to find Mom, Helen, and Ruth huddled together awkwardly on Ruth's bed. Opened on the older woman's lap, with two knobby fingers clinging onto the top corners, was a typewritten letter. From the tense atmosphere and low voices, we realized Ruth had received bad news.

Mom pulled us aside. "Ruth's hometown was bombed, her husband killed, and her home destroyed. She has nothing in Darmstadt to go back to. Her son has been unable to get her released or obtain permission for her to stay in this country. Helen and I have been sitting with her since morning. You two stay with her so we can make arrangements for someone to cover our shift in the kitchen tomorrow. We don't want to leave her alone."

Ruth rested on her bed, her face pale, hands trembling, and her eyes clouded with grief. Eddie and I sat on the floor next to her.

Eddie read from his favorite book that he carried with him, *The Call of the Wild*. His voice was slow and steady.

I found myself under his spell, and the calm look on Ruth's face told me she was comforted by Eddie's voice, as well. Everyone in the building knew of the tragedy and, out of respect for Ruth, spoke softly and quieted their children, allowing Eddie's words to fill the space.

For the next several weeks, Ruth continued to join Mom and Helen in the kitchen in those early mornings, but each afternoon she waited for Eddie and me. We took turns reading aloud. Often, Little Joey, sucking his thumb, waddled over, and crouched down next to Eddie.

At first, Paula simply stood watching.

I smiled and waved for her to join us one afternoon.

She hesitated, then quietly came over, squatting down beside me and resting her small hand on my leg.

An ache distracted me from the reading. *Is this what a little sister would do?* Moments passed before I again became aware of Eddie speaking.

LATER THAT WEEK, a difficult decision was forced upon us. Letters of repatriation arrived. Repatriation was a wartime exchange program between Germany and the United States. It provided for US citizens held in Germany to be released in exchange for individuals of German nationality. Some of the internees included in the agreement were children and spouses who were either US born or naturalized citizens.

At first, no one was interested in going to Germany. They'd come to America for a better life for themselves and their families. They had jobs, homes, churches, and communities they hoped to return to. Or at least, they wished to be free to start over in this country.

For weeks, repatriation was discussed. No one signed up. I heard Dad speaking with Mr. Ridge about it. Part of what made the decision so difficult was not knowing what was actually happening in Germany.

Then, Alex Schultz, a man in Dad's crew, died when an artery in his leg was severed with a saw. Mr. Schultz was well liked, and his death generated a strained mood throughout the camp. What would become of his family? Accepting repatriation may be the way to go, some argued. "As soon as the war ends, we can reapply to return to America," they rationalized. "Many of our sons and daughters are US citizens. We'll surely be allowed to return."

Dave wanted to apply for the repatriation program, but Helen didn't. She spoke of her fear of living in a country at war where bombing was an everyday occurrence and citizens were displaced from their homes, living on what little food they could get. "And the death toll must be climbing," she said. "No one knows what waits for them there." With tears in her eyes, she often stood by the barbed-wire fence as if she was searching for answers.

A few families chose repatriation and left on a train heading east, to then travel by ship to Germany, but we did not know these families well. As winter arrived, Dad and Dave spoke often of the possibility of leaving.

Two weeks before Christmas, my world collapsed. I heard a noise from my room and went outside to find Eddie seated on the ground at the back of the cabin, his knees up, his arms wrapped around them, and his head down resting on his arms. The cold wind rippled his hair. His shoulders shook.

I hesitated, almost afraid to go to him. "Eddie, I've been looking for you. Are you all right?"

Without lifting his head and in a soft voice, he said, "I'll go inside and get the book. It's time to see Ruth."

We went around to the front of his cabin. Obviously, something was wrong. I waited for him to tell me, but he said nothing.

We walked in continued silence to Ruth's building and took our usual positions, me on the floor next to Eddie, Paula beside me, and Joey facing us.

Eddie's voice was harsh and held a trace of defiance as he began to read.

What was wrong?

Hearing his anger, Ruth turned her head to the side and stared down at him. Her brow wrinkled.

Eddie continued to read.

On the way back to our cabins, I couldn't take his mood any longer. "What's wrong?" I asked.

"Dad wants to accept repatriation," he said, his voice full of sadness and fear.

"Why?" A sharp pain stabbed my chest.

"He thinks we could be held here for a long time." Eddie stepped closer and lowered his voice. "We don't know how long we'll be kept in this place, being told what to do, when to do it. This is no way to live. We can't even listen to the radio. We don't have any idea what's going on in the war. Dad said he can't live like this any longer."

"But Eddie." I grabbed his arm. "We're Americans. You were born in Somerville like me. Why would you want to go to Germany? You don't even speak German."

He stopped, his shoulders slumped. "I don't want to go. I don't want to leave. I want to go home to my room and my basketball and comic books. I want to go back to our school. I want things the way they were." He paused then added, "I want to play basketball with my team."

"Your mother doesn't want to go, does she?"

"No. But Dad hates it here. Last night he and Mom got into a fight. He became so angry he shoved her. I was afraid he'd hurt her." Tears filled his eyes. "Dad gets so mad he scares me." Eddie lowered his head and the tears rolled down his face. His glasses slid down his nose. He took them off and wiped his eyes with the back of his hand. "I did nothing to help. I stood there. I thought I was so brave, yet I did nothing."

Pain and sorrow filled my heart. I took his hand. "Your dad scares you? He's always so nice."

"Dad's angry at being here. I've never seen him like this before." Eddie wiped his eyes again. "I feel so helpless. And useless." He gave me a shrug. "Ruth was wrong. I will never be a Paladin. I didn't even stand up for my mom."

I was stunned by Eddie's self-evaluation. Everyone was

changing, reacting to our imprisonment in a different way. Eddie had changed, and I knew one day he would be a Paladin. "You will be." I wanted him to know I believed in him.

That evening, I sat on our cabin steps and gazed at the stars, wondering how much Eddie would change. Wondering how much I would change. What would we be like when we left here? I waited, hoping for a sign from Granddad.

⤮

TWO EVENINGS LATER, I lay on my bed reading and listening to Mom and Dad argue.

"Maybe we should go to Germany until the war is over, then reapply for entry into the US. With Trudy being born here, I'm bound to get re-entry," Dad said. "And especially since you're a citizen."

"What if something happens to you, Karl? Trudy doesn't speak German. I barely speak it. The country is at war. What if we can't stay together? What if you're forced to join the German army? What if you can't come back?" Mom was adamant we would not leave America.

"Edvina, when the war is over, we'll all come back." Dad's voice was loud and angry. "You and Trudy are citizens, so of course we'll be allowed to return."

"And you think the US government will care that Trudy and I are citizens?"

There was a loud thud.

"Look where we are. Look where Trudy is. What makes you think that will change with the end of the war? Germany won't be any better."

Mom's bitter words filled me with fear.

She blew her nose and cleared her throat. "Germany is a dangerous place to be now. Once the ship lands in Wilhelmshaven, the pamphlet said we'd have to make our way to your family home in Freiburg."

I heard her footsteps as she moved to the door.

"The families who chose to repatriate have not been heard from. What do you think became of them?" Seconds passed without a sound. Then the door slammed. The cabin grew silent.

I looked out my window. Mom stood by the fence. The sky gray with clouds.

Was Mom able to read the heavens, to know what the clouds were bringing? They delivered either sustenance or disaster, Granddad had said. I wondered what was in store for us.

A few days after Mom and Dad's argument, Dad announced Dave Gutschmidt and his family were going to Germany. "He signed the papers allowing him and his family to leave the camp next week to be transported to the East Coast for sailing."

"But why? His children are US citizens. The Germans will treat them like traitors," Mom's voice trembled.

Eddie was leaving? I was losing my best friend. My one friend in the camp. I didn't want to believe it. I cried tears that once started would not stop until I was exhausted. I fell asleep.

A gust of wind shook the cabin and woke me. I rose up on my elbows as a streak of light beamed through a window. I felt Granddad's hand on my head. He was with me.

ON THE FOLLOWING Thursday morning, Mom, Dad, and I waited in the administrative building for Eddie and his family to arrive. I paced the hallway, walking back and forth to the door. A bus was waiting to begin what would be a long journey for the Gutschmidts and eight other families who'd chosen to leave.

"Here they come." Dad took my hand and put an arm around Mom.

No one appeared happy to be leaving, not even Dave. Helen and her daughters' eyes were red and swollen, and Eddie looked tired, his eyes dull and shadowy. I wondered if he'd been awake all night.

As she hugged me, Lise kissed my cheek. "Thank you," she whispered.

I flashed back to that horrible night—the night she had been assaulted.

Eddie and I stood close. "Here." He gave me the book he'd carried from Somerville, bought with money he'd earned shoveling snow for neighbors last winter.

"This is your favorite book," I said, surprised he would part with it.

"I want you to have it." His crooked smile returned for a second.

I held the book tightly as if hanging on to our friendship.

Eddie was gone, and I hadn't given him anything. I didn't want to leave America, but at that moment, I envied him. He would be free.

My heart ached. I stared down at the book in my hand

and ran my fingers across Buck, brave and bold, on the cover. *The Call of the Wild* by Jack London. Inside was Eddie's name in large, slanted block letters. I would recognize his letters anywhere. Eddie was left-handed and his letters always leaned. I hugged the book to my chest. The same aloneness I'd felt months ago in Somerville returned.

Chapter 11

The day after Eddie left, the weather changed. We woke to a pounding rain beating on the tin roof and water gushing down the drainpipes to wash away the soil near the buildings. Within an hour, deep furrows were carved into the open ground. The running water made walking difficult as we treaded carefully on our way to the mess hall. The sun was gone. And so was the one friend that had made my life inside the camp bearable.

The nights grew colder, and we were given extra blankets in anticipation of a coming storm. Mothers spoke anxiously about the winter ahead and hunted for catalogs to order coats, gloves, and hot-water bottles to warm the beds of the younger children. Mom placed orders for Ruth and me.

With Eddie gone, my mood matched the weather.

Mom and Dad didn't talk much to me, or each other, except to argue about going to Germany. Whether to accept repatriation was a constant source of friction between them.

Dad remained convinced that we should take the government's offer to send us to his homeland. "But maybe Trudy can stay in America with Tom Sutton at Richmond University. He's a good friend."

"A good friend? Where is your friend now?" Mom asked flinging her sweater onto the bed. "And I will *not* take Trudy to a country where she would be hated."

"Hated!" Dad snapped. "Do you think she is loved here? She's German, Edvina, for God's sake."

Mom lifted her head high, and her face hardened. "Trudy is an American citizen. She was born here, and she will grow up here. If you want to return, then you do so alone."

With Mom's firm stance against leaving, Dad stopped arguing and became despondent—his walk became slower and his smiled faded. The twinkle that had always been there, the spark that was my father, was gone.

The names of families who boarded the train for the East Coast were listed by the date they departed and posted on the bulletin board by the mess hall. Accepting repatriation was the one way to escape the camp, the feeling of indefinite confinement, and the looks of scorn from some of the guards. Looks that amplified our own feelings of shame even though we were guilty of nothing.

⁓⊙∽

"*GUTEN MORGEN, JUNGE ein* (*good morning young one*). Did you come to visit?" was Ruth's greeting along with her smile when I walked into Building Six. I continued to read aloud to her and spent most of each weekend in her building.

Her vision was going, she said, and she rarely worked on the blanket she was knitting for her grandson. Still, she was one of the few people who ever smiled or laughed.

Sometimes I read, and sometimes she told stories about

her life, or recalled one of her favorite folktales her mother had read to her. Except for her son, most of her family was still in Germany, and she worried constantly about them. She spoke of her daughter, her two brothers, Max and Johann, and the town of Welzheim where she'd grown up. She hoped to visit Welzheim, "*nu rein weiteres mal* (*just one more time*)," but feared it too would be destroyed and she'd never see it again.

I continued to spend my days in school or with Ruth and avoided our cabin because of the tension between Mom and Dad.

Ruth spoke more about the Paladins, the twelve brave knights, and how their heroic deeds spawned legends that grew throughout history. "Such people are gifted with wisdom and awareness of right and wrong," she said. "Those who stand for good. They are the guardians and protectors of the powerless who cannot defend themselves."

I didn't believe I was one of them. I had failed Lise and now, I could not chase away my own nightmares. "Eddie will make a good Paladin," I said with a sigh. I missed him.

Breaking my promise to Lise to keep silent, I told Ruth what I'd seen. I'd hoped telling her about that horrible night would relieve some of my guilt. I realized it was the un-Paladin thing to do, but the lid on my box of secrets would no longer stay closed.

With compassion and love in her eyes, she spoke softly. "Such a horrible secret for one so young." She placed her lean hand on my arm. "I understand why Lise stayed silent, and you told no one. Such things are hard to expose. But I believe Captain Nelson would have understood. He understands the humanity needed to guard vulnerable men, women, and children and is aware that monsters exist." She gave me a sympathetic smile and gently squeezed my arm. "You are a Paladin, Trudy. In spite of how you see yourself, you have been given a gift."

I was still doubtful. Perhaps Ruth had read one too many fairytales. In no way could I become a champion fighting for righteousness. She was confusing fairytales with real life.

⌒∽

IN THE DAYS that followed, Ruth took much joy in sharing fables she'd learned as a child. I believed by recalling them, she was transported back to her parents' house and her child-hood, an escape from her current circumstances.

She told the German folktale of Morbach, the monster, a man who had murdered a farmer for his food. Upon seeing this, the farmer's wife put a curse on the man. He turned into a werewolf who was kept from the small village for centuries by the light of a single candle. And even to this day, many houses kept a single candle burning throughout the night.

She told of a beautiful young woman, Lorelei, who, be-cause of a broken heart, threw herself into the Rhine and drowned. Her broken heart survived, continuing to beat in the cold, dark waters, and with its steady enticing rhythm, lured sailors onto rocks in the treacherous waters of Sankt Goarshausen.

My favorite story was of King Barbarossa, who slum-bered on a marble throne, his long red beard flowing like a stream from some hidden source, in a castle deep inside the

Kyffhauser Mountain. The legend promised when the king woke, the world would be free of evil. According to Ruth, even today, many young children spend happy hours in play searching for the magical cave along the base of the mountain.

⁓

IN JANUARY, MR. Ridge surprised everyone and added a German language class to the school curriculum.

After the reports we'd heard of the horrific things perpetrated by the Nazis, I didn't want to learn German, but Dad insisted I should learn the language of my ancestors.

"Why, Dad? I will never speak German!" I shouted. "I hate Germany!"

Dad crossed his arms over his chest. "You won't always be in this camp, Trudy. Years from now, you may want to go for a visit. Get to know your cousins."

This time, Mom agreed with Dad, and this agreement seemed to bring them closer.

I enrolled in the German class. But, without Eddie, I felt detached and uninspired.

As winter settled in, there were more storms. At times, thunder boomed and lightning streaked across the sky. When a storm hit, we stayed indoors as much as possible as rain pelted the hard ground and danced across the camp, digging deep gullies, and making walking without getting our feet wet impossible.

I enjoyed Ruth's fables during those bleak days, but the nights provided me no rest. I dreamed of Lise and the hands that held her captive. In my nightmares, a wall appeared, trapping me, and I became the one whose fingers clawed the darkened barrier. Sometimes, I felt I was drowning in a deep well, frantically fighting to make my way to the surface, but the hand would pull me down into the cold murky water. Shivering, I'd wake.

Hearing my cries, Mom was there to comfort me.

Chapter 12

*T*he winter rains gave way to a spring filled with color. The desert bloomed with bluebonnet, purplish prickly pear, Indian paintbrush, pink fairy-dusters, and rocky daisies whose white rays surrounded a tiny yellow center.

Inspired, Mom retrieved her newly ordered watercolors, creating beautiful works of art, scene after scene. Again, the ever-present barbed-wire fence stood in contrast to the beauty.

The summer of 1944, the beginning of our second year in the camp, brought weeks of suffering. Hot, dry winds from the west whipped clouds of sandy soil into dust devils racing across the prairie into the camp and depositing it at our doorsteps. Layers of dirt pelted our skin and embedded into cracks in the doorways and around the windows.

The smaller children who experienced sunburns, heat rashes, and dry, scratchy throats, and the older adults whose hands cracked and bled seemed to suffer the most. My eyes became red and irritated. Mom flushed them with drops she picked up from the clinic to wash out tiny grains of sand. Scorpions, cockroaches, ants, and grasshoppers invaded our homes, and insects bit our arms and legs, causing us to scratch in search of relief.

Dr. Koch could not keep up with the line of patients waiting each morning, so another section was added to the medical clinic, and more staff was brought in to help.

Mom continued to work in the kitchen, and Dad left the compound each evening to work in the vegetable garden. The camp director had authorized fresh food to supplement what was provided by the government and planting a garden seemed the solution. Dad liked the extra hours outside the barbed wire and brought back wildflower bouquets for Mom.

I spent time with Ruth and Ursula, a girl from German class. Ursula was a small girl. Her arms hung loose at her sides and swung wide when she walked. Her dark eyes saw everything. At times, I became uneasy with her watching me, but nobody else in the class was my age so we stayed together, hoping to form a friendship. Ursula went with me every day to visit Ruth and seemed to enjoy listening to me read. She never offered to read herself, and when I asked if she wanted a turn, she timidly shook her head.

The night sky seemed dull and held no splendor as it had that first year. The camp had changed us.

"Dad, can you read the stars like Granddad did?"

Dad gazed skyward. "Your granddad was a smart man, but maybe he saw what he wanted to see in the heavens," he replied, expressing his own despair.

Was Granddad simply an old man who loved to tell stories? No, I convinced myself, Dad was wrong.

As the summer wore on, we were exhausted by the endless effort that produced nothing—no feelings of accomplishment. The uncertainty and bleakness of the immediate future troubled us all.

The war continued and as news of the German army's atrocities filtered into the camp, some of the guards became more unfriendly and hostile.

Dad and I were walking near the mess hall one evening and I saw the man who'd assaulted Lise.

He glared at me.

Terrified, I wet my pants. With pee flowing down my legs and into my shoes, I cried, embarrassed.

Dad sensed my distress and without questions put his arm around me and walked me back to our cabin.

Once we were inside, he turned to me. "Are you all right, Trudy?" He asked staring into my face.

I nodded.

"Should you speak with your mother?"

"No, Dad. But the way he glared at us scared me."

Dad drew me into his arms for comfort.

Since we'd been in Texas, I'd felt fear, loneliness, and shame, but I'd never imagined being physically attacked before that evening. The absence of my best friend made that feeling more acute, and I stayed close to the other girls at school for safety.

We hadn't heard from Eddie or his family. Mom wrote to Helen's brother asking for news.

Matt replied he'd made inquiries but could not locate them or learn any information about their well-being.

The smothering heat of that long summer finally ended, and cooler nights were welcomed. The sleep we needed, lost by so many hot, sleepless nights, restored energy into our bodies. Our pace quickened as if we had somewhere meaningful to go. Fresh vegetables from the garden enriched our meals and, for the first time, the food was tasty. Life seemed better during these times.

We heard a rumor that the war might soon be over. Hope became infectious. I overheard families taking stock of possessions, and observed them hoarding what could be useful on the "outside." Men talked about possible jobs and seeing groups discussing the best opportunities for employment was common, counting on their fingers the employers who might welcome them back. Dad's job was waiting for him at the university, he said assuredly. He was a teacher and never considered any other career.

After the initial optimism, thinking about a possible end to our status as internees brought additional anxieties. Questions circulated the camp. Could we return to our homes? How would we get there? Were our possessions waiting? How would we be treated by the government and society?

Months passed with no definite news, and talk of the end of the war died. We would not be out of the camp before winter. Before Christmas. Before the New Year. We would not be celebrating our freedom as 1945 began.

꿈

WINTER ARRIVED, AND the first major storm of the season caught everyone in the camp off guard by its severity. An arctic chill had pushed its way south, covering a large portion of the state.

The winds, directly from the north pole, brought freezing temperatures and more than six inches of snow. Icicles hung from the eaves of our cabins. The thin walls with no insulation did not protect us from the cold. I felt I would freeze to death as I lay on my bed fully dressed and shivering under threadbare blankets. Icy temperatures lasted for days, causing pipes to freeze in the kitchen and latrines.

We struggled in the snow and wind to make our way to the mess hall—the cold penetrating our clothes.

Dr. Koch and the two nurses who worked with him stayed busy treating us for colds and flu. The inescapable arctic air strained our bodies and, as before, the young and old suffered the most.

When Ruth didn't show up for meals, I became concerned.

Dad made the walk to her building to learn she'd been admitted to the clinic with pneumonia. Mom requested permission to visit her, and when we did, she offered us a weak smile and reached for my hand. She asked Dad to write a letter to her son, Frederick, in Virginia, and Dad wrote, describing Ruth's condition, and gave it to the guards for approval and mailing.

I spent most of my afternoons at the clinic reading to Ruth and hoping she'd get better. Often, she preferred to talk about her brothers and the games they'd played as children. She'd close her eyes and reenter her childhood, her voice strengthening as she recalled her early life with Max and Johann. "They taught me to play leap-frog." She smiled and placed her hand on her heart. "Johann would bend over, clutch his ankles, and Max stood next to him as I attempted to jump over Johann. If I couldn't make it over, Max lifted me, and then I'd almost fly over." She paused.

I handed her the cup of water by her bed.

"We often played hoops. I was good with the hoop, and so was Max. I'd run alongside him using a hook to roll the wooden hoop. If I couldn't keep up, Max slowed to wait for me. Sometimes the hoop got away from me, and Johann would run it down and bring it back." Ruth paused and reached for another drink. "There was one game I wouldn't play, conkers. It was an autumn activity and played in pairs. Conkers are seeds from the horse-chestnut tree. My brothers would bore holes into the seeds with a knife then thread them onto a cord about a foot long. The idea was to swing the cord toward your opponent so the conkers would hit each other. The contest ended when one conker broke apart. The player with the unbroken conker was the winner. My brothers wanted me to play with them, but I was afraid the conkers would hit me in the face. I was happy watching them play and couldn't help laughing when one conker shattered and the other brother cheered his victory."

❦

RUTH'S HEALTH WASN'T improving. The light in her eyes was dimming, and she often fell asleep when I read.

I worried about her and asked the nurse why Ruth wasn't getting better. I was told we should see improvement soon.

But Ruth was too weak to tell more about her childhood.

"*Ich bin so mude,* (I'm so tired)," she'd say softly and squeeze my hand.

Three weeks after Dad wrote to her son, Ruth slipped away.

I knew she'd gone to heaven before Mom came to tell me.

Like Granddad, she'd come to say goodbye. I felt her fleeting presence when I woke to a narrow ray of light shining through my window.

With Ruth gone, I didn't know how to spend my afternoons. I thought about stopping in to see Joey and Paula but could not bring myself to go into Building Six. Most days, I ended up alone.

Ursula, whose health was poor, missed a lot of school that winter. She was in and out of the clinic. I visited and asked if she wanted me to read aloud to her. She started to reply, but her mother said Ursula needed to remain quiet and sleep as much as possible.

As the activities of the days ceased and nights began, the terror in Lise's eyes and the hatred on her attacker's face tormented me. I continued to be surrounded by anger and bigotry. I was trapped as much by the looks of some of the guards and by them calling my dad a Nazi spy as I was by the barbed wire. Their statements were spoken with such venom that even the younger children, who had no idea what the words meant, were afraid.

The losses of that winter devastated us. With Helen gone and the passing of Ruth, Mom was alone. Each evening, she returned to the fence. She caught pneumonia, and Dr. Koch insisted she be admitted to the clinic. After she was released, she made her way to the fence to stare at the nothingness.

I found her one afternoon clawing at the fence with bloody fingers.

"Mom, what are you doing?" I pulled her away. By now, the guards knew her. And as days passed, Mom wasn't alone at the fence—other internees had joined her silent protest.

Our lives revolved around the weather. We'd suffered the heat and cold and the dry and wet and were left physically exhausted.

Without purpose or direction, I spent most of my time in the warm library.

One afternoon the guard who everyone called Baldy came up to me.

"I see you here often." He pulled out the chair across the table. "You must enjoy reading?"

"Nothing else to do since my friend Eddie is gone."

Baldy leaned forward. "His family go to Germany?"

Tears formed behind my eyes. "Yes."

"I wonder how it's going for them over there," Baldy said. "From what I hear, things are real bad."

Baldy didn't seem to care that I was German. He seemed as lost as I was.

He sat with me and told me about his family.

Baldy was from Ohio and had been married for over twenty years to his high-school sweetheart. They'd lost their nineteen-year-old son, Jason, at Pearl Harbor. Jason had been stationed there one month when the Japanese attacked on December 7, 1941. Holly, Baldy's wife, was still mourning the loss, but Baldy believed nothing could be done except to push on. After this war was over, he was calling the job quits.

"All I want to do is go home and spoil my granddaughters." He leaned back, crossing his large arms over a larger stomach. "I'm opening a little shop."

This was the way life should be, I thought, as Baldy and I relaxed into our conversation. That my family came from

Germany and Baldy's ancestors from Ireland didn't matter. We had no conflict with each other. "What kind of shop?" I enjoyed hearing about his life. Having a normal conversation distracted me from my current environment.

He smiled and ran his hand over his bald head. "I'm good with engines. Can fix anything with a motor."

"Are you leaving Texas and going home?"

This time he laughed. "I'm not cut out for this empty land. I like the congestion and noise of the city."

I stood. "It's time to go to supper."

He got to his feet, his heavy frame moving slowly. "Take care of yourself."

I was at the door when he called to me. "Wait up. Is your mother the artist?"

I nodded hesitantly.

"I saw a watercolor of the camp. A real nice sunset. The light seemed realistic, like the desert here. I thought I might get one to send my wife. Let her know I'm thinking of her." He grinned. "I'm willing to pay the going price."

I was surprised, but Baldy's statement renewed my spirit.

After supper that evening, Baldy approached like a friend, ignoring any division between guard and internee. "Mrs. Herman," he called and joined us outside the doorway. "Hi," he said to me.

"Hi, Baldy."

"Mrs. Herman," he repeated. "I wonder if I might buy one of your sunsets to send to my wife? I know she'd love it."

Mom straightened, suddenly taller. "You want to buy one of my paintings for your wife?" An expression of disbelief crossed her face.

"Yes, ma'am, that's right." Baldy gave her that same friendly grin he'd given me in the library.

"Well, of course. Come by tomorrow before supper, and I will show you the sunsets. You may choose which one you think she might like best."

With Baldy's purchase validating her work, Mom was happier and began going to the fence again, not to hopelessly stare off into the distance, but to paint. She stood at the fence painting the ever-changing landscape—the barbed wire appearing on each canvas.

Chapter 13

*F*inally, an announcement was made. The war in Europe was over. The Axis powers had been defeated, but during the process, many European cities had been destroyed or badly damaged by the relentless bombing.

Celebrations by both the guards and internees erupted. Men, women, and children rushed out into the camp, cheering and hugging. But the initial joy ceased as reality set in, and questions were asked. What would become of us? Would the government transport us back to our homes? How would we be treated?

For over two years, our emotional lives had been like a roller coaster, moving from possibilities to bleakness, hope to despair. Granddad had been right; the heavens are linked to our lives. I thought of the severe contrast in weather the clouds brought, and we endured.

Each of us carried scars from those years—the legacy of our internment. We suffered deep wounds at knowing our families had been selected by our government and identified as "enemy aliens." Of the millions of German immigrants and US citizens of German ancestry, both naturalized and natural-born, between eleven and twelve thousand had been interned.

Many of us had lost faith in the American system. Citizens from all over the world risked their lives to come to this country and to join the dream. Now, to the internees, America was flawed. The American ideals and principles deserted us.

The adults spoke of prejudice, of being destitute, of not finding employment to support families, and of not being able to overcome the hollowness and dejection that smothered us.

I was so troubled by the changes in Mom and Dad, that only now did I become aware of the even more drastic changes in me. The innocent child from two years ago had been replaced by a disillusioned adolescent. An adolescent who'd lived through a war—the weapons of actions and words. As we prepared to leave Texas, I no longer knew who I was. For days, I parked myself in front of the small, round mirror, inspecting the tall, blonde teenager with Granddad's hazel eyes. *"Who are you, Trudy Herman?"* I asked the reflection.

The answer was complex. I was an American. I'd lived over two years inside an internment camp in my own country. I was a confused, bitter, frightened teenager.

⌒⟋⟍⌒

WE RETURNED TO Somerville, to our home that had been seized and sold. A family named Johnson invited us inside.

Dad had simply told them we were thinking of building and would be interested in their floor plan, but I knew he and Mom wanted to see it one last time.

Viewing the changes and following Mrs. Johnson from room to room was difficult.

In the kitchen, Mom opened the door to the broom closet and there on the inside wall were marks signifying my age along with my height; AGE 5, 3'7", AGE 6, 3'10 ¼", AGE 7, 4'. My heart fell to my stomach, and tears burned my eyes. A part of me was being left behind. Before long, this information would be forgotten. I looked up and Mrs. Johnson was walking toward my room. When she opened the door, I wondered if my tooth-fairy pillow was still there, hanging on the inside doorknob. Seeing more changes would be too painful, so I said I'd wait for Mom and Dad by the front door.

When we left, a few of the neighbors stopped and stared as if we were strangers. No one called a greeting. Across the street, Maggie's house seemed different. Smaller. The doors and blinds were closed.

Our next stop was the university. Dad was confident he'd be offered a position. Instead, he was told the university did not employ German parolees who had been classified as enemies of our country. Besides, too many unemployed Americans needed jobs.

Our German friends fortunate enough to escape internment, such as those who had no ties to the homeland and thus avoided scrutiny, were still afraid to associate with us. They worried about their own employment being slowed by post-war prejudice.

Our non-German friends were baffled by our situation. Joe Taylor, an English professor, and his wife offered us the use of their basement until Dad could find work.

Dad tried to explain to the Taylors what had happened, but it was difficult, since we hadn't been given a reason for our internment.

Matt gave us the boxes and portrait he'd stored. He also gave my parents money. He'd sold several pieces of our furniture once he'd heard the house was being forfeited. But he, too, he said, was afraid of losing his job due to existing bias.

Along with the stigma of internment, we had to start over. We learned to hide our confinement from people we met and tried to forget our time in Texas.

"This is a pivotal moment in our lives. The choices we make now will determine our future." Dad said to Mom and me. "A new day, and new memories to be made."

Several families we knew from the camp felt compelled to change or shorten their names, and others simply lied: "It was another family" or "that's such a common German name," they said.

I struggled to follow Dad's lead and move forward. But the face of Lise's attacker still brought me nightmares. I was haunted at times by the pure hatred I'd seen and was burdened by the enormous guilt I carried over my inaction to help Lise. Most of all, I was full of resentment.

I had been treated like the enemy, and that treatment was deeply embedded inside me. I felt like an outsider in America in 1945.

Chapter 14

*J*n late November, Dad accepted a job with Global Insurance in Duluth, Minnesota. We arrived along with a blizzard—cold winds raced down from Canada leaving over a foot of snow behind. We rented a smelly, drafty, one-bedroom house parked on an alley behind our landlady's larger home. The small house with dark furniture, faded wallpaper, and scuffed wooden floors was left to Mrs. Downs when her mother died a year earlier. The smell of sickness and urine permeated the space and still lingered under the disinfectant used to rid the rooms of what remained from the last years of the older woman's life.

I slept with my face buried into the recently purchased pillow and bedding and learned to control my breathing, taking shallow breaths as I curled up on the lumpy brown sofa. Fear overwhelmed me. *How long would we be stuck in this cramped, cold place with Dad at a job he didn't like? When would the nightmares go away? Would we ever be normal again?* Trying not to wake Mom and Dad, I lay quietly as tears of hopelessness inched down my face.

The house odors encircled me, and I burrowed my face deeper. Those odors had seeped into my hair, skin, and clothes, and I worried others might also be able to smell them. Last week, in my eighth-grade geometry class, Mrs. Banks had stood in front of the classroom, sniffed the air, her nostrils widening, and with a look of total disdain, glared at Toby Hayes seated beside me. Then she shifted her gaze, her expression relaxing as she smiled at some of the more popular, conventional students. She judged Toby on his unkempt appearance and failed to recognize the boy within. From the expression on his face, Toby guessed her thoughts and shrank, his body becoming slighter and his chair larger—reduced from the person he was to the person she saw, small and insignificant.

I could guess how Toby felt. I, too, felt hollow and inconsequential, but inside the barbed wire, I'd learned to hide my feelings and pretend. I had listened to Ruth's stories and legends and now became one of her Paladins when I needed to escape—a Paladin with inner strength and a resilient heart, both qualities lacking in the frightened, resentful girl I'd become.

Mrs. Banks never suspected the foul odor that filled her classroom came from this small house, a house that had been visited by death. Or that the stench was carried to her classroom by a tall, blonde, hazel-eyed, well-read girl who appeared normal. This teacher was not interested in knowing her students; therefore, she never glimpsed beneath the surface.

I was almost fifteen. I'd once longed for the moment when I'd join that special group of indestructible teenagers. When the world was ours. When I could dream of accomplishing the impossible. A special group who saw the world filled only with opportunities.

Yet, I was different. Bitterness and anger lived inside me,

and I felt my world teetering on a narrow ledge, yanked off-center by extreme events that began when I was eleven, changed by a madman hungry for power and domination.

I felt helpless, as I often had these last three years. We'd lived two of those years in a controlling society, following orders and rules of the camp. The last year had been spent struggling to adjust to a normal life.

I was forgetting much of my life in Somerville. Forgetting the details, the little things—and special things—the things I once cherished and held dear. They were vanishing, one by one, like the railcars we'd passed on our way to internment—railcars parked on a siding, uncoupled, and left to rust, forgotten.

My fingers clutched the wooden angel Granddad whittled for me—the one tangible treasure I had from him, an anchor, connecting me to my childhood.

༄

THE SMALL HOUSE filled quickly with our memories and ghosts. Through the thin walls, I heard my parents' voices, especially my father's. He was comforting Mom after a nightmare invaded her sleep. Dad led her to the door, calmly reassuring her she was safe. They stood in the opened doorway, breaths curling from their lips reminding me of Granddad's pipe smoke. Fear knotted inside me. I heard Mom admiring the layers of snow glistening in the moonlight, her voice thick with tears.

"It's gone," she said, her hands shaking.

Mom was searching for the barbed-wire fence.

Dad wrapped his arms around her shoulders. "Yes, Veenie. It's gone," he whispered.

It was true, the barbed wire was gone, but a fence remained. I knew that Mom felt its presence. I felt it, too, and at times, when my Paladin shield was down, and I was most vulnerable, the fence seemed to move a little closer.

⁓

MOLLY DOWNS, OUR landlady, was a friendly, talkative, loud, heavy-set woman. Her daughters had moved away, but she spoke of them often. One daughter moved to Chicago and the other to San Francisco. Both were teachers, as was Mrs. Downs. Fortunately, Mrs. Downs taught at my school and each morning gave me a ride.

She'd back her 1936 Ford slowly out of her garage and wait for me to open the car door and jump in, making sure my feet were placed on the dark towels she kept on the floorboard. As she drove, she repeated her story of how thoughtful her husband had been to leave her this respectable car with its inverted grille and three horizontal chrome side strips, each carefully polished to a bright shine. On snowy mornings, I wished he'd taught her to drive on snow and ice. If there had been an overnight snowfall, she drove down the center of the road at twenty miles an hour, a foot on the brake, leaning forward and peering out the windshield, retelling her story. Still, I was grateful I didn't have to wait for the bus in the freezing temperatures.

Mrs. Downs helped Mom find customers, mostly Mrs. Downs's own sisters and friends, and Mom spent her days sewing. Listening to music on the radio, she bent over an ancient treadle Singer sewing machine that belonged to Mrs. Downs's mother mending and finding ways to enlarge wool skirts that were a little too tight or lengthen those that were too short. Mom saved her money to furnish the home she yearned to own.

"You don't have to take in sewing, Veenie," Dad told her. "We're managing to put away a bit each month. And with what we already have, we'll be able to buy a house when I find a teaching position."

I believe Dad was concerned about Mom's emotional fragility.

Mom lifted her head from the scarred, well-used machine. "What would I do with myself if I didn't work?"

Dad smiled. "You could paint."

Mom stiffened, and her lips pressed tightly together. "I'm fine, Karl," she said softly.

"We might yet be reimbursed for our house. And we still have most of the money Matt received for the furniture he sold. Why don't you and Trudy go on a shopping spree, have some fun?"

Dad, the optimist, was always encouraging.

At the expression "shopping spree," I moved to Mom's side. "Shopping would be fun. I need some boots." Years had passed since Mom and I had shopped, unless you counted going through pages of the Sears & Roebuck catalog as a shopping trip. Mom could copy any item I found in the catalog; therefore, she made most of my clothes.

Mom removed the sleeve of the brown jacket she was mending from under the needle of the sewing machine. She held up the jacket, shook it out, and checked the stitching. Satisfied, she rose and picked up a hanger. "If we go shopping, we might even buy you a few books." She ran a hand over her blonde hair, now streaked with gray.

Several times that winter, Mom interrupted what she was doing and went to the kitchen window. She watched as large snowflakes floated to the ground and blanketed the alley in white, decorating the trees across the alley and the wooden birdhouse hanging from a branch.

Fresh snowfalls seemed to fascinate Mom. One day I asked, "What are you looking at?"

"Trudy, the barbed wire is gone," she said in the same matter-of-fact voice that told me it was snowing.

Tears stung my eyes. I didn't know what to say. This was not the mother I remembered, this woman, so frail it seemed like light could pass through her. The moment caused me to recall the strong, kind, generous woman who tried to help others.

Years ago in Somerville, a young postman dropped the neighborhood mail into a puddle and much of it had gotten wet. Mom found him sitting on our front steps trying to dry the letters with his handkerchief. He told her it was only his first week on the job, and he wasn't sure he'd be able to continue. Mom invited him inside, helped him spread out the mail before the fire, and served him a cup of coffee and a biscuit with butter and jam.

She explained to the young man that everyone has days where things go wrong, but it's important to keep moving forward—for tomorrow could be a great one.

I went to the window, wrapped my arm around Mom's

waist, and leaned my head on her shoulder. We gazed out at the snow-laden tree at the end of the alley and the blue jay on the wooden fence beyond. "It's a pretty view," I said.

"When we buy a house, I want a place without a fence." Her voice was barely above a whisper.

"Let's take a walk," I suggested. "Make footprints in the fresh snow."

Mom stepped back. "I don't know, honey." She gazed out the window, a cautious look in her eyes.

"The winds are not strong now. It might be a good time to get out." I encouraged.

Four inches of snow had fallen overnight and the alley, a passageway of white, was bright and sparkly in the sunlight. We dressed for the cold, opened the back door, and stepped off the tiny porch. Mom stiffened, took a deep breath, and surveyed her surroundings like a runner planning her strategy while waiting for the signal to start the race.

We walked side by side down the alley toward the street, and I realized for the first time I was taller than Mom. The air retained a heavy silence except for the sound of Dad shoveling Mrs. Downs's driveway, the shovel scraping the pavement in a persistent rhythm.

As we approached the A-framed birdhouse hanging from a low branch, a breeze blew the snow in our direction.

Mom jumped back and smiled as she brushed the back of her gloved hand across her face. Water droplets stuck to her lashes, outlining her large, round, hazel eyes. Our eyes. And Granddad Weber's. This was one of the few times I saw my mother as a young girl. The pictures on Granddad's mantel, although brown and faded, had shown her face to be so youthful, it had been challenging for me to imagine that the girl was Mom.

She laughed.

Surprised, I wiped my eyes on the sleeve of my coat and held my breath. This was the Mom I was missing. The strict, but loving, Mom who'd held my hand when I was a child. I reached over and took her gloved hand in mine.

"Let's walk around the block and see how Dad's doing."

Chapter 15

The winter of '47 set record cold temperatures and more than eleven feet of snow fell along the north shore of Lake Superior. The tiny house was never warm. However, I often found Mom staring out the window, and hoped she was admiring the scenery and not reliving our lives inside the barbed wire.

The junior high in Duluth seemed foreign after the school in the internment camp, but I made a friend at the school that winter. Joyce McNair and I were paired by Mrs. Banks on a math project. Joyce was kind, and although I occasionally caught her curious glances at the gaps in my knowledge of events of the last three years, she never once asked about my life before moving to Duluth.

Maybe in time I would have told Joyce about Somerville but never the barbed-wire fence. That lid was tightly closed. I hoped those memories would become fainter, like photographs fading in sunlight.

A year earlier, Joyce had moved in with her grandparents. Her parents died in a car accident, and she was lost and lonely, too. With her help, I learned about popular fashions. She and I went shopping and added new clothes and colors to update my wardrobe. Joyce pronounced the right shade of pink made my skin glow. We visited a beauty salon for haircuts and learned make-up tips. For the first time, I felt like a teenager.

Joyce invited me to spend evenings with her, and we rode the bus to her grandparents' farm north of town. There, we listened to music, the top-ten musical hits on the radio, and practiced new dance steps.

On a couple of Saturdays, we rode the county bus from the farm to the theater in Duluth and saw the movies *Double Indemnity* with Barbara Stanwyck and Edward G. Robinson and *Mildred Pierce* with Joan Crawford.

Dad spent evenings at the city library going through newspapers searching for a teaching job. He said he wanted to return to the classroom where his heart belonged.

I believed he was also searching for more than a job. He was searching for his place in the new post-war America.

⤳⤳

ON A SUNDAY morning in March, the sun shone bright after two inches of snow the previous day, Mom rose early to surprise Dad with a peach kuchen, his favorite. The aroma filled the small house as she filled their coffee cups.

Dad rubbed his hands together, anticipating a slice of the hot pastry, and smiled. "That smells great, Veenie."

As Dad picked up his fork, the doorbell rang.

"That woman has the nose of a bloodhound," he said softly.

I opened the door to find Mrs. Downs on the porch.

"Trudy, I'd like to pick up Janet's jacket. I'm seeing her later today."

Janet was Mrs. Downs's sister.

I went to get the jacket Mom had mended the day before. Mrs. Downs followed, stopping at the painted sunset Dad had hung to brighten the narrow hallway. Leaning forward for several seconds then stepping back and turning her head for a different perspective, she seemed to study the scene.

"This is a lovely watercolor." She leaned forward again, examining the desert sunset, her nose practically touching the colors. "Who did this?"

"It's Mom's," I said with pride.

"Edvina!" She raised her voice.

I smiled. Mrs. Downs's normal voice was as large as she was.

"I didn't know you were so talented," she said. "I must have Paul, my nephew, take a look at this. He owns Morgan Art Gallery on Third."

"Do you think he'd be interested?" Mom asked skeptically.

"I'm sure he would. It's very good."

"That would be nice. If you really think he might want to look at my work," Mom said and opened the cabinet to pull out another cup. "Do you have time for a cup of coffee, Molly?"

Mrs. Downs took a deep breath, and her eyes focused on the kuchen. "I could drink another cup." She removed her snow boots, coat, and scarf, and joined Dad at the table.

⹀

Two weeks later, Paul Morgan came to meet Mom and view her watercolors. He was friendly and the two of them got along well. Impressed with Mom's paintings, he selected twenty and laid out a plan to host a showing. After figuring out the details, and insisting Mom ask more for each painting than she or Dad ever thought possible, he hosted a two-day show at his gallery. Five paintings sold. The dark ones, those where the barbed wire loomed large over the brown and gray compound, sold best.

On the last day of the show, a representative from St. Paul's well-established Travis Gallery agreed to take four watercolors on consignment.

With the money from Mom's paintings, my parents talked of buying a house in Duluth. Living here, Mom could continue to paint and work with Paul. Then, before they even began the search for a place, one of Dad's former colleagues at the university scheduled a job interview for Dad at a high school in his home state of Mississippi.

On April 10, Dad took the train to Three Rivers, Mississippi, then a bus to Willow Bay for an interview. He was offered a teaching position in math and accepted, delighted to be getting back into the classroom. Before leaving Willow Bay, he met Pricilla Davis, a woman desperate to sell her home that had sat vacant and deteriorating for years. He purchased the vacant Southern-style house with the money he and Mom had saved.

❧

EXPERIENCED AT PACKING, we boxed up our belongings and were ready to leave by the end of the school year in May.

Busy planning our move, I failed to notice the changing weather. Green trees and yellow-red buds, a result of warmer temperatures, had transformed Duluth into a beautiful place to live. Looking down from the sunny hilltops, I saw freighters drifting in the now ice-free port on Lake Superior.

Before our departure, I rode the bus one last time to visit Joyce. She'd been a good friend and ally during a difficult transition in my life—from a lost youth to a genuine teenager, from an internee to a schoolgirl. We hoped to see each other again and promised to write.

For a second time, we had coffee and kuchen with Mrs. Downs. She, too, had been a good friend. Working with Mrs. Downs's nephew, Mom had regained much of her confidence and was now eager to begin a new life.

❧

DURING ANOTHER BEAUTIFUL sunrise, we once again waited for a train to take us to our new home. The day supplying warmth for growth and renewal, I thought of Granddad, the spring garden, and his anticipation of fresh vegetables at his fingertips.

I tried not to concentrate on my fears and instead, created images of the small town of Willow Bay. On a Mississippi map, Dad showed us its location on the Pascagoula River in the southeast part of the state.

Mom was thrilled to have a place of our own, a Tara, she'd said, perhaps like the manor in *Gone with the Wind*.

I hoped this would be an easier transition than the previous one and longed for a place where I would gain strength and spirit like the Paladin I pretended to be—a safe place where painful memories and fears would eventually perish.

This journey would be different from the dreadful one to the camp, I told myself. The war was over, Dad was with us, and the weight and fear had been replaced by optimism. Maybe Mom's nightmares and her images of the barbed-wire fence would be left behind. I prayed that my own nightmares would be replaced with visions of Granddad, the rocking chair, my small carved angel resting on his knee, and the circles of smoke rising from his pipe.

I was anxious about what lay ahead.

The train station and platform were crowded, not with people overwhelmed with humiliation and shame, but with the chatter of smiling couples, families, and servicemen. I examined a group of uniformed soldiers waiting for the train, looking for the guard who'd attacked Lise and whose face had been twisted with hate. I needed to see him once more, to find out if that hatred consumed him. Granddad taught me good was in all of us, and I felt if I saw the guard's animosity was vanishing, then the emotions leaping around inside me would someday melt away.

I closed my eyes. The world had changed. We had changed. Prospects for our future had brightened.

I heard the rumble of the train moments before I saw it steaming into the station, the coal black engine grinning at me, the same large dragon that sped us toward the barbed-wire compound, the marching guards, and the daily roll-calls had returned to carry us to a new life.

A man stood back to allow Mom and me to board first. We were eager and ready for the journey to begin. We were a family looking forward to our future. Dad's arrest and our internment were unknown and no one cared who we were, where we'd been, or where we were going.

I thought of the Japanese American internees and wondered how they were blending into post-war America. Toby Hayes, the unkempt boy from Mrs. Banks's classroom, slipped into my mind, and I wondered if he'd learn to play the pretend game.

"Here we go," Dad said, sliding into the seat next to Mom.

Dad was acting like memories of the internment camp no longer existed for him.

As I fell into the rhythm of the speeding train, memories I'd suppressed resurfaced like a stone, solid and heavy, and I couldn't deny or erase them like Dad had done. *Did ghastly memories lay heavy inside Mom as well?*

Before long, dark clouds and shadows of doubts appeared as they had three years earlier. My heart thumped as the pursuing memories refused to fade. I stared out the window, watching the sky grow darker while the stone in my stomach grew heavier. *How much living would I have to do before I could read the heavens as Granddad had done?*

The things we remember from our childhood are surprising: our favorite birthday party, a single Christmas gift, or a fight with our best friend. Or even some of the people and places we encountered during those years, like annals of time, remaining alive in our memories. On my way to a new town, I knew that I would never be completely free from the memories of the camp and the resentments that burned within, forcing their way to the surface of my mind at a time I was most defenseless.

Chapter 16

*M*om and I were impatient to see our new home.
On the train, Dad drew a floor plan, both the
downstairs and upstairs, indicating inside walls, doorways,
and windows.

Mom seemed able to visualize it, but as hard as I tried, I
could not picture rooms from rectangles and squares drawn
on paper.

"Are you sure you want to make a trip to Rob's and buy
furniture before seeing the house?" asked Dad.

Mom gave a firm nod. "If one of the school board members recommended Rob's, I can't see any harm in checking it
out. If we want, we can buy a few things now. We still have
some of the money Matt gave us and what I earned sewing.
Maybe the gallery in Minneapolis will sell one of my watercolors soon."

We got off the train at Three Rivers, left our overstuffed
bags at the station with a friendly, heavyset porter who easily
hefted the luggage onto a cart, and then caught a taxi to Rob's
Second-hand Furniture on the outskirts of town.

Mom selected a pink-and-brown flowered sofa she insisted looked brand new, a large brown upholstered chair, a
kitchen table and chairs, and beds. In the store window was

an upright Kimball piano. Mom's gaze kept returning to it. She never spoke of the piano left behind, the one her father bought when she was fifteen and the beautiful world of music had been open to her. She'd used that piano for hundreds of lessons before Matt sold it.

I often wondered what became of our personal belongings left in Somerville. Several times I thought of asking Dad but couldn't bring myself to do so. I feared the answer might rip apart scars from the wounds of loss that were beginning to heal.

The furnishings were purchased and arrangements made for delivery the following day. We picked up our luggage and caught a Greyhound bus to Willow Bay.

Soon, rolling countryside lush with green crops and bright flowers, many I'd never seen before, traveled by my window as the bus rambled along a two-lane road. Majestic homes built on acres of fertile land caught my attention, and though I was unable to visualize my own home, in these stately mansions, images of spiral staircases, polished wooden floors, trunk rooms, gardens, orchards, and ice houses from the eighteenth century danced in my head. I imagined walls covered with beautiful tapestries and hallways lined with family portraits.

"We're here." Dad said. His voice breaking into my daydream and transporting me back to the present.

There was no bus depot in Willow Bay, a small town of fewer than three thousand residents, and the bus had stopped at a corner by the courthouse. The two-story red brick courthouse with four white pillars stood tall and proud across Main Street from Riverside Park.

Stepping off the bus, we were met by flower beds and vibrant pots of flowers full of color placed throughout the park and along the street. The blocks of one- and two-story buildings were also brick with white trim, most with awnings advertising the names of the businesses within. Next to the courthouse stood an office building with accounting and law firms listed on a wooden placard. Farther down the block, I could see a hardware store, a pharmacy, and a red-and-white–checked awning marking the Marigold Cafe.

The end of May brought heat to Willow Bay, reminding me of the heat in Texas, except this humid air weighed heavy on our shoulders. Our clothes clung to us, making it harder to move. As we stood in the sun, the luggage at our feet, I swatted at fat insects swarming around me. Heat from the concrete sidewalk burned through the soles of my shoes.

Squinting against the bright sun, I gazed up at the court-house and saw the image of an eagle carved into the façade of the building, its wing-span covering half of the front of the narrow courthouse, and the declaration EQUAL JUSTICE FOR ALL sculpted into the plaster below. "Look, Dad." I pointed to the words and the eagle above them.

"What?" He turned in the direction I was pointing. "Yes, I hope so."

"Welcome to Willow Bay." A tall man walked toward us, a wide smile spread across his tanned face. He stretched out a large hand to Dad and nodded a greeting to Mom and me. "Hope your trip was good." He pumped Dad's hand enthusiastically. "You're in for some hot weather, I'm afraid. It's early this year. So, let's get you out of the sun."

Mom and I were introduced to James Foster, the town's

pharmacist and a school board member. He'd offered to give us a ride to our home located on the east bank of the river.

"Mrs. Herman, let me have that." James Foster said and took the brown, tattered suitcase Mom had dragged along to the internment camp, the suitcase she'd had since her honeymoon.

Mr. Foster ushered us along the sidewalk. "I have a daughter your age. She's lookin' forward to meetin' you." He spoke slowly, and with his drawl, his speech sounded odd.

We made our way toward Mr. Foster's car. In front of Mabel's General Store, Dad stopped to speak with Joe Thompson. This time we were introduced to an elderly man with a mouth full of chewing tobacco and a smile exhibiting large yellow teeth but welcoming nonetheless.

"Everybody calls me Joe, you hear?" He stood to shake hands, then fell back into his chair positioned under the store's awning in the shade. He propped his feet on a wooden pop case and leaned his chair back against the brick wall of the building. Tobacco stains covered the front of his blue shirt. When he spoke, Joe shifted the wad of tobacco into his jaw, forcing a cheek to protrude. Joe and his wife, Mabel, owned the general store, and Joe was also a member of the school board.

As we headed out of downtown, we drove past two blocks of one- and two-story brick businesses that sat along both sides of the street. A small number of people flowed in and out of the stores. We took a left onto River Road that led to the bottom lands and older homes near the river. As we started downhill, two large estates came into view. Mr. Foster explained they belonged to families who had been living here for over a hundred years. One belonged to a former United States Senator who'd died in a car accident three years earlier. The senator's daughter lived there now. The second estate, belonging to the Logan family, produced much of the area's tobacco.

Southern oaks draped in Spanish moss, like the pictures I'd seen in books, lined the street. We passed three more homes, and Mr. Foster described the families who lived in each, but I barely heard his comments. I was daydreaming my way through the past to Scarlett O'Hara and Rhett Butler.

Mom put her hand to her mouth and her eyes widened as our home came into view.

Placed well back from the road in a grove of oaks and red maples sat a white, two-story house with green shutters.

"Oh, Karl. It's beautiful," she said and scooted forward on her seat.

Two columns, one on each side of the front door, rose tall from the veranda to the roof. Half a dozen steps led from a gravel walk up to the veranda that ran the entire length of the house, a large home compared to the small deteriorating one we'd been living in.

Mom's expression soon turned to one of joy. But for some reason, I became fearful of the new place and worried our previous ghosts may have shadowed us here. I wondered what our lives would be like inside this home. *Was this a place to restore us?*

"The weeds are overgrown and the house itself needs a lot of work and paint, but it sure is nicely situated." Mr. Foster said as he held the steering wheel with one hand while the other arm relaxed out the open window. "There's one other piece of property farther down this way toward the river, and its owner is Jackson Dalton. A widower, he's approachin' eighty. He's known to be ornery, but he's nice enough. Can be a good neighbor if he takes a likin' to you. I'm sure Pricilla told you that." He glanced to Dad for confirmation. "You see, I went to school with Pricilla Davis, the former owner of your home."

Mr. Foster smiled as if remembering a secret.

"How long did she live here?" Mom couldn't take her eyes from the house.

Mr. Foster placed both hands on the steering wheel. "Pricilla? She was born here. In that very house." He slowed and waved to a woman bent over a yellow rose bush. "That's Miss Walker, a neighbor. I'm sure she'll be callin' on you once you're settled."

We were near the end of the road when Mr. Foster turned right and the car rolled up a gravel lane to the edge of a walkway stopping near a dry-looking shrub with one green branch covered in tiny buds. He got out and opened the trunk to unload our luggage. "They're deliverin' your furniture from Twin Rivers, are they?" He set our luggage on the corner of the veranda.

Dad nodded. "Yes. It will be delivered."

"Well then. I must be goin'." He took a step back. "You got yourselves a real nice place here."

I waited anxiously on the gravel drive as Mr. Foster drove away. Then, we walked to the steps to enter our new home.

FROM THE OUTSIDE, the stately house appeared to have been built in prosperous times and had survived declining ones. Though weathered and in poor condition—peeling paint, hanging shutters, and loose boards—two tall oak doors, each with an oval stained-glass window inset, and a wide entrance welcomed us.

Inside, oak floors, a massive brick fireplace in the living room, and floor-to-ceiling windows, showering the woodwork with sunlight, created a time-honored Southern elegance. High ceilings and a carved wooden bannister led to the second floor where large bedrooms and wide windows again embraced the sunlight, which shined on scarred woodwork and yellowing, flowered wallpaper.

The house had been built in the late 1800s and updated shortly before Miss Davis unexpectedly relocated to the coast several years back to take care of her ill sister. Since then, the home had been left to deteriorate. Nonetheless, the kitchen had relatively new appliances and cabinets and countertops, a large, white porcelain sink, and bright green linoleum that stood out beneath dust and grime.

The green linoleum reminded me of our kitchen floor in Somerville, the floor I was sweeping when we heard the knock on the door the night our home was searched and Dad was taken away. I shivered, trying to shake away those memories.

Best of all, as Mom requested, there was no fence. The backyard was full of bushes and dead and dormant plants. A birdbath lay broken on the ground beneath a tree, and a rusted set of gardening tools leaned against the house. Someone had failed to place the tools in the shed now overgrown with blackberry vines. Behind the blackberries and shed stood a row of cypresses, a barrier between us and the high bank of the river.

∽

MOM AND I spent our first days cleaning. We arranged the furniture, and washed and rehung the white cotton curtains embroidered with bright yellow flowers left behind in the kitchen and the teal ones in my bedroom. Mom worked with a contentment I had not seen since before the internment camp, and I often paused to watch as she cheerfully established a new home.

On Mom's dresser, Grandma Rose's silver mirror, comb, and brush took their place in the center—proud showpieces of our past. When I saw Mom cleaning them with a soft cloth one morning, my eyes filled with tears. We had survived.

"Trudy, a piano would go there perfectly," Mom said, her hands on her hips, looking toward the small area off the living room.

With light reflecting down into a circle on the floor, I was reminded of an enchanted dwelling from a fairy tale.

I moved closer to her. "It would be good to have the house filled with music." I laughed. "I miss my piano lessons."

"Oh, Trudy," she smiled. "But maybe someday we can get one." She gave me a wide grin. "The house is beautiful, isn't it?" She leaned in, bumping my shoulder with hers. "I love it, Trudy. It's perfect. Your father knew exactly what we needed. I'm glad we were able to get it."

Mom and Dad had agreed to save their remaining money

for "the unexpected." I'd overheard Dad say that if one of Mom's watercolors at the Minneapolis gallery sold, we might be able to buy a car; otherwise, we had to watch what we spent.

Mr. Samuels at Dixson's Hardware gave Dad credit, and Dad got tools, lumber, and paint. Later, while he was measuring the dimensions of the veranda, our neighbor, Mr. Dalton, who lived on the farm at the end of the road, came by to introduce himself. From a window, Mom and I watched the two of them standing close in the pathway, gesturing to different parts of the landscape as they spoke.

Mr. Dalton stood straight, his short, stocky stature not reflecting his age. He pushed his hat high on his forehead showing a line from his tanned leathery face to the white skin usually hidden beneath the hat. He tucked both hands into the bib of his overalls and, from time to time, leaned to one side and spat a stream of yellowish brown liquid through the air.

"Chewing tobacco." Mom frowned.

"Yuck." I laughed. Chewing tobacco was one of the many things I experienced in Willow Bay.

⤳⟋

THE NEXT AFTERNOON, I took a walk to check out the trail to the river. I strode slowly across the field behind our house, stopping to pick flowers for a bouquet for the dining table and cattails for the tall clay pot left next to the kitchen door. Before long, I learned I shared the fragrant blossoms with honey bees. When I reached for a buttercup, one of them landed on my left hand. Without thinking, I slapped at it, and it stung me.

Mom pulled the stinger from my hand and made a paste of baking soda and water to coat the swelling red spot. By suppertime, my entire hand was so swollen and stiff that my fingers wouldn't bend.

While I was setting the table with one hand, Mr. Dalton knocked on the door. He came to give us the name of a man who would cut the weeds and plow enough land behind the tool shed for a garden should we want one.

Mom invited him for supper.

"Why, thank you, ma'am. I do get tired of eatin' alone," he said, removing his hat.

As we ate, Mr. Dalton spoke of the history of Willow Bay. The small town had once been an important settlement along the river, a location perfect for sending commercial goods to towns upriver or cotton downriver to the Mississippi. The river commerce had sustained the town's economic growth, however, the prosperity declined when steamboat trade was replaced by the railroads that bypassed Willow Bay.

After everyone had eaten, Mom and I rose to clear the table.

Mr. Dalton watched us for a moment. "You might want to get one of those colored women to do that kind of work for you."

Not seeming to understand to what he was referring, Mom asked, "What kind of work?"

He glanced around the room. "Your domestic work."

"There's not that much. I can manage fine." Mom poured him another cup of coffee.

"Well, now." Mr. Dalton lifted his cup. "They need the work. Not much else for colored folks to do here." He turned to address Dad. "Sure would be good if you could afford to offer one a little work." His gaze shifted back to Mom. "Give yourself a break."

"Oh," Mom said.

She sounded somewhat unsure about the whole concept of colored help.

"It's something to think about," Dad replied, filling the awkward silence.

✿

NOT USED TO the heat and humidity, I had difficulty falling asleep. Cooler weather was heading toward us according to the weather report; however, tonight, not even the slightest breeze moved the cotton curtains though the window was wide open. My cotton gown was damp, and perspiration trickled down my neck feeling like one of those crawly bugs that swarmed together and scratched at the window screen when the bedside lamp was on.

I lay on my back, arms out to the side, listening to the faint whistle of a train speeding south to the gulf.

In spite of a fresh future, I still felt empty and lonely.

Tears rolled down my face as I tried to recall childhood memories, some so far away they were difficult to recover. I could barely remember some features of my room in Somerville. Or what happened to the box of cream-colored stationery, my last gift from Granddad, or the pretty marble lying on the windowsill to catch the light. I could no longer call to mind the sounds of the ocean or vaguely visualize two friends gathering seashells.

For some reason, my thoughts settled on Eddie and our time with Ruth. Dear Ruth had been such a kind woman. Even now, Eddie did not know she was gone, or that the letter approving her release from the camp arrived a week too late.

I picked up Angel from my nightstand and for the first time in weeks, I felt Granddad's presence. I closed my eyes and imagined the two of us sitting in rockers on his porch while I told him about Willow Bay.

Chapter 17

*T*he work of setting up our new home was nearly complete. The house was free of the accumulated dust and cobwebs from years of sitting empty, the furniture was in place after several attempts in different locations, most of the repairs were done, and Dad was scraping the outside walls, preparing to paint.

In the afternoon heat, one room stayed cool, the small enchanted one off the living room with light shining from a row of high windows. That's where I spent time reading. Mr. Foster had stopped by with the ninth-grade summer reading list and books from the school library.

I placed eight lemons on the counter for Mom to make lemonade and then joined Dad at the breakfast table. As Mom poured herself coffee, we heard a noise on the back stoop. I went to the screen door and peered out. A black girl sat on the stoop next to the wooden barrel of last year's geraniums. I stared. She was beautiful with flawless brown skin, dark eyes, full lips, and a pretty, oval face. She stared back as she got to her feet, her large eyes reminding me of the frightened deer Dad and I had seen on the riverbank two days before.

"Hi," I smiled.

Dad walked up behind me.

The girl stepped back until her legs were against the wooden barrel, not able to back up any farther. She wore a faded pink dress, but her feet were bare. The dress, tight around her slender chest, was torn under one arm. A flowered scarf was wrapped around her head and tied in a knot at her forehead.

"What's your name, Miss?" Dad asked.

"I's be Ellie Mae, sur."

"Do you need something?" Dad place a hand on my shoulder.

"I's clean tha house fer the missus."

"You looking for employment?"

Mom joined us.

The girl frowned, her eyes shifting from Dad to Mom.

"You want a job?" Dad tried again.

Ellie Mae smiled, a gorgeous smile. "Yes, sur."

Dad took a step back. "Well, Ellie Mae, we're about to have breakfast. Would you care to come inside?"

Her head jerked up, and her large, round eyes widened. She took a step toward us, looking again like the frightened deer. "Youse be wantin' me to work?"

I smiled and opened the screen door inviting her inside.

She stayed where she was but gave us a big grin.

"We can't offer you much. What did you have in mind?" Mom asked.

"What 'bout two quarters and a pound? That's what my cousin gits from Mr. Preston."

"A pound?" Mom frowned.

"A pound of somethin'. Don't mutter what. Sugar, coffee,

flour for bean biscuits or spoon bread. My mama be partial to bean biscuits." She eyed Mom.

Mom glanced at Dad. "Dalton sent her?"

Dad nodded. "Most likely."

"I believe we'll be able to accommodate you. Come in," Mom said.

I pushed open the door even wider. It banged against the side of the house.

Ellie Mae shuffled her feet a couple of times, not willing to come inside. "Youse ain't ate. I's wait out here." She sat on the stoop to wait.

"I'm not sure what to do with her," Mom said after she was seated at the table.

"Maybe she can help with the housework," Dad suggested and took a drink of coffee.

Mom's fork clanked on her plate. Her forehead creased. "I'm not sure I have enough housework for the both of us," she whispered, but her voice filled the room. "Maybe she can help with the house painting and gardening."

"Whatever you want, Veenie."

As soon as they took their last bite, I went to the door. "Come in." I held the door open.

Dad left the room.

Mom stared.

Ellie Mae came slowly into the kitchen. She was about 5'9", slightly taller than me. She shifted her weight from foot to foot.

She appeared alert, her thin body straight.

Ellie Mae's gaze darted to the food on the table.

"I hate to waste food, but I cooked too much. Could you

possibly eat something while I make a list of chores? That way, I won't have so much to store in the refrigerator."

Ellie Mae smiled, and her eyes shifted from Mom back to the table. "Yes'um, I's could do that. I's surely could."

"Give her a plate and a fork, Trudy." Mom went to the desk in the corner of the living room to make a list.

I filled a clean plate with cold scrambled eggs, the remaining sausage patty, and two biscuits with jam, and placed it on the table.

Ellie Mae picked up the plate and fork and went out to the stoop, balanced the plate on her knees, and ate.

I'd never been around black people. I had never even spoken to one before. The only one I knew was Negra Jones, who stocked the shelves and swept the floor for Mabel at the general store. He was friendly, always nodding to me when I went in to pick up items for Mom.

I was curious about Ellie Mae, and clearly so was Mom.

Mom didn't say much but continued to glance at Ellie Mae through the screen door. Each time I reached for a dish from the table, I saw Mom at the desk with a puzzled look on her face waving her pencil around.

"What if she shares your chores?" Mom asked.

I nodded. "That's fine."

"She can help you weed the garden and that will give your dad time to get the house painted and the shutters back on before school starts." With that decision made, Mom wrote *garden.*

Ellie Mae came in and put her plate by the sink. Gardening was the single item on Mom's chore list. The three of us stood there, not knowing exactly what to do.

"Don't youse weary," Ellie Mae said. "I wash clothes."

Mom wrote down *laundry* and returned to the kitchen. "Then let's strip the beds and wash the sheets."

"Yes'um," Ellie Mae said.

Ellie Mae helped Mom push the washer Miss Davis had left behind into the kitchen and hook the hose up to the faucet. "Rollers is mighty worn," Ellie Mae said as she wiped the washer rollers with the rag Mom handed to her.

Dad and I spent the morning on my studies. He insisted I'd lost critical fundamentals while being schooled in Texas and was determined to help me catch up. I knew I would have no difficulties with schoolwork, but entering high school, a thought that used to excite me, now terrified me. I was new and had no friends. No one should enter high school without a friend.

Dad and I discussed the book about the French Revolution I had not yet finished, and the ascent of Napoleon Bonaparte in 1790, while Mom and Ellie Mae stripped the beds and put the sheets into the washer.

Ellie Mae was precise with her work, and it was noon before the sheets were washed and flapping in the breeze on our new clothesline.

When it was time for Ellie Mae to leave, Mom pulled the sugar from the cupboard. "This is all I have," she said, speaking more to herself than me. "I should have placed an order with Mabel, but I was hoping your dad could find a car. A car would make getting around and picking up what we need much easier. I hate to have so much delivered."

Mom smiled. "Thank you, Ellie Mae. We got that chore out of the way for the week. Here's your pound, and here's your money." Mom offered Ellie Mae the sugar and quarters.

Ellie Mae stepped back wringing her hands, her head down. A tiny curl had slipped out from beneath her scarf. "No, ma'am," she said, "the job ain't finished."

"Well, it's your first day, and I think you've done enough for one day."

Ellie Mae frowned and slowly moved backwards to the door.

"Here's your pound and money," Mom repeated.

Ellie Mae shook her head and stared at Mom for a moment before shifting her gaze to Dad, who'd walked into the kitchen. "I's not work a week," she said before opening the screen door and leaving.

We'd never had help inside our home or been around a black person. I wasn't sure what to do, or say.

Mom released a long breath. "I need a list of chores for tomorrow." She stood in the doorway watching Ellie Mae walk down the road. "I didn't want her in my home when I first saw her, but she did an excellent job with the bedding."

Dad reached up and patted Mom's shoulder. "Just shows you shouldn't judge too soon. So, what will you do with her?"

"She certainly looks like she needs the work. But honestly, I don't think I can keep her busy."

"We've hired her?"

"If it's all right with you," Mom answered and headed for the desk that held the list she'd written earlier.

⌖

COOL BREEZES FROM the north pushed the hot air farther south into New Orleans and the panhandle of Florida, leaving us with warm days and comfortable nights. Mom and Dad now enjoyed evenings on the veranda.

Ellie Mae returned every morning, and the number of chores she was given did not matter—she was there until evening. After finishing her inside chores, she helped Dad and me in the garden. Often, Dad painted, leaving the hoeing and weeding to Ellie Mae and me. Once the garden was in shape, Dad gave us brushes and explained how to paint the window shutters he'd laid across sawhorses he'd found in the shed.

For several days, Ellie Mae and I painted the shutters for the upstairs windows before starting on the backyard cleanup. There, we pulled the partially rusted cans, buckets, and a one-handle wheelbarrow from the overgrown ground, cleaned them, and filled each container with soil. Next, we planted black-eyed Susans and petunias. In the front of the house, we helped Dad plant azaleas, nasturtiums, and roses. In a matter of weeks, we'd made the Davis place ours.

Chapter 18

*T*he first weeks in Willow Bay were busy and tiring as we completed the task of creating a home. But by June 21st, the heat and humidity returned and left us even more exhausted. With little to do, I longed for school to start as I dragged myself about the house. I was restless, bored, and lonely.

On a hot afternoon, I went to my room and grabbed Jack London's *Call of the Wild*. I knew the story by heart, but holding it helped me feel less lonely. "Mom, I'm going down to the river." I stepped out onto the veranda.

At the end of the road was a well-worn path that led to a low bank on the river. A large willow tree hung over the riverbank, providing a perfect spot to rest in the shade reading and reflecting. I figured I needed a little of both.

"Wait." Mom had grabbed the hat from the back of the closet door. "Wear this. You don't need to sunburn. And make sure you're wearing shoes."

I went barefoot around the house and hated the hat Mom insisted I wear. She'd found it upstairs when we'd first moved in. It was straw, with a wide brim. With that thing on my head, I looked like Huck Finn. I took the hat from her hand and turned to leave.

"Trudy, why don't you take Ellie Mae along? I worry about you being on that river by yourself. You can sit in the shade and read, but I don't want you swimming without your father there."

Ellie Mae raised her head from her dusting and turned to me.

"All right." I lifted Eddie's book to show Mom I'd listened. To me, the book would always belong to Eddie, even though he'd given it to me.

I glanced around and Ellie Mae had disappeared. "Ellie Mae!" I called.

"I's here." Her voice came from the side of the house.

It took me awhile to realize Ellie Mae would not use the front door. She'd left by the back.

We walked past Mr. Dalton's henhouse, his chickens scattering across the yard as we got near, and continued down the path toward the river.

Ellie Mae swung a large stick, striking the weeds and bushes along the way. When the path narrowed, she walked behind me.

The whack, whack, pause, whack on the bushes became a musical rhythm. I stopped and turned. She bumped into me.

She was only a little taller than me, but her legs were longer as was her stride. Everything about her was long and slender, even her fingers.

"What are you doing, Ellie Mae?"

"I scart away snakes."

I stepped closer to her. "What kind of snakes?" I asked, searching for movement at our feet. "Cottonmouth and copperhead?" I shuddered.

"Yes'um. We's plenty of them. We's also has garter and milk snakes."

"There's a snake named milk?" I asked, surprised.

"Yes'um. My mama told me."

I walked with my head down, looking for movement in the weeds. I hated snakes.

No one was on the riverbank when we arrived. I removed my hat and collapsed down under the tree. Branches bowed low, skimming the surface of the water shading the bank all the way to the river.

Ellie Mae stood watching me. "Are youse goin' for a wade?"

"Yes, let's." I grinned, took off my shoes, and tossed them next to the hat. We waded into the water. Thick mud squeezed between my toes.

"We's mud snakes, too, but they's don't bite peoples."

I laughed. "I think you're making that up."

Her eyes widened. "No, ma'am."

Surprised, I asked, "Why'd you call me ma'am?"

She shrugged.

She seemed unaware of the strangeness of a girl close to my age calling me ma'am.

⁓

WE WADED OUT into the water. Insects buzzed around me, and I swatted at them while squatting down allowing the water to move up my legs until it touched the hem of my shorts.

Once we were cool, we went back to shore. I picked up the book and held it to my chest. I missed Eddie and my eyes filled with tears.

Ellie Mae nodded like she understood my loneliness and looked away.

Two weeks ago, I'd begged Dad to check again with Helen's brother, Matt, for news of Eddie's family. I wanted to know Eddie was safe. But Matt wrote he had not heard a word even though he'd filed a formal request into their whereabouts and had written letters to the few people he knew still in Germany.

Sitting in the shade with Ellie Mae reminded me of all the times I'd sat with Maggie in the park in Somerville. Overwhelmed by sadness, I took a deep breath, forcing the memories down, shoving them back into my box. I didn't want to revisit my past. I brought my knees up and placed the book against them.

"Youse readin'?" Ellie Mae's voice interrupted my thoughts. When we were together, we rarely spoke. I didn't know what to say, but I'd become comfortable in her presence.

I opened the book. "Have you read it?" I stared down at Eddie's name spelled out in the large, black slanted letters and once again I fought against the memories.

"Naw." She avoided looking at me and instead focused on the flowing river.

I wondered if something there held her attention.

"It's my favorite. I've read it a hundred times." I flipped the pages. "Would you like to hear it?"

Ellie Mae straightened and spun around, searching both banks of the river. She grinned. Her white teeth flashed. "You'ns don't know nothin' 'bout the ways here."

I closed the book letting it fall onto my lap. "Did I do something wrong?"

She shrugged. Several minutes passed in silence as we listened to the sounds of bees and insects buzzing over the flowers and water. Iridescent dragonflies darted about, landing for seconds before taking flight again.

"Do you want to hear the story?" I asked a second time.

Ellie Mae scooted back against the tree and nodded.

"Chapter one, Into the Primitive," I read.

After four chapters, we cooled off in the river again. As I was splashing water over the insect bites on my arms and legs, Mr. Dalton appeared on the bank with a fishing pole over his shoulder and a bucket of bait in his hand.

He waited to speak until we got back to shore. "You been playin' with that colored girl?" His eyes were like spotlights focusing on my face.

"I was reading," I replied defensively.

"Hum." Without another remark, he walked farther down the riverbank.

With a knowing look, Ellie Mae said, "We's best go." She picked up her stick and headed up the trail. As we walked home, she let out a cry.

I was sure she'd been bitten by a snake. "Where is it?" I yelled, jumping back.

She lifted a foot upon a log and wincing, pulled out a sharp piece of glass. Blood dripped from her cut.

I helped her hop home.

"Mom!" I called as we entered the back door. "Ellie Mae's foot is bleeding."

Mom rushed into the kitchen. "Sit here." She pulled out a chair from the table and then hurried to the sink for a basin of water. "Put your foot in here," she ordered. "What happened?"

Ellie Mae looked at Mom, then slowly placed her foot into the water.

"She stepped on a piece of broken glass," I answered, looking down at Ellie Mae's foot, wondering when the wound would stop bleeding.

Mom went into the bathroom and brought back a bar of soap. "Wash your foot with this."

After Ellie Mae's foot was clean, Mom put iodine on the cut and bandaged it. "Might as well wash the other foot." She carried the washbasin to the sink for fresh water.

"Trudy, see if you can find a pair of shoes for her to wear when she walks through those woods to and from home," Mom said and placed the clean water in front of Ellie Mae's feet. "What size do you wear?" she asked.

Ellie Mae didn't answer.

Her feet were longer than mine, but Ellie Mae could fit into a pair of Mom's shoes. With her new shoes tied on her feet, her stick in her hand, and a slight limp, she headed down the road toward home.

Chapter 19

*E*llie Mae arrived at eight and waited on the back stoop until we'd eaten breakfast before removing her shoes and entering the kitchen. Then, with a plate piled with leftovers, she went outside to eat, either on the stoop or on a large stump located down the dirt path behind our house. From the stump, she had a view of the river.

Mom's routine was to clean the kitchen right after breakfast, but she began leaving the dishes in the sink for Ellie Mae. Washing the breakfast dishes became Ellie Mae's first task and was added to her list of chores.

During the mornings, I worked on math problems Dad prepared for me and then spent the rest of the time reading in my small, enchanted room. The books on the ninth-grade reading list were interesting. So far, my favorites were *The Pearl* by John Steinbeck and *The Secret Garden,* which I'd read while in the camp with Eddie. Reading diverted my mind from the loneliness I often felt.

After lunch, there was nothing left to do. Overwhelmed by the humidity, I tried to convince Dad to take me to the river to swim. If he couldn't go, I got permission from Mom to go wading with Ellie Mae. I took a book along and read aloud.

One afternoon, on the way to the river, we stopped and sat close together on a large stump, sucking on orange Popsicles and watching logs float over the rapids. A long brown snake slithered out from under a bush, and we both jumped onto the stump, clinging to each other so we wouldn't fall or drop our Popsicles. We watched the snake glide across the ground to a flat rock to warm itself in the sun. Cool drops of orange soon ran down my leg, but I was afraid to let go of Ellie Mae to wipe them away.

"What should we do?" I whispered into her ear.

"It's not poison. I's chase it away."

The sounds of scurrying animals and chirping birds filled the silence. A paddle boat skirted around a waterfall, moving closer to the other bank. Logs floated along in clusters. Still, she didn't move.

Finally, I realized Ellie Mae was as afraid of the snake as I was. That fact struck me as funny, and I couldn't stop laughing. She clung to me so I wouldn't fall. Moments later, we saw Dad walking toward us. Ellie Mae stiffened, dropped her arms to her side, and her Popsicle splashed to the ground. She swayed, almost falling. I jerked on her arm and went over backward. Ellie Mae landed on top of me. I looked up, and Dad stood over us.

Ellie Mae leaped to her feet and pulled me up.

"Are you girls all right?"

"We saw a snake." I pointed toward the rock.

Dad lifted an arm to shade his eyes. "That snake won't hurt you. With all the noise you two were making, I'm surprised you didn't scare it away." He turned back to us. "I'm going fishing. You girls want to come along?" He held the fishing pole over his shoulder and the bait in a small dented bucket he'd found in the shed behind the house. Dad wore overalls when he worked on the house and in the garden. He also wore them fishing and used the bibbed pocket to carry a fruit jar of ice water.

Dad had changed since our move here. Although his hair had turned a little gray and his face had a few more lines, he was much the same now as he had been when I was a young child—a swift smile and gentle manner. But I wondered if at times he, too, was haunted by memories.

"Thanks, Dad, but I don't want to sit and swat insects all afternoon." That's exactly what Ellie Mae and I did when we sat on the riverbank and read.

Ellie Mae wrung her hands and shook her head. "No, sur."

"Well then, I will see you girls later." Dad continued down the path.

I had noticed that whenever Dad joined Ellie Mae and me, she got nervous. "Ellie Mae, don't you like my Dad?" I stuck the last of my Popsicle in my mouth, enjoying the frozen flavor on my tongue.

Today was extremely warm and sweat rolled down my back. I wiggled my torso to free the skin from my damp blouse and sat down on the stump.

Ellie Mae sank to the ground beside me and bowed her head, following a column of ants at our feet. "Oh no, I's like him."

"Then why don't you like being around him?"

She slid a foot over the anthill, destroying all signs it ever existed. Tiny ants scurried around in all directions.

"He talks five-dollar words," she said quietly.

"What?" I had no idea how her answer explained anything.

"Your Pa. He talks five-dollar words. Everybodies says so." She lifted her foot and tiny ants rushed out of a small hole. "Everybodies says, 'that Mister Herman talks big words.' That's why I's come to work here."

Surprised by Ellie Mae's comment, I leaned back so I could see her face. "You knew about us before you came looking for work?"

"Yes'um. Everybodies knows you'ns. We's don't get too many peoples from up north."

"You wanted to work for us?"

"Yes'um. And Mr. Joe told my mama youse might want a worker."

"Why did you want to work for us?" I was confused. What had Joe said about us?

"I's never met anyones from up north," she said with a wide smile.

Not knowing how to respond, I stayed quiet but thought of how others might judge Dad's speech. As a young German, he'd learned English from a teacher who'd lived in London. Though I was puzzled about why Dad's way of speaking would be a matter for discussion, I pushed that thought aside and decided to read.

Sitting comfortably together with our backs against the stump, I pulled out the book I'd stuffed into my pocket earlier. "Do you want to read?" This meaning, "Do you want me to read to you?"

Ellie Mae nodded eagerly.

⮜❧⮞

LYING UNDER THE willow tree on the riverbank or sitting under the red maple in our yard, me reading and Ellie Mae listening filled many of our afternoons. After *The Call of the Wild* and *The Small Rain*, I selected *Blue Willow*, a book I'd bought in Duluth. The story was about a lonely girl without a home, the way I'd felt in that tiny house on the alley. I thought Ellie Mae might enjoy it.

When I read, Ellie Mae usually sat against a tree with her head back and eyes closed. Sometimes, she'd stretch out on her back, her hands behind her head, legs crossed at the ankles, carefree. Her pretty, oval face showed no signs she was even listening, but I knew she was. When I paused, she'd open her eyes and turn to me, her forehead wrinkled. I wondered if my pause forced her attention away from the imagined world of books back to her real world.

"Is Janey for real?" Her first question came halfway through *Blue Willow*.

"No. She's a made-up person."

"She seems real." Ellie Mae rose and nodded toward Mr. Dalton's place. "He's real enough."

I wondered what she meant, but before I could ask, she went inside and returned with two glasses of water. "Here," she said.

I took the glass. "Thank you."

"Where's you from?" She settled back on the grass.

"I was born in Somerville, just north of Richmond, Virginia," I answered, taking a long drink of water, then holding the cool glass to my cheek to hide my uneasiness. I became nervous when someone asked questions about my past.

She glanced at me. "Your pa wasn't, was he?"

"No." I answered, still ill at ease.

"You'ns different. Your pa talks different." She pulled her dress down to her knees. The hem had been let out to make it longer, but there was nothing she could do to loosen the strain on the fabric around her waist and chest. "I's never been out of Lee County."

"You've always lived here?"

"Yes'um."

"You're lucky to have had a place to call home." My uneasiness caused a parade of worries to pass through my mind. When would Mom be able to sleep through the nights without worrying that a fence might materialize to trap her? Would I make friends? Would I ever be asked on a date? I remembered Maggie and me watching Patricia and Gordon hold hands in the park. What would a kiss be like? "Have you ever been kissed?"

"Yes'um."

I started to ask if she had a boyfriend.

Just then, Mom came onto the veranda. "Girls, please go to the garden and bring back any ripe tomatoes and green onions you find. I need them for supper."

We headed to the garden, admiring the roses we'd planted along the way. Later, when Ellie Mae and I entered the kitchen carrying two red tomatoes and half a dozen green onions, I heard Mom speaking with someone in the parlor. We put the vegetables in the sink.

"Let's go see who's visiting." I waved for Ellie Mae to follow me.

Mom was seated in a chair across from a stranger. "Trudy,

come in and meet Miss Walker, a neighbor." She turned back to the other woman who was wearing a blue flowered dress and a large straw hat that covered her head and part of her face. A yellow rose stuck out of the hat. "And this is . . ."

"I know who she is," Miss Walker snapped. She pushed her thick-lensed, wire-framed glasses up on her nose and scowled.

Ellie Mae slipped out of the room.

"Pleased to meet you, Miss Walker." I gave her my biggest smile, hoping to hide my resentment of the tone she'd used when she spoke of Ellie Mae.

"Trudy, is it?" Her voice was pleasant now.

"Yes, ma'am."

"Would you like a slice of zucchini bread and a cold glass of lemonade?" Mom offered.

Miss Walker adjusted her hat, touched the yellow rose, repositioning it, and then smoothed her dress over her knees. "That would be nice, *Edveena*. I wouldn't mind a little refreshment. Not at all."

Miss Walker added a long 'e' to Mom's name.

Mom gave me a wink. "Well then." She rose.

"I'll get it, Mom," I spoke quickly, wanting to escape the pucker-faced woman. She had plenty of wrinkles, but I was sure none were from smiling.

"Isn't the girl much help?" Miss Walker asked Mom.

"The girl?"

"That colored girl," Miss Walker said by way of explanation.

Mom bent forward and stacked the magazines on the coffee table. "Don't know what I'd do without her. With so much to do to get this place in shape."

"You've done a fine job. You have it looking like . . ."

I retrieved the wooden tray tucked into the side cabinet.

Ellie Mae opened the refrigerator for the pitcher of lemonade Mom had made after breakfast.

As we prepared the tray for serving, Dad came inside empty-handed.

"Didn't you catch anything?" I asked.

"Nothing biting except the insects. They swarmed me today. I'm half eaten." He saw the tray laid out with Mom's best napkins. "Do we have guests?"

"Miss Walker. You should meet her!" I giggled.

Ellie Mae snickered as her bare feet pattered across the kitchen floor to place the lemonade on the tray.

"Let me wash my hands, then I will take the tray to the parlor."

When Miss Walker left an hour later, Dad walked her home to look at the '39 Ford she wanted to sell.

$$\backsim\!\!\!\!\!\backsim$$

DAD RETURNED WITH a black sedan.

Excited, Mom and I ran out to meet him.

"Since her brother is gone and she doesn't drive, she said she had no need for this old car. What do you think?" Dad asked. "She said we could pay her whenever we could get the money together."

"It's very nice, Karl." Mom stuck her hand through the open window and ran it over the back of the passenger seat. "Let's go for a ride and see how it runs."

"Now?" he said with a wink.

"Why not?"

"Get in, ladies." He laughed.

"Come on." I called to Ellie Mae.

She shook her head and sat on the edge of the stoop.

                                      ◦⌒◦

ELLIE MAE AND I spent many afternoons together. We pulled weeds from the garden, scraped and painted window shutters, and completed the household chores on Mom's list. We also waded in the river or sat on the large stump sucking Popsicles and watching the clouds, sometimes trying to discover images or read our future. I told her about Granddad and how he read the heavens, telling me "good things are coming" or "a storm's brewing."

She talked about an aunt living in Mobile who also predicted the future.

I read and she listened, sometimes making a remark or asking a question. Yet, we spoke little of our personal lives. I knew nothing about her home or family. I still felt ignorant of the ways of Willow Bay and wasn't sure what I should ask.

Chapter 20

*T*he end of June brought beautiful nights, black skies filled with brilliant stars, and not a cloud to block the exhibition. Without a curfew, I was free to explore the heavens.

Unable to shake the deep loneliness that had plagued me the entire day, I strolled to the edge of our drive, away from the house and the artificial lights, to look at the stars and talk to Granddad.

I stood with my head back, gazing at the vastness of the heavens, my heart heavy. "What are the constellations you taught me, Granddad?" I asked.

First, I began counting on my fingers, Big Bear (Ursa Major), which houses the Big Dipper, and was easy to find. Second was Little Bear (Ursa Minor), host of Polaris. Third was Cassiopeia, which lay on the other side of the north pole opposite the Big Dipper, and fourth, . . . I couldn't remember. Tears stung my eyes as I tried to recall. My memories with Granddad were important to me, but I felt this part of my childhood gradually fading and was afraid it would soon be lost forever.

"You contemplating the heavens tonight, are you?" a voice asked.

Mr. Dalton and his Irish setter, Lady Belle, had wandered up behind me.

I wiped my forearm across my eyes and turned.

Lady Belle marched over and sniffed my legs and shoes and licked my hand.

"I was looking for the constellations Granddad taught me. But I can only find the Big Bear, Little Bear, and Cassiopeia. I can't remember the others," I said, heartbroken.

Mr. Dalton nodded, seeming to understand how important it was to me. He placed his hands inside the bib of his overalls and leaned to his left side, spitting a mouthful of tobacco juice onto the road.

"Well now, let's see. There's Cepheus, the king, but it isn't visible now, and Draco, the dragon."

"What about Orion?"

"Nope." He rocked back on his heels. "Orion's not in view now either. The best time to see it is in November and December, but by this time of year, it's completely gone from the night sky."

"Do you study the stars, Mr. Dalton?"

He watched Lady Belle head into the trees at the edge of his driveway. "Pearl loved the stars. We spent many a night surveyin' the sky." His voice trembled.

I didn't know what to say. Pearl was Mr. Dalton's late wife. I'd thought of Mr. Dalton as a person without feelings, much less romantic ones for a loving wife. Had I been wrong about him? "Granddad studied the stars, too, but I'm starting to forget what he told me about them." My voice sounded childlike even to my own ears.

"Well, Missy, you'll have plenty of time to learn." He

shifted his stance to gaze at me. "The stars will stay the same. You are the one who will change." He whistled for Lady Belle. "Night, Missy," he said, slowly walking away.

Lady Belle trotted by his side.

∽👁∾

AFTER THREE DAYS of cooler and drier weather, the hot, humid air returned and settled over us milking the strength from our bodies as the small town planned its Fourth of July fireworks celebration. Mom suffered most from the heat and carried around a small fan that simply stirred the hot air and accomplished little.

On the Fourth of July, Mr. Dalton came by for a visit. He and Mom were rocking on the veranda with frosty glasses of lemonade as Dad and I left for the town's celebration.

Red, white, and blue banners decorated the storefronts on Main Street across from the park. Large posters of war heroes were displayed in windows, and American flags waved from awnings. Families lined the sidewalks, ready for the sun to set and the fireworks to begin.

We saw Mabel and Joe standing outside their store.

They waved for us to join them. "How's *Edveena* handlin' this humidity?" Mabel asked, pulling a handkerchief from her ample bosom to wipe the sweat from her neck. "Lordy, how we're all sufferin' this summer."

Mabel, too, spoke Mom's name with a strong accent.

Dad smiled. "She's uncomfortable, so we left her and Dalton on the veranda drinking cold lemonade."

"She needs to have that girl workin' for her make up a

pitcher of some good iced tea. That might do the trick." Mabel stuck the limp handkerchief back into place.

"We'll do that," Dad said. "She could use some relief. And how's everything going with you, Joe?"

Joe, who had difficulty walking because of a knee injury, held on to Mabel's upper arm. "Fair to middlin', I'd say."

Mabel grinned and gave Dad a wink. Everyone knew Joe loved to complain about his health. "We'll try to meet up with you in the park, won't we, Joe?" Mabel wore a flowered dress and red lipstick, the red coating one of her front teeth. Her pink scalp peaked out between short, tight, gray curls.

Joe, a bit older, carried a cane, but I'd never seen him use it. Every time I saw them together, he was holding tightly to Mabel's arm.

"Be an honor," Joe said. "You look mighty pretty tonight, Trudy. Have a beau already?"

"Oh, Joe." Mabel shifted her body around to face me. "I do believe your hair is getting lighter from all this sun, don't you?" Mabel asked and leaned her head to the side to check out my hair.

Joe tugged on Mabel's arm, ready to move on.

"I see Reverend Taylor. Let's go hear the latest news." Joe moved forward on his own. The reverend was a main link in the town's news and gossip, and Joe was essential in passing both along.

While Mabel ran the general store, Joe sat by the door in a tall, wooden chair, chewing tobacco and spitting into a Maxwell House coffee can, ready to talk to each person entering or leaving.

And as Dad once laughingly said, "If the reverend and Joe

know the news, it's no longer a secret." That's how the whole community knew Dad had *chosen* to leave the university and move to Willow Bay to teach. The same news chain let Dad know that the people here were thrilled to have a teacher with his experience.

We moved along the sidewalk toward the hardware store. While Dad talked with Max Samuels, who worked at the store, I hurried on to the soda fountain in the back of the drug store. As I entered, a very cute boy looked up from behind the counter.

"Hi," he greeted. "You must be Dr. Herman's daughter." He smiled.

I nodded. He was tall and had a great smile. "Yes," I said, feeling a bit tongue-tied. "I'm Trudy." I blushed and hoped it wasn't noticeable.

"I'm Steve Foster. You've met my dad." He picked up a white dishtowel and wiped his hands, side-stepping to the freezer full of round ice cream containers. He picked up a scoop and gave me a grin. "What would you like, Trudy?"

I ordered one scoop of chocolate in a cone.

He grabbed a cone from a stack placed bottoms-up and reached into the case.

I felt I should say something. "Are you in high school?" Once the question was out, I was embarrassed. Of course he was in high school. Mr. Foster told us his son was a junior.

He grinned again.

A very nice smile. His brown eyes sparkled, with specks of hazel, from the overhead lights. "Yep. I'm a junior. Dad said you will be at the high school, too." He wrapped a second napkin around the cone and offered it to me.

"Thank you." I reached into my pocket and walked to the cash register to pay. "Did you get a reading list?"

He laughed. "Mrs. Weston, our librarian, makes sure every student at school gets a list. She insists reading is the way to improve our grades. I'm almost finished with the junior list. The books are pretty good this year. Yours?"

"*The Pearl* and *The Secret Garden* are my favorites so far. Have you read them?"

He leaned on the counter, his muscles visible beneath the T-shirt. "*The Pearl* I liked, but don't believe I've read the other one. I was probably too busy readin' Jack London."

I licked the ice cream to keep it from melting over the top of the cone. "I've read all of Jack London's books, too."

"You have?" He straightened and stared at me. A big smile crossed his face and his brown eyes sparkled. "Which was your favorite?"

My breath caught. I swallowed. "*The Call of the Wild*. I must have read it a hundred times." I held the cone away from my body afraid the chocolate would drip on my clothes.

"It's my favorite, too," he said as a family entered. His attention focused on them.

"I'd better go." I took a step back, almost knocking over a stand of cards, and hurried out.

Mr. Samuels was gone and Dad stood waiting. We walked across the street to the park where a large crowd had gathered on the grass—families sitting on quilts, boys chasing each other and girls talking and laughing together. I felt lost and wished I'd stayed home with Mom. But if I'd stayed home, I wouldn't have met Steve. I forced a smile, hoping to look normal.

I licked my ice cream, and Dad spread our quilt under a white oak.

He pointed to families he'd met and told me what he knew about them. "It's important to remember people's names," Dad said, using his teaching voice. He waved to a couple crossing the street.

I looked around for Mabel and Joe and saw them talking with a younger couple in front of the courthouse. They had not made it to the park.

"How do you remember everybody's name?" I asked, crunching on my cone.

"Association. See the man wearing the straw hat with the red-striped band around it? He reminds me of a dandy; therefore, I can remember his name. Randall, Randy Dutton. Randy always wears that hat. His wife, Ellen, is a very nice woman. They have three small boys."

I caught the last of the ice cream on my tongue. "What's a dandy?" I asked, my mouth cold from the ice cream.

Dad chuckled. "A dandy is a bit of a show-off."

Mr. Dutton, his wife, and boys searched the park for a place to sit. Mrs. Dutton carried a quilt over her arm with the colors of the American flag.

Beyond the Duttons at the end of the park were restrooms and drinking fountains. "I need to visit the restroom."

Dad nodded and shifted his position. "I could stretch my legs. My joints are bothering me tonight." He got to his feet. "We might run into Mabel and Joe on our way there, tell them where we are sitting."

We walked through the park, weaving around families squeezed together, most on quilts like ours.

Dad nodded to each group.

I smiled.

We were near the concrete-block building when some-one called Dad's name. Dad turned, and James Foster rose to his feet next to a woman and two girls crowded around a small cooler.

Mr. Foster owned and ran the Bay Drug Store. Dad liked him, and he'd been friendly and helpful when we'd first ar-rived.

Except for Steve at the soda fountain, I had not met Mr. Foster's family. He had a daughter, Brenda Sue, who would also be entering high school. I ran my hand over the front of my beige shorts. I was nervous. *What would Brenda Sue think of me?*

"It's good to see you and your daughter out tonight. Edvina's not used to this heat, I hear."

The two men shook hands. "She'll be fine. It's the humid-ity," Dad said.

James Foster was about Dad's age, but his receding hair-line made him look older.

"Don't think you've met my family." He lowered his hand, resting it on the shoulder of a slim woman with short, dark, curly hair. "My wife, Betty." He nodded toward dad. "This here is Dr. Herman, our new math teacher. He taught at a univer-sity up north for several years. We're lucky to have a teacher of such experience. Our first PhD to teach here in Willow Bay." Mr. Foster spoke loudly and people around us turned to watch and listen.

Dad squatted and stretched out his hand. "My name's Karl. Nice to meet you, Betty."

Her smile reminded me of Steve's.

"Nice to meet you, too. James has been telling our son that he'll be lucky to get into one of your advanced math classes. That boy needs to be challenged to get prepared for the university." She turned, examining the crowd. "Where is he? He should have closed the fountain by now."

Betty waved her hand toward the two girls seated next to her. They were happily sucking on grape Popsicles. "This here is Brenda Sue. You and Brenda Sue are going into the same grade." Betty looked up at me with a smile.

Brenda Sue had her mother's brown hair and dark eyes and her father's long face. Her face, like his, appeared kind and friendly. The pink sleeveless blouse she wore was from Sears. I'd seen it in the catalog and longed for it. She held her Popsicle away from her so the drops fell onto the grass.

"Hi," she said. "I wanted to call you, but Daddy said I should wait awhile, give you time to settle in. Do you like movies? *The Bishop's Wife* is coming, and we plan to see it." She tilted her head slightly to include the girl sitting beside her. "Would you like to go?"

"I love Loretta Young," the other girl said. "Don't you?"

"Yes. I love movies." I thought of Joyce and wondered what movies she'd seen since I'd left Duluth.

"I'll call you then," Brenda Sue said. "Daddy said you moved into the Davis place down in the bottom. It's pretty down there."

I liked Brenda Sue right away. "The flats are nice."

Dad put his hand on my shoulder. "Our daughter, Trudy," he said to Betty.

"Well, Trudy," Betty grinned, "this is Brenda Sue's friend, Charlene."

Charlene's eyes roamed over me, taking in my clothes and hair.

I felt her appraisal and was glad my blush was hidden in the fading light. "Hi."

"Hi." She stuck the Popsicle into her mouth.

Charlene was gorgeous. Her hair was light, almost blonde, and even in the growing darkness, I could see her perfect features.

With a shrug, she dismissed me.

"Do you have the reading list?" Brenda Sue asked.

"Yes, your dad brought it to me. And the books."

"Have you read all of them?" Charlene asked.

Her tone had been sarcastic. "Not yet. Do you have a favorite?"

She snickered. "I read a couple. Figured that was enough. After all, the books are boring."

At that moment, I wasn't sure I'd like Charlene. Her flippant attitude about reading was unfamiliar to me. I loved reading. So did Eddie and Joyce. A dull ache grew in my chest. *How would I fit into Charlene's world? What if I was unable to hold onto the false disguise I wore, the Paladin I pretended to be, and revealed the scared, insecure girl within? What if I didn't fit in here, in Willow Bay?*

"Let's get back before the fireworks start." Dad straightened. "It was nice meeting you." He said to Betty, Brenda Sue, and Charlene, then shook hands again with Mr. Foster.

"I hear you've been doing a little fishin'. Have you caught any of those smallmouth bass?" Mr. Foster asked.

"No bass yet. But I haven't given up," Dad answered.

Mr. Foster laughed.

"Give our best to Edvina," Betty said in a sincere voice. "I'll pay her a visit soon."

"She'd like that." Dad stuck his hands in his pockets.

"Bye," I said as we walked away, toward the restrooms.

Joyce and our trips to the movies were still on my mind when I came out of the concrete building. I stood, waiting for my eyes to adjust to the darkness and saw Dad helping a young black boy fill a jar with water from the drinking fountain marked WHITES ONLY. The fountain under the faded COLORED sign was broken, dangling at an angle from the building.

I was pretty sure the white folks in town wouldn't take kindly to Dad helping this boy to water from the white fountain, and the young boy's face held a look of fear and surprise when Dad gave him the filled jar.

He grabbed it from Dad's hand and ran away.

Dad waited until the boy disappeared into the shadows before strolling over to me letting out a long sigh. "It's hot and the other fountain isn't working." He lowered his head in determination and walked away.

I glanced into the shadows and saw Mabel and Joe walking toward the concrete building. I waved to them, then rushed to catch up with Dad.

∽

AS DAD AND I were returning to our quilt, I saw a section of the park closer to the river was now crowded with black families. They clustered together, parents serving food and drinks to the little ones. These children played catch with a baseball like the children on the white side of the park. And a group of young girls held hands while moving in a circle, singing "Ring Around the Rosy."

"I'll go see if Ellie Mae's here." As soon as the words escaped my lips, I realized what I'd said was impossible. Blacks and whites were separated and did not socialize.

Dad sat and scooted back against the base of the tree. "Come here." His expression was serious. He patted a blue square on the faded quilt that once belonged to Mrs. Downs's mother.

I joined him and wrapped my arms around my knees. "What, Dad?"

"Listen, Trudy." His expression was sober. "The color of someone's skin is not the determinant of the type of person they are. You should look at the individual. Many people don't because of their own history or absence of understanding. Few even know people of other races."

I nodded but wasn't sure I understood. I surveyed the park. The white and black families were clearly separated, as surely as if a barbed-wire fence stood between them. I'd never thought much about prejudice except how it pertained to me. Now, I recognized what Ellie Mae was telling me when she said Mom, Dad, and I were different.

I knew about segregation. For over two years we were interned, separated from other Americans, and confined inside a fence. We had been called to meals by a demanding bell and expected to line up for roll-call morning and night. We'd lost our freedom. But until now, I never gave a thought to the prejudice that existed elsewhere. I frankly never grasped the fact that other people were segregated, separated, and controlled in a similar fashion.

"Dad." I paused, not sure what I wanted to ask. "We are in the same park, waiting for the same fireworks, and celebrating the same Independence Day. So why don't we wave hello?" Across the park, I saw several black men who worked at the stores in town, even Negra Jones, who stocked the shelves for Mabel, and who, she said, she couldn't do without.

Dad shook his head, his lips pressed tightly together. "I guess people see only differences instead of how we are alike."

"Why?" I asked.

"Good question. I don't know, Trudy. These are good people, but this way of life is what they know, and they somehow justify it in their minds. Others are afraid, so they do nothing."

As darkness replaced the soft light of dusk, lightning bugs appeared, blinking on and off like tiny beacons. Many more people joined those of us already here, and anticipation for the fireworks grew.

My thoughts still on our discussion, I asked, "What's going to happen, Dad?" The strangeness of this reality re-awakened the fear that had filled me when we were in the camp.

"I don't really know, but change is bound to come. America is a young country, not yet two hundred years old. The end of slavery is a fairly recent event in our history. I believe reform will take place over time."

Around us, families with children crowded together and the ones who had not sought a space to sit, stood at the back of the park. I wished Mom had come to celebrate with us.

At night, I continued to explore the heavens for warning signs and then often lay awake listening to the sounds of insects banging against the window screens beside my bed. Occasionally, when the air was crisp, I could hear the splash of water as small animals slid from the shore into the river. I prayed that these clear, starry nights foretold a fresh beginning.

However, in spite of a safe home and beautiful surroundings, my nightmares persisted. I dreamed of the soldier, his eyes full of disgust and rage, and Ruth's face as her body weakened. I dreamed of Eddie and his family living in a destroyed city. Rumors were that many of the repatriated families may have been killed by the bombing after they crossed into Germany, never reaching their hometowns. In my dreams, when the bombs fell on Eddie, he slowly disappeared into the flames of the aftermath. I'd wake with my body coated in sweat. Many times, I climbed out of bed, pulled back the cotton curtains, found a bright star, and talked with Granddad. Some nights when I woke, I found Mom sitting beside me, telling me that it was just a bad dream.

Mom had nightmares, too. There were nights when the barbed wire closed in on her. When she couldn't sleep, she'd leave her bed and stand on the back stoop, looking out over the open field, or walk to the bench Dad built overlooking the river, and wait for a streak of morning light to appear. Occasionally, in her dreams, she said she could hear the guards' footsteps as they made their rounds in the camp. She told us one morning she would be healed when all she heard was the barking of a lonely dog or the chirping of crickets.

The fireworks began, and these thoughts fled my mind at the sight of the sky filling with bursts of dazzling lights and colors signifying America's independence. And ours?

Chapter 21

The following Sunday morning, we followed Mr. Dalton up five narrow concrete steps and through the white double doors of the Willow Bay Community Church. The buzz of conversations momentarily stopped as all sixty or so members of the congregation turned in unison for a glimpse of the new teacher and his family.

Mr. Dalton greeted several families as he made his way slowly toward the large cross hanging between two long, narrow windows.

Joe waved for us to join him in a pew near the front, and he and Mabel slid closer together to make room. Mr. Dalton continued toward the altar and took one of four chairs. The other three chairs were filled with older men staring expressionlessly toward the congregation.

"Welcome, *Edveena*," Mabel smiled, shifting her ample figure into a more comfortable position. As she twisted about, gray hair escaped the hairnet pinned on her head and fell down her neck. "It's nice to see you out and about. I'm glad you're feelin' better. But like I say to Joe, that humidity can get to anybody."

"It's good to be out. Willow Bay is a lovely town." Mom placed her handbag on her lap before sliding across the bench leaving room for Dad and me.

Joe chuckled. "I hear you've won over Dalton. He brags about your cookin' every time I see him, and he can be a hard person to get along with, that's for sure."

I noticed Joe wore a starched white shirt and, unlike the blue ones he wore at the general store, not one stain was visible.

"And that Henrietta, his housekeeper, is an excellent cook." Joe winked at Mom. "I think Dalton likes the company. He was always a sucker when a pretty woman was involved."

"We do enjoy having him, and it's nice having another person at the table who appreciates my cooking." Mom smiled at Dad.

Mr. Dalton often dropped in at suppertime and last week brought Mom a bouquet of wildflowers.

Dad teased she had an admirer, but Mom said Mr. Dalton simply enjoyed eating.

"Do you knit, *Edveena?*" Mabel asked. "A few of us get together ever-so-often at . . ."

Reverend Joshua D. Taylor, who'd been leaning over the pulpit talking with a man sitting in a front pew, raised his hands, and the loud conversations became whispers. With his hands pointing skyward, he began the service.

Mom reached for the hymnal stuck in the pocket of the pew in front of us as everyone stood.

Reverend Taylor called out a page number and led us in song.

The church had no pipe organ or piano to keep us in tune, and voices, many loud and off-key, filled the large building.

After three hymns, everyone took their seats.

Reverend Taylor picked up a glass from the dais and took a drink. Seconds later, he raised his voice and began his sermon on greed.

As the sermon got underway, the reverend became animated, and soon he was shouting, marching back and forth, wiping sweat from his forehead with a large handkerchief he'd pulled from his back pocket.

Between gulps of air, the affirmations streamed out so fast I found myself unable to keep up.

Restless, I squirmed in my seat and tried to figure out the letters carved into the back of the pew in front of me next to the torn hymnals. After several minutes, I guessed the letters "lo" and presumed it was a declaration of love.

Bored, I looked among the hats decorated with flowers, searching for the Fosters. I'd hoped to see Brenda Sue again. I had not heard from her about a movie, and not one soul without gray hair lived along our road except me.

I let my mind wander as my eyes aimlessly roamed over the parishioners. These Southern women seemed relaxed in their world. They strolled unhurriedly in their decorated hats and flowered dresses, their days endless and each minute as important as the next—cutting a rose or flowers for a bouquet, sitting on their verandas with family or friends, or best yet, talking with a stranger. They loved to tell the history of their town, especially the days when steamboat passengers stopped in Willow Bay and enjoyed a rest and a meal at the

Grand Hotel. Willow Bay had been significant back then, and they had been a part of that stately past.

Dad was right. These were good people who were clinging to times past and a way of life that was slipping away. They were anxious about their future, the same as me.

After what felt like hours of his screaming and restless noise from the congregation, Reverend Taylor calmed and ended his sermon.

I had not heard his remarks on greed.

And neither had Joe. Next to us, Joe was asleep, his head bobbing on his thick chest and his hands folded together resting on his swollen stomach.

The couples in front of us had either stared out the windows at the sun, thinking little about the sermon being yelled from the pulpit or were in a trance, no doubt letting their minds wander, too.

Most of us stood for another hymn before the service ended. Joe remained seated and Mabel took his arm to help him to his feet.

Mom bent down and put her hand under his other arm.

Joe leaned forward and slowly stood. He patted Mom's hand. "That was a mite helpful."

Mabel introduced us to Mary Jean and Millard Perkins, who sat directly in front of us. "The Perkins have three boys, who are allowed to stay in the back of the church and no doubt sneak out when no one is looking." Mabel shook her head and frowned making it clear she didn't approve of such behavior.

Smiling at Mabel, Mrs. Perkins explained that she ran herd over the three boys while Mr. Perkins was the local postmaster. Mrs. Perkins had worked at the county library on the north edge of town, but after the third boy, everything became too much for her. "I hope to get back to work before long." She clutched her husband's arm.

"Miss Gracie is here today, too. She's practically your neighbor." Mabel pulled down on her dress to straighten out the wrinkles. She ushered Mom and me across the aisle to the front pew toward a woman in a large black-and-white polka-dot hat with a bouquet of white flowers on one side. In the middle of the bouquet was a red rose. The woman's navy dress flowed down her slim figure, and the white shawl thrown over one shoulder displayed a small blue anchor on the corner, as did the white gloves she wore.

Miss Gracie Faye Butler lived at the end of Lee Street, a half mile from town, where the river had carved a U into the flat, fertile land. "I had my eyes on the Davis land for years. Hopin' my son would pick it up." She smiled.

"Miss Gracie is the largest property owner in Latimer County, and her father was a US senator for many years," Mabel said proudly. "He was highly thought of in these parts. Highly thought of. Goodness, his name is still respected around here."

Miss Gracie's posture and manner spoke of confidence, and her expression was that of a person familiar with power. Yet, she was as gracious to the country folks who said good morning to her as she was to the town's leading citizens and business owners.

Many couples came over to shake hands and ask about her health.

I watched the greetings and realized Miss Gracie, too, was well respected.

I liked Miss Gracie straight away. A playful twinkle shone in dark eyes that clearly missed nothing, and her graying hair was swept up under her hat, exposing striking features.

We said our goodbyes to both Mabel and Miss Gracie, as they discussed Joe's health, and walked over to join Dad. As we approached the group of men, I overheard Mr. Dalton say, "She appears to be a good worker all right, but you have to be careful with them."

"Dalton's right. Those negras can't be trusted," said the man standing beside him.

"Now, now," Joe declared. "Her daddy's done work for us. He was as fair as they come. Why, gentlemen, he fought for us in the war." He turned and limped back to join Mabel, who was now talking with Reverend Taylor.

Mr. Dalton nodded to Mom and me as we approached. "Well, well, here's your family, Karl. I better let you get home; you'd be wantin' your Sunday dinner."

"Edvina, why don't you and your family take your Sunday meal with me?" Miss Gracie had slipped up behind us. "And it's always a pleasure to have your company, Jackson."

Mom hesitated and glanced at Dad. "All right with you, Karl?"

Dad introduced himself. "We'd love to join you, Miss Gracie."

Miss Gracie took Mom's arm as the two walked toward the door. Mr. Dalton, Dad, and I followed.

The bright sun had heated the concrete steps and sidewalk as we left the coolness of the brick church. A leaf floated toward us, landing at Mr. Dalton's feet. For some reason, Duluth drifted into my mind. Last week, Mom had gotten a letter from Mrs. Downs who wrote how much she missed us. Apparently, her new tenants made too much noise for her taste. And Joyce, in her last letter, said her grandmother was ill. Joyce was going to live with her aunt in Michigan.

Miss Gracie's black Cadillac rested at the curb. "Jackson, ride with me," she said as her black chauffeur opened the door and helped her into the back seat.

Mr. Dalton stepped in beside her.

Oak Grove, Miss Gracie's estate, sat at the end of a long drive lined with large oaks. Broad steps led to a wide veranda. Eight soaring columns extended across the front of the white residence with blue wooden shutters to filter the southern sunlight. A white, laced-rail balcony allowed guests on the two upper floors to venture out and enjoy the flowered grounds.

The entrance was dark and cool. The wooden floor, covered by a well-worn blue-and-yellow flowered rug, shone around the edges as if recently waxed, and a wide staircase curved to the left. The entry itself was the size of our kitchen.

A large black woman with a huge smile greeted us at the door. "Welcome to Oak Grove," she sang. Her voice was deep, her words musical.

"Good afternoon, Miss," Dad said.

She took his hat and hung it on a hook inside the door. "Call me Tulah."

"Nice to meet you, Miss Tulah. Today will be another hot one out there."

"That t'is sur, that t'is. Tulah's just fine," she sang.

Dad wiped the sweat from his forehead and neck.

"How do you keep this place so cool?" Mom pressed the front of her skirt with her hands.

Tulah laughed. "We's keep everythin' closed up tight." She pointed to a doorway. "They's in the parlor."

Miss Gracie stood in the doorway with the hint of a smile on her face. Her hat was missing and her gray curls were neatly combed back. "This way." She motioned.

The parlor was like a room from a magazine: dark wood and red velvet, brass lamps and porcelain vases, portraits along the walls, and an enormous brick fireplace in the center. Above the fireplace was a portrait of a man with dark eyes, like Miss Gracie's, and a long face.

I immediately felt I'd been transported back to the time many of the people here fondly recalled—a time of stately homes and riverboat highways.

Miss Gracie stood next to me as I paused before the hand-carved mantel and stared at the man's stern face.

"That is my great-grandfather, Joseph. He was a power-ful man. Look at those eyes. They show his determination to make this land prosper." She placed her hands on my shoulders and turned me to face her. "I see a determination in you." She smiled and turned away. "Take a seat, everyone. Tulah will bring refreshments soon." Miss Gracie walked across the room to sit in a winged-back armchair supported by dark, wooden-clawed feet.

What did she see in me? Not the strength of a Paladin. I'd failed that test.

Light bounced off the polished brass lamps and shiny woodwork. The room gleamed wealth, power, and influence.

"This is a beautiful home," Mom said. "You have magnificent pieces. I don't think I've seen anything like this."

"Well, thank you, Edvina," Miss Gracie smiled. "What an interesting name."

"I was named after my great-aunt. She was gone before I was born, but I heard lots of stories about her. Papa loved to talk about family."

"Keeping family history alive is a good thing to do." Miss Gracie turned to Mr. Dalton and Dad. "Heard you two often go fishin'." She folded her hands in her lap. "Do you remember the days, Jackson, when I was your fishin' companion?"

The idea of Miss Gracie and Mr. Dalton fishing together was incredible and disbelief must have shown on my face.

Miss Gracie laughed. "Jackson and I grew up together, didn't we, Jackson?" she said as if reading my thoughts. "You'd be surprised the mischief we got into."

I realized why she was the only person to call him Jackson and wondered what Mr. Dalton was like as a boy.

Miss Tulah entered the room carrying a large silver tray holding five glasses of mint iced tea. She offered a glass to Mom.

"This looks wonderful, Miss Tulah," Mom said. "I haven't quite mastered the art of making good iced tea."

"I told them to hire some help. That's a big place they have," Mr. Dalton explained to Miss Gracie.

Miss Tulah nodded. "There's a secret to it, that's for sure," she sang.

"Would you consider sharing that secret?" Mom asked.

Miss Tulah smiled and nodded. "It's the cane sugar."

"Cane sugar?"

"I's show you sometime if you wants."

"I'd like that. Thank you." Mom took a drink and closed her eyes. "This is delicious."

Miss Tulah looked pleased.

Miss Gracie grinned at the conversation between Miss Tulah and Mom.

Mr. Dalton scowled.

Miss Gracie looked at me and winked. "Trudy, I think you might be good for Jackson—teach him what's happening in this century."

Mr. Dalton looked at her and scoffed.

Miss Gracie laughed.

The talk turned to politics as we sipped tea from tall, frosty glasses. Opinions differed on the direction the country should head now that the war was over. And President Truman? Well, they were saving judgment on him for now.

"This can't be an interesting subject for you, Trudy. The library is through there if you'd like to take a look. I hear you're a reader."

I blushed. What else had Miss Gracie heard about me, and who had she heard it from? Her knowledge of the new teacher and his family was obviously thorough. I wondered just how thorough. "Thank you." I rose.

She pointed to the library. "If you find a book you'd like to read, you're welcome to borrow it."

As I walked away, I heard her say, "Jackson and I somewhat agree on the direction. We disagree on how to proceed. What is your opinion on . . . ?"

The library was cool like the entrance and parlor. Two walls were covered with books from floor to ceiling, and a movable ladder that slid along a wooden rod rested in the corner. Tall windows behind a large desk overlooked a flower garden, and the room was filled with the scent of magnolia.

The African Queen by C. S. Forester caught my eye. As I pulled it from the shelf, Miss Tulah entered.

"Youse lookin' for a special one?"

"No, ma'am," I said. "I've been wanting to read this one, but I'm working on my reading list for school."

Her dark eyes examined me. "Ellie Mae says youse reads a lot." She did not move, her feet together and her posture rigid with pride as she stood by the door.

"Do you know her?" I asked wondering how she knew Ellie Mae.

Miss Tulah ran her hand down her white apron. "Her mather's my cousin."

At that moment, I was struck by how little I actually knew about Ellie Mae. I didn't know if she had siblings, a sister, perhaps, or brothers. What were her parents like? I'd overheard Joe say her father fought in the war. Though Mr. Dalton hadn't used her name, I knew that after the church service, the men had been talking about her.

I'd asked Ellie Mae about the ways of Willow Bay for my own selfish purposes, for my own survival, because I needed to learn about life in this Southern town where many of the residents clung to a past glory that had been the old South when cotton was high.

"Youse ain't her friend." Tulah's voice broke into my thoughts.

Stunned by her words, I didn't know how to respond.

Tulah turned on her heels and left me alone in the large room.

The social line had been unmistakably drawn, and I was more confused than ever.

Chapter 22

Heat radiated from the sidewalk as I walked past the construction tape blocking a section of the theater being remodeled. It was hot and humid, and I hoped we'd soon adjust to this heavy humidity. My blouse stuck to the skin underneath and my tight bra was uncomfortable.

A pot of cheery red geraniums rested in a wooden box next to the ticket window, their faces leaning toward the sun. I bought my ticket and stood next to the building in the shade, waiting for Brenda Sue and Charlene to arrive.

Two girls in line behind me bought tickets and came to rest against the brick wall next to me.

"Hi," one of the girls said. She gave me a friendly smile.

"Hi." Before I could say more, I heard someone calling my name.

Steve and a short, blonde girl came toward us.

A burst of jealousy shot through me. Steve was as handsome as the first time I'd seen him behind the soda fountain. And the girl with him was cute—not a single freckle on her pixie face.

"Hi," he said as he flashed his gorgeous smile. "Brenda Sue stopped at the pharmacy to see Dad. She won't be long."

"I'm Audrey." The short blonde introduced herself.

"Hi, I'm Trudy."

"Your dad is the new math teacher?" she asked.

The petite, little Audrey was a good five inches shorter than me, with a lively smile and friendly manner. Her short legs were tanned and her blouse was my favorite blue. I wanted to shrink. "Yes," I mumbled, feeling like a giant.

"Welcome to Willow Bay," she said with a friendly smile.

Being with Steve made me want to dislike her, but she seemed pleasant, and I was unable to stir up any hard feelings toward her, except envy.

A boy with glasses came over to join us. "You goin' fishin' tomorrow afternoon?" he asked Steve. "Hi, Audrey. Is this the new girl from up north?"

"Trudy, this is Joe Gillett," Steve said.

I felt as if Joe's eyes took in my height and freckles. My back slid slowly down the wall, inch by inch.

Audrey laughed. "Joe won a fishing competition earlier this summer and now fancies himself an expert."

"Hi." Joe moved to my side.

Oh no. He was also shorter than me.

`"You going to the movie?"

"She's waiting for Brenda Sue." Steve said in a sharp tone.

Audrey glanced up at him and raised her eyebrows.

"What do you fish for?" I asked, as Joe relaxed beside me.

His face brightened. "Bluegill and smallmouth bass. You fish?"

I nodded. "Dad and I fish in the river near our house. I haven't caught one yet, but Dad caught a bluegill recently when he went with Mr. Dalton."

"Where on the river do you fish?" Joe straightened. His smile widened, revealing a nice mouth.

"I'm not sure." I shrugged. "Not far from our house."

"They bought the Davis place," Steve said.

Joe smiled. "Wow! That's a nice piece of land. And real close to the river."

"Are you kidding?" Audrey groaned. "She's surrounded by old folks."

"They're nice," I mumbled. I felt the need to support my neighbors even though I agreed with her.

Joe lowered his voice. "You don't know them well. Mr. Dalton is always complainin' about somethin' or other. And no one has ever seen Miss Walker smile. She doesn't say much, but when she does, she's criticizin' someone."

Sunlight flashed in my eyes so I edged closer to Joe to get away from it. Steve turned away, and I assumed he wanted to get inside the theater and was looking for Brenda Sue.

"Miss Gracie is nice. Not a person in town has anything bad to say about her," Steve said.

"What do you think of Mississippi?" Joe asked as he removed his glasses and wiped them with his shirt.

"I haven't seen much of it. Except for Willow Bay, I've only been to Twin Rivers."

Joe altered his stance and opened his mouth to say something more.

"She hasn't been here long." Steve interrupted.

I wondered why Steve was acting strange—telling Joe about me before I could.

Audrey swatted at a yellow-jacket buzzing around her head.

Steve glanced at me, then at the line to the box office.

"Go on. Get a good seat," I encouraged. A steady stream of people had been entering the theater for the Saturday matinee. "I'm sure Brenda Sue and Charlene will be here soon."

Steve nodded and smiled. "See you later."

They got their tickets and went inside.

I was glad they'd gone. I was nervous around Steve, especially with Audrey holding his hand.

⚬ᕽᕽᘔ

FINALLY, BRENDA SUE and Charlene arrived, bought tickets, and we entered the theater. Large fans behind tubs of ice cooled the dark interior, and I was relieved to be out of the heat.

"Sorry we're late. Mom wanted me to give Dad a list to pick up at the store to save her a trip into town." The Fosters lived five miles north of Willow Bay on cotton land. Mr. Foster had told Dad he and Steve loved horses so they kept a few around. Apparently, Steve once dreamed of going on the rodeo circuit.

"I didn't have to wait long." I followed Charlene down the aisle. "I saw Steve and met Audrey and Joe."

Charlene chose three seats on the end of a row halfway to the screen. "Steve is here? He brought Audrey?" She questioned. "I don't know what he sees in her."

Oh no, I thought. Charlene likes Steve, too. I stared at her. She was so pretty—long lashes and silky hair curling around her face.

"Audrey's nice," Brenda Sue replied.

A loud noise above us caused me to look up.

Three black teenagers entered the balcony from a large window half-covered by a dark shade.

I watched as they settled into seats.

"They sit up there." Brenda Sue whispered in my ear.

"Why are they coming in the window?"

She and Charlene gave me questioning looks. "That's the colored entrance," Charlene said curtly.

"The window?"

"And the fire escape, of course." She tilted her head. "How else could they get inside? A door for them doesn't exist."

The WHITES ONLY sign above the door of the theater flashed into my head. I'd hardly noticed it. Would I even be aware of this prejudice if not for Ellie Mae? Could I have ignored it? Been blind to it? It felt like a rock rolled in my stomach and I held my breath. "Not a door for them?" I repeated, feeling sick.

To me, sharing a door made sense, but, of course, I'd never thought much about race or nationality for that matter before the war. Before Dad was taken away, I never imagined I would be hated because of my German heritage. Now, I knew better—nationality and race were central to how society judged us.

I sensed a stir and heard more commotion above us. Two more black teenagers climbed through the window.

I had trouble concentrating on the movie. My mind flashed through memory after memory like the motion picture on the screen: my classmates failing to see me, Maggie forgetting me, Dad being arrested because he was German, the guards giving us orders, Ruth reliving her childhood as

~

her body and spirit declined, the look on Lise's attacker's face, and, recently, the rusted water fountain, with the ugly sign taped above, hanging from the wall.

Charlene's comments played like a record over and over in my head. I sat immobile, unable to grasp a clear thought.

"That was really good, wasn't it?" Brenda Sue asked as we headed into the lobby.

"Isn't she great? She has gorgeous skin." Charlene gushed.

"She's so beautiful." I agreed.

Brenda Sue lifted her hand to my hair. "If you curled your hair and used a conditioner to make it shiny, you could look like her. You have nice hazel eyes. Don't you think so?" she asked Charlene.

Charlene shrugged.

Actually, Brenda Sue was just being kind.

I was flattered nonetheless and decided to experiment with hairstyles before school started. "Thanks," I said. "I like your hair short."

Brenda Sue wore her thick, frizzy hair right below her ears, but it looked good on her.

She crossed her eyes. "This stuff is always a mess. I can hardly get a comb through it and that's on a good day."

We laughed. I liked Brenda Sue's ability to poke fun at herself.

"So, you don't have any brothers or sisters?" Charlene pushed her shiny hair away from her face.

I shook my head. "You?"

"Oh, yes. I have two younger sisters. They're terrible. You're lucky."

"I've always wanted a younger sister."

"Be happy you don't have one." She stepped aside as a group of laughing girls rushed by. "They get all the attention."

"You should have a brother." Brenda Sue waved to a pretty redhead. "Mom thinks Steve's perfect."

Charlene searched the lobby. "Did Steve already leave? At least he's nice to you. My sister, Jeannie, wore my favorite shoes and ruined them."

Something shifted in my chest. What in heaven was wrong with me? I didn't want to think about Ellie Mae. I didn't want to think of her walking from Lowland through the woods without shoes. Life wasn't fair. I wanted to enjoy my new friends without guilt. After all, who was I to question why a doorway couldn't be shared? Or fret about a girl without shoes? I was fifteen. What happened to my carefree teens?

We said goodbye with promises to call.

"I need to go," my voice broke. Tears burnt behind my eyes as I hurried away. I was heartbroken. At that moment, I knew I would never be the happy-go-lucky girl I was at eleven. Ruth had been right. The camp had changed a young innocent girl into a teenager who recognized wrongs.

Chapter 23

*H*umid, lazy days continued. We were lucky to get a breeze up from the gulf and left our doors and windows open with screens to protect us from the swarms of mosquitoes, bees, and flies. Mom joined the knitting circle at church, and most of Dad's days were spent with his new colleagues preparing for the coming school year.

Brenda Sue and I talked on the phone every day, usually planning a time to get together. I loved the days she invited me out to their farm. Dad dropped me off, and Brenda Sue and Steve drove me home. Mr. Foster had bought Steve an old clunker to drive to work at the soda fountain, and Brenda Sue and I benefited from Steve's chauffeuring.

While at the farm, Brenda Sue and I usually went horseback riding. My first time was on a horse named Lucky, and my stomach was full of butterflies and fear from lack of control. But soon, I enjoyed the feel of the wind on my face and through my hair and the freedom of flying above the land and into the trees. A meadow full of yellow wildflowers where Brenda Sue stopped to pick a bouquet for her room became one of my favorite spots. I also learned that yellow was Brenda Sue's favorite color.

Occasionally, we walked the gravel road to Charlene's. I

met Charlene's father, Pete Rowlin, who was a barber. He was tall with a head of thick, dark hair. Her mother, Wanda, worked in the office at the elementary school. Charlene's mother and two sisters looked like her, blonde and pretty.

Charlene wanted to be a beautician and after high school planned to attend a beauty school up in Jackson. She knew about the latest fashions and styles. One afternoon, we lay on her bed and looked through magazines. We found a hairstyle that the three of us agreed would look good on me. With Brenda Sue's encouragement, Charlene cut my hair and showed me how to curl it. I loved my new layered look.

"Your hair looks exactly like hers." Brenda Sue held up the magazine so I could see the model.

Suddenly, I was reminded of the time I'd cut Maggie's hair and her mother had been upset even though Maggie herself had liked her shorter hair. A sadness slipped over me, and I wondered if Maggie ever thought of me.

Charlene had made a conditioner from mayonnaise and egg whites for her own hair and used it on Brenda Sue's. Thirty minutes later, Brenda Sue's frizz was gone, and her hair hung softly around her ears. Both Brenda Sue and I were grateful and agreed Charlene would make a terrific beautician.

My favorite days were when Steve, Brenda Sue, and I went horseback riding. That didn't happen often since Steve spent much of his time working on his car. Something was always wrong with it.

I liked Steve better the more we were together. He was smart, funny, and handsome. And Charlene was right, Brenda Sue was lucky to have him for a brother. When he couldn't go riding with us, he was still able to drive me home.

And he often drove Brenda Sue into town or dropped her off at my house. She and I walked into town for ice cream cones, waded in the river, or stayed in my room drinking lemonade and dreaming about what high school would be like.

One day when I went to visit, Brenda Sue wasn't feeling well. Complaining of cramps, she said sitting on a horse was the last thing she wanted to do. She insisted Steve take me riding.

The sun warmed our backs as we rode along a ridge. I pulled my hat low on my head to avoid sunburn or, more freckles. I was nervous being alone with Steve and worried about saying something stupid. He seemed relaxed next to me as we trotted downhill and alongside a creek. Water, sparkling in the sun, flowed over and around rocks in the creek bed. Steve headed up onto a rocky ledge, and I followed.

"Nice view from here, isn't it?" He pulled back on the reins and adjusted his hat.

Overlooking a vast valley, I could see for miles. "Mississippi is so flat and green. It's really beautiful."

He smiled and nudged his mount forward, down into a ravine where the creek bubbled into a tiny pool. "Let's give them a rest."

We dismounted and walked our horses to the water. Steve took a seat on a rock, and I sat on a patch of grass closer to the pool, hoping to cool off. Perspiration trickled down my chest.

"That ride was longer than I thought it was goin' to be."

His words were slow and perfect, except for the dropped g. Everyone in town ignored the g. But when Steve spoke, it was nice.

I blushed, hoping he couldn't read my thoughts. Right now, all I wanted was to stop blushing when he spoke to me.

The air was still, nothing stirred. The horses swished their tails, shifting positions to fight off flies to no avail. The flies continued to swarm.

"Have you traveled much?" Steve slid to the ground, using the rock for a backrest.

I smiled to myself as he adjusted his hat again, a habit of his.

I thought about the three places I'd lived before coming to Willow Bay. "No, not a lot. We planned a trip to Washington, D.C., but weren't able to make it."

"But you also lived in Texas and Minnesota." He said, his face shaded by his hat. "Dad told us. He was impressed your dad wanted to teach high school here in Mississippi."

My stomach knotted when he mentioned Texas. "Oh, yes, we did." My voice a whisper.

Steve crossed his long legs at the ankles. "What's Texas like?"

My whole body tensed and the sun became hotter. Think. Think, I told myself, tightening the lid on my box. What would I say if we'd lived in a small town in Texas? "Areas of Texas are dry and hot. Everything turns brown there during the summer. And big, creepy tarantulas can sneak up on you." I used my hands to demonstrate exactly how big. "The nights are warm and beautiful, the stars clear and bright." I immediately felt embarrassed. A dreamer's answer, I thought. "But in the winter and spring, it's beautiful."

"And Minnesota?"

I laughed at this question. "Duluth, where we lived, is cold."

"That's it?"

"People in Minnesota are kind and extremely helpful and friendly. We were there less than a year, and the winter was horrible. Lots of snow and cold weather. I mean, really cold."

He placed his hands behind his head looking more re-laxed. "I take it you didn't like either."

I took a deep breath. *How much do I say without arousing curiosity?* "I was young, and leaving our home near Richmond was hard. I loved it there, but, of course, that was all I knew. I was born there."

"I've lived here all my life." He lifted his head and looked around like he was searching for something special he could identify. "It's nice, I love the land, but I long to travel. I want to see what the rest of the country is like—see the world." His upper lip lifted on one side in a shy grin. "You're the only person I know who pronounces the *g*."

"I noticed." I laughed.

"Have you read all your assigned books?"

I knew he meant on the ninth-grade reading list.

I nodded, wondering what he would think of me. "You?"

The horses whinnied, and he gave them a quick glance, his profile showing his strong features. "Yes. I love to read. I take it you do, too."

"I guess I do. I've always read."

Steve gave me several curious glances.

I held my breath. Somehow, I knew he wanted to say something and was working up to it.

A serious expression crossed his face, his brows furrowed, and the firm set of his jaw told me whatever he wanted to say was important to him.

I sat quietly, not knowing what to expect. I was more nervous. I wanted our friendship to grow.

He took a deep breath. "Brenda Sue said you were surprised about the colored entrance at the theater." He studied his boots, a sober look still on his face.

I slowly released the breath I'd been holding and wondered why my reaction at the movie theater had been discussed. "I'd never seen people climbing through a window to enter a building." The words were true, but weak. Surely others in this small town must think the situation of teenagers using the fire escape to enter the movie theater strange? I wanted to ask what he thought but remained silent.

"Are things that different here in Mississippi?"

I was uncomfortable. I didn't want to endanger Brenda Sue's friendship or Steve's, or their parents'. "I can't really say, Steve." I let out a long sigh. "I simply didn't know about the entrance." The rock in my stomach inched forward. My chest tightened with guilt. I thought of Eddie and Ruth and the legend of the Paladins. What would they think of me? Then I felt Granddad's hand rest on my shoulder, giving me courage.

I stared into Steve's eyes, my expression challenging, my anger flaring. The rock flew loose. "Yes, Steve. I reacted to the injustice of teenagers not being allowed to use an open door because of skin color."

There. I'd taken a stand, and it felt good. Granddad's hand gave my shoulder a reassuring squeeze.

Steve inspected his boots again. "I knew you would."

My mouth opened. "Y-y-you did?"

He rose slowly, and his long legs took three steps to the

stream. "Trudy," he sat down next to me, "not all of us Mississippians are blind to these injustices, especially we younger ones, even though we are raised that way. We also see the wrongs. Right now, we don't see what can be done. That's one reason I want to travel and go to college up north so I can learn what the rest of the country is like." He studied me for a moment. "I would like to help bring about change someday."

My heart lifted. "That's good, Steve." What would he find in other parts of the country? Enlightenment? "But a lot of change is needed, because prejudice has many faces."

I didn't want to have this discussion with Steve. I didn't want these feelings to overpower me, drag me back.

He reached for my hand and took it in his larger one, his gorgeous brown eyes focused on my face.

I straightened, thinking he might kiss me.

He didn't. Instead, he spoke softly. "I won't tell others, Trudy. But be careful. People here are unforgiving. They hold tight to their beliefs and prejudices."

⁓

I LIVED A double life. One with Brenda Sue and Charlene, and one at home with Ellie Mae.

When Ellie Mae and I were alone, our days continued as before. We worked side by side, as was our habit, and in the hot afternoons, we read together.

Taking a break from canning green beans one afternoon, Ellie Mae and I took biscuits filled with ham and cheese and walked down to the bench Dad had built overlooking the river. We ate silently watching the birds and muskrats hunt for food. A blue jay landed next to us, and we dared not move until it flew away. Ants swarmed around crumbs that fell from our sandwiches, and flies constantly took bites. We spent a good deal of time swatting them away.

I'd forgotten I had Angel in my pocket until she fell out on the bench between us. "Is that yer dollbaby?" Ellie Mae asked.

"What?" I didn't understand what she meant.

"Yer dollbaby." She pointed to Angel.

I held Angel toward her to give Ellie Mae a better look. "Granddad whittled her especially for me when I was little."

Ellie Mae nodded, understanding. "I's have a lucky penny. My pappy give it to me."

We remained quiet. My thoughts were with Granddad, and I assumed Ellie Mae was thinking of her pappy.

Quite often, when Ellie Mae and Mom were busy and my chores finished, I walked to the bench alone and reflected on Steve's comments. "Be careful," he'd said. I was as uncertain, as before, how I should behave.

Sometimes, while I sat contemplating my inner struggles, a sandhill crane would swoop in and stand quietly in the mud on the riverbank, its brown feathers unlike the white whooping cranes we saw in Minnesota. Still, the bird reminded me of Joyce and her grandparent's farm.

One afternoon, Mom handed us a bucket and asked Ellie Mae and me to fill it with raspberries. Berry vines covered Mr. Dalton's fence, and he'd told Mom she was welcome to as many berries as she wanted. I grabbed my straw hat and headed down the road with Ellie Mae, swinging a bucket, beside me.

Willow Lane was the name of Mr. Dalton's farm. The house stood huge and white against the green of the willows that lined the gravel path to his veranda. I'd overheard him tell Mom the house had been built by a great-uncle shortly after the Civil War.

I knocked on Mr. Dalton's door.

Ellie Mae stood on the lawn with the bucket in her hand.

Henrietta, Mr. Dalton's black housekeeper, answered. "Miss Trudy." She glanced toward Ellie Mae and gave a slight nod of recognition. Henrietta was short with a friendly face and a perpetual smile.

"We're here to pick raspberries," I said.

She laughed. Her body shook. "I's make him jam every year. He's jest don't want to waits until I gits around to it. He's bein' ornery, plain and simple."

I liked Henrietta. "We'll make sure he gets a jar of jam."

We picked berries all afternoon returning home with a full pail. I had taken off my hat to cool my head and forgotten to put it back on. My red face and neck burned while Ellie Mae's pretty, brown skin had not changed. I was envious.

Mom pushed cold glasses of lemonade at us and gave me a towel soaked in vinegar and water for my skin.

I was hot and miserable throughout the night.

The next morning, Ellie Mae brought milkweed, made a paste, and spread it on my face. As the redness and pain receded, more freckles trailed across my nose and cheeks—no amount of scrubbing faded them.

Chapter 24

*L*ess than two weeks remained before the first day of school, and I talked incessantly about what to wear. I laid out an outfit, and then changed it daily. I wanted new shoes and begged Mom to order a pair for me.

I was nervous about entering high school, more so than when I'd started school in Minnesota. I was different now and my life was different, unlike what it had been in Somerville and Duluth, and I did not yet understand it or the conflicting parts of me.

Dad seemed to sense my apprehension.

"You're ready, Trudy," he said without taking his eyes from the newspaper in his hands.

I stood in front of the bookcase that covered one wall of the living room and, unable to find anything I wanted to read, moved to stare out the window.

"And youse look happy, too," Ellie Mae said.

I had not heard her enter the room. I turned. "Aren't you a little excited to start back to school?"

She gathered up plates and glasses from the coffee table.

Mom had baked a raspberry pie and brought Dad and me slices along with glasses of milk.

"I's finished with school," she said.

"You're out of high school?" I questioned, disbelief in my voice. Of all the hours we read together, Ellie Mae never volunteered to read, and I'd never asked her.

"No's, the high school's too far a walk." She stood by the table, balancing the dirty glasses on top of the stacked plates.

"But Ellie Mae . . ."

"Thank you, Ellie Mae. I'd planned to send those dishes to the kitchen with Trudy," Dad said, then returned to his reading.

Dad was still uncomfortable with Ellie Mae cleaning up after him.

"Yessur." She slipped from the room.

I glanced questioningly at him. "Dad?"

"Ellie Mae is not allowed to attend Willow Bay schools. The next township over has a colored high school." Dad folded the paper.

I knew Ellie Mae attending my school was impractical. Still, the fact she couldn't attend high school at all was so unfair.

"Dad, I thought everyone had access to public schools."

"Supposedly, yes. A 'separate but equal' law exists, which means colored schools are to be equal to white schools. But access is another matter entirely."

I dropped down onto the sofa, saddened. I'd heard the emphasis in Dad's voice when he said the word "supposedly" and recalled the broken drinking fountain in the park, and the strange entrance to the theater. Oblivious to her situation, I'd pranced around the house for days talking about what dress to wear on my first day of school. Now, I felt ashamed of my actions.

The more I thought about Ellie Mae, the angrier I became. Part of me felt guilty. I would be going to school and on to college like Dad. I might even teach someday while Ellie Mae would remain in Willow Bay cleaning someone else's home, barely earning enough to keep her family from starving.

I hated to admit it, but a part of me wished Ellie Mae had never entered our lives. If not for her, I could have pretended I was unaware of the bigotry and not think about racial segregation.

That she couldn't go to Willow Bay schools or she'd be stuck cleaning other people's homes wasn't my fault, nor was the fact she was black.

I straightened upright, stricken by a painful reality. Maggie wasn't at fault my parents were of German heritage or that my uncle was a scientist in Dusseldorf or that Dad had been interned. Yet, her actions had hurt.

I got to my feet and, with long strides like Ellie Mae's, headed for the river. The path made from feet stomping the weeds ran along the east bank of the Pascagoula River and close to the willow tree at the end of our property. I picked up a long stick and whacked at the bushes, daring a snake to wiggle out. I was ready to pound anything that moved.

I knew I had a right to dream about my future, to imagine going to college. But didn't Ellie Mae have the same right? We were both Americans. We lived in a free country. Then why was Dad taken away, and why was Ellie Mae's life restricted? What I said to Steve was correct. Injustices occurred throughout the country.

At times, I wished I was more like Brenda Sue and

Charlene. They only knew their own world and had never once that day looked up toward the hot balcony designated as the colored section of the theater.

I sat on the bench, hating all the wrongs I was forced to recall because of the struggles Ellie Mae faced and wished I was a Paladin.

I stayed on the bank listening to the water ripple over a log jam that had drifted downriver until the insects drove me home.

Later, in my room, my fingers caressed Angel's smooth wooden body, up over her carved chin and tiny ears. She looked so small now, but back when Granddad carved her, I was small. I fell back onto the bed, weary and alone. My emotions flew around like a lost bird searching for true north. I did not know which direction I was headed. My eyes closed and, from pure frustration, a tear ran down the side of my face into my new hairstyle.

I fell asleep, and in my nightmare, I was back inside the barbed-wire fence searching for an opportunity that would allow me to escape to freedom—a tiny crack, a pinpoint of light, an opening I could break apart. But clouds hung above and dark eyes filled with hate reached for me, and no matter how hard I tried, I could not stop my body from being dragged away from the speck of light I longed for. I opened my mouth to scream, and a large hairy hand covered my face. I clawed at the hand until I heard a roar from my lips.

When I woke, Mom was beside me.

"Trudy, you're okay, you're safe." She rubbed my shoulders. "Someday, we will be released from the fears of our past."

Chapter 25

On September 3, 1948, a warm day with flowers and trees holding tightly to the colors of summer, I entered high school. A dream come true. Excited and anxious, I showed myself as a normal teenager. The past—the barbed-wire fence and the dark eyes of the man who still invaded my sleep—would cease to haunt me. I felt confident. The war was over, and the fifties were right around the corner. America was moving forward, and so was I.

Thanks to my home studying, I did not dread school-work. Actually, I looked forward to it. I took a deep breath and smiled. Four years of high school in Willow Bay were ahead.

Twenty-one noisy ninth-graders, laughing and talking loudly, squeezed into Miss Baker's homeroom to receive class schedules and locker assignments. I tried to remember faces so I could place them later.

Brenda Sue, sitting at a desk between Charlene and me with her lips pressed tightly together, took my schedule from my hand.

"Let's compare." She ran a finger down both sheets, and then gave me a relaxed smile. "They're identical. We have all of our classes together." She handed back my schedule and turned to Charlene. "Let's see yours." Charlene was in neither our math nor PE class.

Miss Baker was our English teacher, and she made it clear the first day that she didn't like "any foolishness." "I expect this to be a good year for all of us," she said. "We are on this upward journey together." Her voice was soft, yet commanded our attention. Slender and pretty, her dark hair pulled back with a ribbon and big blue eyes behind wire-rimmed glasses perched low on her nose, she roamed the classroom. With a kind smile, she nodded as she passed our desks. On the white blouse buttoned tight around her neck, she wore a small rose pin over her heart. The pin was a gift from the man she loved and lost in the war, the whispers stated.

Mr. Tucker was my algebra teacher. In math, free books were given only to those who could not afford to purchase one.

"We're getting new math books this year," he said. "And the school district is short of funds, so remember, those books will be passed out tomorrow."

After the bell rang, Mr. Tucker called to me. "You did well on the review problems." He sat his heavy frame on the edge of his desk. "Clearly, you've had some good math teachers along the way." He chuckled.

Dad was right. I was prepared for my classes and, with Brenda Sue and Charlene by my side, I finally believed I could fit in.

Physical education was a challenge, however.

"We'll play basketball, not for competition with other

schools, just for the exercise. After drills, you'll be assigned to teams." Mrs. Adams announced.

I was tall, which meant most of my classmates expected me to do well. I had good eye-hand coordination, but for some reason, I couldn't sink a basket. The ball rolled around the rim before falling to the floor.

Most of these same students were in one or more classes with me where I excelled academically, therefore, they were tolerant and even encouraging.

The person who acted most disappointed in my basketball skills was Mrs. Adams. She seemed determined I do well and continued to assign me to different positions.

We reported to homeroom each morning for fifteen minutes for announcements and attendance check, and then from there went to our first class. Walking the hallway gave me a happy, peaceful feeling. I'd found my place. I wanted to laugh aloud. The dark shadows were fading. Soon, they'd be completely gone.

High school was everything I'd hoped it would be, and the days passed quickly. Life was perfect. October arrived with less humidity, but the temperature stayed warm.

Betty, Brenda Sue's mother, and Mom canned sweet potatoes and collard greens. Betty's garden supplied an abundance of both this year, and she was committed to providing cans of food to the Christmas relief box at her church.

Ellie Mae was happy to help, and Mom sent jars of each home with her.

Dad, Mr. Tucker, and Paul Conway, the other two math teachers, got along well. The men welcomed Dad to their small department, and Dad was glad to be teaching again.

The school buzzed with talk of a Halloween party. The Future Farmers of America grew pumpkins for carving and volunteered to decorate the gym. The area became a haunted mansion with ghosts floating from rafters, large black spiders, and lots of gray skulls and slimy eyeballs. The Future Homemakers of America members made cookies, brownies, and punch to sell. The money collected was to be shared between the two clubs.

Discussions about what costume to wear filled our days. We decided to be flappers. Charlene's mother had two flapper dresses in black and one in silver. Brenda Sue chose the silver, and it looked great with her dark features. Charlene helped us with our hairstyles and makeup. I was thrilled to be going to my first high school party.

Entrance to the gymnasium was free; however, each trip through the haunted house cost a dime. The fact that Steve was there without the cute Audrey lifted Charlene's mood, and mine, too.

The noise was deafening. The Andrews Sisters singing "Boogie Woogie Bugle Boy" along with screaming from those making their way through the haunted house made conversation nearly impossible. Once through the haunted house was enough for me. I did not care for the headless bodies, bloody corpses, or slimy eyeballs, and an uneasiness settled into me.

Brenda Sue, Charlene, and I stood in a line with others from our classes, ate treats, and waited for our chance to enter the pumpkin-carving contest. The dance floor was crowded with mostly juniors and seniors. The sophomores and freshmen hung around the games.

At eleven o'clock, festivities were over, and a group of

students was invited to Joe's barn. Joe and his friends were not ready for the party to end. Charlene wrangled us an invitation, but the people I recognized making their way to the parking lot were either juniors or seniors with a few younger students mixed in. All thirty or so students were dressed in costumes, and not knowing many of them well, I struggled to tell who was hidden behind a full mask. Everyone piled into the pickups and cars, even sitting on laps, and headed east.

"Joe is a junior, and his family is one of the few in the area who hasn't suffered financially from the war." Charlene whispered into my ear as we rode crammed in the back seat of a Chevy.

The state's economy had been hit hard with the fall of cotton prices, but the war had brought manufacturing plants and jobs, and Joe's family owned one of the plants.

"Joe would be a great catch," her voice low in my ear.

As we walked into a dimly lit barn, I wasn't sure what to expect. "I'm Nobody's Baby" was playing loudly, and voices and shouts of laughter rose over the music. Paper cups of punch were shoved into our hands. One swallow and the liquid burned my throat. I set it aside on a table made of long planks placed atop bales of hay.

The Lone Ranger, who I did not recognize, pulled Charlene onto the crowded dance floor.

Brenda Sue took a seat on the hay, talking with Linda Cramer from our English class.

I moved to join them.

A skeleton grinned, grabbed my hand, and pulled me toward a circle of students. I knew the moment he touched my hand, Steve was behind the mask. He led me to the game of

"Spin the Bottle." An empty 7-Up bottle was spun in the center of the small circle and whoever the bottle pointed to when the spinning stopped, the spinner grabbed that person's hand. Shouting, chanting, and laughter followed them as they went behind the bales of hay. Moments later, the pair rejoined the circle.

I squatted, along with others, and within seconds, the bottle pointed to me. Shouting and laughter rang out. "You've got a flapper," someone yelled, referring to my costume. "Have her dance for you."

The skeleton had been the spinner. Steve bent over, gripped my hand, and pulled me to my feet. We walked hand-in-hand behind a stack of hay.

I could see his eyes and mouth behind the mask.

He smiled and placed one hand on my shoulder, the other on the back of my head, and leaned toward me.

Nervously, I held my breath and closed my eyes. His warm lips pressed softly against mine.

He smiled again, took my hand, and led me back to the circle. Not a word passed between us.

After that, the bottle did not connect the skeleton and me again. In fact, it didn't point to me for a second time that entire night. I knew it was all a game, and Steve was seeing Audrey, but that didn't matter. I'd been kissed, and it was nice.

⌒∽

WHAT GIRL COULD have imagined the euphoria of that memorable Friday night being crushed on a bright Saturday morning?

I had slept well and late, and woke happy to simply lie in bed and relive the party over and over in my mind. Finally, getting out of bed, I stood in front of the mirror over my dresser checking for changes. I looked different. I was different.

I closed my eyes and touched my mouth with my finger, feeling Steve's lips against mine. I blushed, leaned forward, and checked my freckles. They were fading. I ran the brush through my hair and pulled it back into a ponytail. Mom and Dad would want me to share the evening's events, and I was deciding what to tell them when I entered the kitchen.

They sat at the table reading the *Biloxi News.* I smelled bacon, Mom's way of celebrating my first teenage party.

"Good morning, sleepyhead." Mom greeted with a knowing grin.

I hoped she couldn't read my thoughts. "Morning, Mom." I opened the refrigerator to grab the bottle of orange juice.

She rose and went to the sink to pour out her cold coffee. "Get four eggs for me, Trudy," she said. "Did you have a good time? Your daddy and I would like to hear about the party."

I handed the eggs to Mom and then turned to pour a glass of juice.

Mom screamed. "Karl! Karl!"

I turned in time to see the eggs leave her hand and crack onto the floor. Four large yellow yolks stared up at me.

Mom whimpered and crossed her arms over her body.

I reached forward and wrapped my arms around her.

She was shaking, her arms tight across her chest.

I looked out the window and felt the fear explode in my stomach. Tears stung my eyes.

The garage door had been painted with large, black,

zigzagging letters—branded like the cattle we'd seen in Texas. Each letter was sharp and distinct and as clear as the bold, black numbers on the buildings inside the camp. The words were unmistakable, but my brain refused to process the message.

I heard Dad move next to me.

"What the hell were they thinking?" His voice was loud and rigid. "This is unbelievable."

"Nigger lover," Mom read aloud. "Oh no, Karl. How terrible." She cried and rubbed both shaky hands over her pale face as if to erase the words.

I knew the dreadful wounds of prejudice inside her had been ripped opened.

"Hold breakfast. I'll get rid of it." Dad hurried out the door.

Mom and I stared out the window, unable to move. We could not walk or even turn away. Dad held a paint can in one hand and a wide brush in the other. With each stroke of the brush, the dark malicious letters became lighter and lighter until they were concealed beneath the paint.

The letters vanished, but a vision seared within us, and the effect knocked loose our hidden fears of being marked.

We sat at the kitchen table, the food untouched in front of us, as Dad explained. "Daniel Harvey, the principal at Latimer County High, called Nathan and said he'd heard we'd gotten new math books this year and asked if they could have the used ones. Nathan spoke with Principal Walker who suggested he contact the superintendent's office. Nathan talked with Sally Crawford, a secretary there, and was told to handle the situation as the department saw fit. That's exactly what we did. Two of Latimer's teachers drove over the week before school and picked up the books." Dad pushed away his untouched plate and picked up his coffee. "I never thought our decision would cause this type of reaction, and I doubt Nathan or Paul did either. They've been at the school for years."

In silence, I drank my juice, and Mom and Dad emptied their cups. I could hear Mr. Dalton's chickens clucking on their nests; otherwise, the morning was quiet. Sunlight filtered through the sheer yellow curtains over the sink, bathing the kitchen in a pale gold. One side of Dad's face was in the light, the other in shadow.

For the second time, Dad looked stricken. I'd seen fear cross his face before, but not this. This was more than not knowing what lay ahead. His eyes said he suspected our future would be filled with adversities. I was afraid Dad might not remain strong. What would Mom and I do then?

My heart pounded. What would happen now? Again, we had been labeled. I prayed for inner strength.

"What should we do?" Mom asked. "Will we have to leave again?"

"I think it's best if I give Paul and Nathan a call. Talk with them."

"I promised Miss Gracie Trudy and I would come by this morning. She has a few things she wants to donate to the Lafayette County Historical Museum, and Trudy and I were going to help her select the exact pieces to give them." Mom picked up her cup, saw it was empty, and placed it back on the saucer. "Some of the clothing may need a little mending, and I said if all that work was too much for Tulah to do before next week, I would help."

Dad pushed away from the table and walked to the window. With his back to us, he said, "Go visit with Miss Gracie. I don't think we should change anything. A bunch of kids could be responsible."

He turned toward us. "You didn't see anything when you came home, did you, Trudy?"

I shook my head. "No, Dad."

"Did Betty drop you off?"

"Steve, Brenda Sue, Charlene, and I were together. Steve drove. I didn't see anything though.

He nodded. "I was reading late, but . . ."

The phone rang.

$\mathcal{B}$y the time Mr. Tucker and Dad finished their conversation on the party line, most residents of Willow Bay knew the three math teachers had been targeted by vandals.

Nell Dutton, the telephone operator, who listened in on calls but sometimes had difficulty hearing over the crackling lines, often passed along inaccurate information. This was one of those times. Paul Conway's place had not been touched.

Instead, Miss Baker's front door had been defaced, and she'd called the police.

At 9:45 a.m., Police Chief Harry Castle drove his black Chevy up to the front of our house. WILLOW BAY POLICE gleamed in white block letters on the side. The car door opened and the lawman, a solid, middle-aged man chewing his gum energetically, slowly climbed out and walked to our door.

"I'm Chief Castle, Mr. Herman. Might I have a word with you and your family?" He stood in the doorway glancing around the room.

"Of course, come in, Chief Castle." Dad stepped back,

allowing the chief to enter. "This is my wife, Edvina, and daughter, Trudy."

"Howdy, ma'am." Chief Castle nodded and removed his hat.

The cowlick at the front of his hairline caused his blond hair to stick up. He ran his hand over it.

"Could I offer you coffee?" Mom asked.

He moved farther into the room. "Don't mind if I do. Thank you, ma'am."

Seated on the sofa we'd bought only months earlier, the chief took a sip of his coffee. A grin spread across his face. "This is mighty good. Kitchen work is not one of my skills." He took another drink, then straightened and cleared his throat, his face solemn and official. "Looks like we've got a mess here."

The chief crossed one leg over the other knee. "Minnie— Miss Baker—was frightened when she saw those awful words on her door and called me. I spent the best part of the last two hours with her, talking and listening, helping her settle down. She's calm now. The only thing we can figure is that whoever did this is not a student. The students know who the math teachers are. And that's the only department that got new books." He looked down at his pant leg and plucked at a nonexistent thread. "What made you all decide to give those books to *them?*"

I held my breath. Did the chief blame Dad? I glanced at Mom and saw her face was relaxed. I assumed she believed Chief Castle would handle the situation fairly.

"Have you spoken to Mr. Tucker about the donation?" Dad asked.

The chief cleared his throat. "Yes, sir, I did. Nathan said after contacting the superintendent's office, you three made the decision together."

Dad leaned forward and placed his forearms on his thighs. "That's right. We had no use for those books. I, for one, was glad the county school could use them. The content is fairly current and according to Nathan, they are newer than the books that school used last year."

The chief nodded. "Like I said, we have a mess here. Most likely the vandal is someone in the community who's unhappy with the decision you all made. Last night offered him a chance to let you know."

The chief's gaze shifted from Mom to me. "Did you two see anything?"

We assured Chief Castle we saw nothing unusual.

I worried about what would happen next. How would my friends react? I wanted to get away from the situation. "May I go to my room?" I asked no one in particular.

Dad nodded.

Saddened, I slowly climbed the stairs. As I closed my bedroom door behind me, I heard the chief and Dad making their way to the kitchen, probably for a slice of Mom's apple pie.

❧

"WE HEARD," WERE Brenda Sue's first words when she came to the phone Sunday afternoon. "I tried to call you yesterday but the line was busy. Were you scared? Daddy said he would run by to check with Dr. Herman today."

I didn't want to talk about this new nightmare. I wanted

to return to those past weeks of happiness. "The party was great. Didn't you think so?" Halloween seemed so long ago.

"Did you hear? Larry Williams asked Charlene to the football game next Friday night."

Even though I knew it was unlikely Steve would ask me out, I was glad someone else had caught Charlene's attention. "Was he the Lone Ranger? What did she say?"

"She said she'd let him know Monday at lunch."

"I saw you dancing with Dracula. Did he ask you out?"

"Oh, that was Eugene Gates. He's a sophomore, but I've known Eugene since I was in first grade. He's nice. But no, he didn't ask me out."

"He's cute. Would you date him?"

"I guess so, if Mom and Daddy would let me. They say I can't go out with a boy by myself until I'm sixteen. But I could double-date to the movies if you got a date." Brenda Sue's voice grew louder with excitement.

I took a deep breath. Maybe Steve would oblige. I held the phone with my shoulder and crossed my fingers on both hands.

I wanted to keep talking about school, the students, and my first party. For as long as I spoke about the happy memories, the dark ones couldn't rise up and overwhelm me.

Chapter 27

*W*eeks passed, our lives were much the same as before. I settled into myself and returned to the Trudy I had created, the previous scared girl hidden.

November arrived, then Thanksgiving was days away.

"Henrietta is going to roast a big turkey," Mr. Dalton said like an excited child waiting for Santa.

He'd invited us to share Thanksgiving dinner with him. He'd also invited Miss Gracie. Henrietta was right. Food was not the main reason Mr. Dalton often ate with us. He didn't like to eat alone, plain and simple.

"I invited Minnie to join us for turkey, but she's havin' company of her own," Mr. Dalton said when he dropped by with the name of a man who was setting up a Christmas tree lot the day after Thanksgiving. "Here you go." He gave Mom a notecard. "Trey Austin, the lot owner, is the grandson of our former mayor."

Mom had called Miss Baker the day after the Halloween party to offer support, and this initiated a friendship between the two of them. Miss Baker had come to supper twice since the incident. Both times, Mr. Dalton had been a guest as well, and the two of them disagreed on many social mores.

Mr. Dalton believed women should be homemakers and not work outside the home.

Miss Baker laughed at the idea, which made for spirited conversations, yet they both seemed to enjoy debating different points of view.

The week after Thanksgiving, Miss Baker spoke of the internment of Japanese-Americans during the war and assigned a five-page paper on what conditions were like inside those internment camps. My heart pounded as she talked about the subject. I sat stiffly in my seat, staring down at my desk while listening to Miss Baker's words. "The Japanese-Americans are the only group interned by . . ."

My head swam. The room became hot. *What about us? Didn't eleven thousand five-hundred people of German ancestry matter? Could the act of interning eleven thousand be ignored? Were our circumstances and numbers not important enough to mention? I had been reduced to a name inside a folder on Mr. Ridge's desk, and no one cared. Was no one listening?*

I forced myself to recall happy childhood days with Granddad and feigned an interest in the subject. During the entire assignment, Miss Baker never mentioned the internment of German-Americans. No one did. That internment was unknown to them, and I was glad, while at the same time, that lack of knowledge also troubled me.

That week was a difficult one, and even though we hadn't heard from him and didn't know where he was, I shared it with Eddie. I was surprised how much I wrote during those days—telling him how I felt and what I was doing. I wrote that no one in America seemed to know that we had been sent to an internment camp. I wrote I wanted him to come home so maybe we could attend the same university. I wrote how much I missed him.

I was glad when the assignment was over, and the class moved on to a different topic.

❦

CHIEF CASTLE DROPPED by once a week to report progress on the vandalism case and to stay for coffee.

Dad chuckled after the chief left. No progress had been made.

The words disappeared beneath layers of paint, and everyone pretended they had never been written. No one wanted to talk about what happened, and no one wanted to talk about the real issue. Neighbors disagreed over the word "discrimination." Family members held different opinions about segregation, and in Willow Bay, I was learning cases such as this were rarely discussed openly.

Miss Baker and Mr. Dalton were guests for Sunday dinner. Mom had invited Miss Baker to join the knitting group at church, and Miss Baker and Dad enjoyed a friendship at school.

Mom, Miss Baker, and I were cleaning up the kitchen when Chief Castle came by, ready with an imaginary weekly update.

He accepted a cup of coffee and a slice of pecan pie. When the time came for Miss Baker to leave, the chief jumped to his feet and volunteered to drive her home.

Mom remained standing on the veranda, having said goodbye to Mr. Dalton.

The chief and Miss Baker were already gone.

Dad moved to one of the rockers, and I paused in the open doorway. Sunlight warmed my face. Mild breezes blew up from the gulf, the warm temperatures unusual for late November.

"Did you see that?" Mom asked.

"What, Veenie?"

Mom picked up her cup from the small table between the two rockers and went to sit on the veranda, her feet planted on the top step. "You two didn't notice anything this afternoon?" Mom was better at reading people than Dad and me.

"What did we miss this time?"

I heard the laughter in Dad's voice.

"You two." Mom shook her head. "It's Chief Castle and Minnie."

I walked outside and took the rocker next to Dad. Once Mom finished her coffee, I'd promised to help make cookies for the church bake sale.

"What about Miss Baker?"

"I believe they like each other." Mom emptied her cup and sighed.

"Isn't he too old for her?" I liked Miss Baker but wasn't sure of my feelings for the chief.

"That's between them." Mom relaxed back against a column. "A gorgeous day for this late in the year, isn't it? But I think cooler temperatures and rain might be on their way."

"Nathan says you're doing well in algebra. Actually, he said you were one of his best students." Dad crossed one ankle over the other and rocked slowly back and forth.

I nodded. My thoughts were on Miss Baker and Chief

Castle. I wondered if Mom read more into their relationship than was there.

I glanced at Mom. She and Dad seemed content, enjoying the weather and the new life we'd built here in Mississippi. The sound of barking dogs floated on the afternoon breeze. A peaceful sound, one that allowed individuals to let down their guard.

⌒⟁⌒

SINCE SCHOOL STARTED, I hadn't seen much of Ellie Mae. After I got home in the afternoons, I spent time in my room completing homework. And by suppertime, she was gone.

The second Monday in December was a teacher conference day. I slept later than usual and woke to the sound of music.

Ellie Mae turned the radio to jazz as soon as she arrived each morning if it wasn't already on. She loved music as much as Mom, and Mom often listened to music and news throughout her day.

I crawled lazily out of bed and went downstairs for a glass of juice.

Ellie Mae was not in the kitchen.

"Where's Ellie Mae?"

"Oh my, is it that late?" Mom lifted her head from the morning paper. "I was reading about a snowstorm in Richmond."

"Isn't Ellie Mae here?"

During the months with us, Ellie Mae had arrived promptly at eight each morning since Mom preferred to cook breakfast. The clock showed the time as close to nine."Let's walk out to see if she's on her way." Mom folded the paper.

We waited on the stoop, willing her to appear. I imagined her walking toward us with her long, graceful stride as if she hadn't a care in the world.

Mom stepped inside, and I heard her pick up the phone. "I should call your dad," she said, but instead, she set the receiver back in place. A moment later, she returned to the stoop.

"Maybe I shouldn't bother your dad with this. She'll be along soon." Mom placed an arm around my shoulder. "This is such nice weather we're having again. I don't miss the cold and snow we faced in Duluth last year. I think poor Mrs. Downs is feeling the cold a bit more this year, though. Did you read her last letter?"

"No. I saw it on the coffee table. Is she all right?"

"Oh, she's fine but that car is giving her problems." Mom gave my shoulders a squeeze. "In the next couple of years, she will need a new one. What story will she have to tell then?"

I continued to watch the wooded path. "She's never late, is she?" I was speaking of Ellie Mae.

"Something must be wrong. I'm calling your dad." Mom stepped inside.

Waiting on the stoop, I searched the sky. "The heavens is awake," I said to Granddad, "bringing us blue sky and sunshine." A perfect day for standing on the riverbank fishing, watching dragonflies skim the surface of the water, and frogs snatching unsuspecting insects. I wondered if Granddad liked to fish, and if so, why he never took me.

"I miss you," I whispered.

Mom stuck her head out the door. "He's on his way." She turned back to the kitchen.

I heard her open the refrigerator. Mom loved her new home, especially the electric stove and large Frigidaire refrigerator.

Now, if only the nightmares would stop. A few nights ago, I'd heard her tiptoeing through the house to the veranda.

When Mom was disturbed by her memories of the camp, viewing the stars and moon, and listening to ordinary night sounds seemed to soothe her. Those nights, she spent several hours on the bench overlooking the river or on the veranda where the squeaking of a rocker singing *it's safe, it's safe, it's safe* reassured her all was well.

⌒〇〇

DAD PULLED UP to the stoop.

At that moment, I realized we didn't know where Ellie Mae lived.

When Mom had asked her, she'd answered, "Lowland, back yonder in them trees," and motioned toward the dirt path that led away from the paved road. To come to work, she took the path, a shortcut, through the small forest that separated Willow Bay from Lowland, the black community that sat on the low riverbank northwest of town.

Dad and I set out to find her. We went north through Willow Bay and took Roberts Road for several miles before turning left onto a dirt road leading to Lowland. Four miles later, we drove through a community of small wooden buildings standing high off the ground reminding me of pictures I'd seen of stilt houses built over water in Asia. Porches were filled with black faces watching us. We stopped in front of a grocery market with signs attached to the windows and outside walls advertising familiar food items: Campbell soups, Kellogg Corn Flakes, Orange Crush, and several Betty Crocker selections alongside Lucky Strike and Camel cigarettes.

"Stay in the car. I'll find out where she lives," Dad said as he got out and rushed up the steps.

Two black men came outside, stepping aside to let Dad enter.

A minute later Dad reappeared, and a store clerk accompanied him to the porch. "Not far." Dad stuck the key into the ignition, started the engine, and pulled forward.

After several miles, we stopped again. "Here," Dad said.

I stared out the window at the weather-beaten shack, not much bigger than the tiny family cabins at the camp in Texas. The roof of the porch leaned to one side unevenly like a bowed old man resting precariously on a cane—one mishap and he'd tumble to the ground. Broken furniture, rusted buckets, and washtubs cluttered the porch. A swing, once painted green, hung off-center by chains from the ceiling, two links missing from one side.

A small child sucking a thumb, dressed in panties and nothing else, appeared in the doorway, the door half-closed behind her.

We got out of the car and walked to the edge of the porch.

The child disappeared inside and closed the door.

A tire swing, hanging from an oak branch to the side of the house, caught my eye. A gift for the child?

"Ellie Mae!" Dad called. We waited at the bottom of the sloped steps, rotten and broken from time and use.

In Willow Bay, one rarely climbed steps onto a porch without calling out and waiting for permission. Not exactly verbal permission but more of a nod, an acknowledgement that the visitor had been recognized and welcomed.

The door opened slightly and the child reappeared. Tight curls clung to her scalp, and I wasn't sure if the child was a girl or boy.

Ellie Mae walked up behind the child and peeked out. "Howdy." She opened the door a little wider.

"Is everything all right here?" Dad asked.

Ellie Mae stepped out onto the porch and shifted her eyes to me. "My ma's feelin' real poorly."

The blurry-eyed, small child scooted closer to Ellie Mae's side. Flies bunched around her nose and mouth. Her tiny hand batted them away, and her dark eyes fixed on Dad and me.

I moved closer to Dad. The situation was disturbing, and I could barely keep my feelings in control. I felt rage for the ragged poverty Ellie Mae lived in, paired with an intense desire to help. I had never, in the hollows of my mind, realized or imagined such poverty existed only a few miles from my home.

I felt Dad shifting his weight from one foot to the other.

"What can we do to help?"

Ellie Mae glanced down at the child clinging to her dress and then back to us. "Youse wanta see my ma?"

"If I may." Dad placed a foot cautiously on the bottom step.

"Youse wanta come inside?" Ellie Mae backed away from the door.

"Wait here," Dad said quietly. He went up the steps and disappeared through the doorway.

Ellie Mae followed.

I climbed the steps and sat on the porch, my feet resting on a broken board.

The child, a girl, walked to the edge and stood next to a post, her eyes focused on me. She had Ellie Mae's round face, dark eyes, and smooth skin. "I'm Trudy. What's your name?"

She pulled the thumb from her mouth. "Hattie Benson." She stuck the thumb back between her tiny teeth.

"Would you like to sit here, Hattie?" I patted a board next to me.

Without speaking, she inched closer, her bare feet covered with scratches.

I hesitated, then placed a hand on her shoulder.

She smiled, her tiny teeth white and perfect.

"How old are you, Hattie?"

She blinked and again removed the thumb from her mouth.

I felt her hand touch my hair.

She took a handful and pulled it toward her. She smiled again and stroked my hair.

"Do you know how old you are, Hattie?" I didn't know what else to ask, and remembered Baby Joey from the camp enjoyed telling everyone his age.

She opened her hand wide. "Five," she said.

"Five. Wow, you're a big girl." My voice broke. My baby sister or brother would have been five.

Perhaps Hattie sensed my sadness for she leaned into my side. I felt her slight, warm body press against mine, and my arm tightened around her slender shoulders.

Ellie Mae came out and stood beside us. Her feet were bare, and her dress stained.

Over my shoulder, I looked up at her face. "Is Hattie your sister?"

"She's my sister's youngin. Wilfreda drowned last year."

"How horrible. I'm sorry," I stammered. "I didn't know." Of all the hours I'd spent with Ellie Mae, she never talked about her family. I was ashamed I had not asked.

Dad stepped out and placed his hat on his head. "We'll be back," he said to Ellie Mae.

She nodded as Hattie stood and clung to her legs.

No words were spoken between Dad and me as we drove home. We were lost in our own thoughts about the world we'd encountered.

$$\sim\!\!\infty$$

MUSIC FILLED THE room. A waltz played, and Mom sat on the sofa looking through quilt patterns.

I paused, taking in the comforting scene.

Mom got to her feet when she saw us. "Is something wrong?"

Dad gave a heavy sigh and took off his hat. "Do we have any food we could take to the family? I think they're suffering from malnutrition, and there's a child. I didn't even see a place for a garden, so I suspect no food has been canned or put aside. Lord knows what they eat."

He followed Mom to the kitchen.

I trailed behind Dad. He didn't appear as alarmed by what we saw as I was. He'd seen such places before, but I struggled to understand, to retain my balance as my worldview was tumbling. I slowly realized that at the camp in Texas, we always had hope and believed an end was in sight. I wondered if poverty was endless.

"How many live there?" Mom asked. She opened the refrigerator and took out several eggs and a jar of blackberry jam and then turned to Dad. "How much?"

Dad stepped to the stove. "Could you scramble a few eggs with potatoes?" He took three potatoes from the bin.

Mom pulled an apron from the door of the broom closet. "It's that bad, is it?"

Dad pulled out a chair from the table. "Yes. Pretty bad." He gazed at me. "Are you all right?"

Mom placed a cup of coffee in front of him.

"Thanks," he said. "Trudy looked into the face of poverty and its devastating consequences today."

"Oh, Trudy." Mom came over, pulled me into her arms, and squeezed tightly.

I fought back tears and sank against her.

"Let's get busy," She said softly after a moment.

Mom fried potatoes, eggs, and onions and put them in a bowl, and I sliced leftover breakfast biscuits into halves and smothered each half with butter and jam.

Once the food was packed, Dad rose and picked up the box. "Come on, Trudy. I don't think I should go there alone."

"Here's a little milk to take." Mom handed me half a quart of milk.

Again, we rode in silence. My chest hurt from distress, but now I couldn't cry. For the first time, I realized poverty and starvation was a way of life for many black residents of

Willow Bay. I wondered what would happen to Hattie. Or Ellie Mae. We were in the internment camp because of our heritage, and Ellie Mae was here because of her race.

In my eighth-grade US history class, the teacher had spoken of poverty. I'd sat at my desk and stared at the pictures of gaunt bodies and empty stares, not actually seeing real people. I'd failed to understand what the word truly meant. Poverty wasn't merely the lack of food and shelter but also the lack of opportunities and change.

∽⟋⟋∽

ONCE HER MOTHER was well, Ellie Mae's routine did not change. She arrived each morning with a smile. We never spoke of my visit with Dad, but Mom often sent food home with her—a dozen eggs here, a sack of flour and a sack of potatoes there. Mom also increased Ellie Mae's wages.

Dad learned that Ellie Mae's father, Luther Washington, served in the 761st Tank Battalion and was killed in Europe during the war. After Mr. Dalton confirmed the information to be true, Dad spoke with Joe about Luther, who'd performed odd jobs for him and Mabel over the years. The two men worked privately, writing letters to Washington, D.C., asking for any survivor benefits of service members killed in the war to be sent to Luther's widow.

More than a month passed before the army found Luther's records. After that, more weeks of waiting. Dad and Joe wrote two more letters before they received confirmation from a Colonel T. J. Bridges that compensation would be mailed to Luther Washington's family.

Chapter 28

*M*id-December brought cold temperatures and morning frost. However, I was happy not to contemplate weeks of shoveling snow as we'd done in Duluth, and the heavy coat Mom and I bought there hung unused in the back of my closet.

At the high school, Miss Baker was in charge of the Christmas program, as she had been for the past six years, and asked many of us to participate. Charlene won a part in the play, and Brenda Sue and I helped with the stage sets. For days, I spent after school hours painting scenes Mom had sketched on cardboard, stringing lights and garland, and hanging wreaths and stockings above a mock-red-brick fireplace Brenda Sue had so meticulously painted.

One afternoon, five of us were adding the final additions to the sets before leaving for the day, gossiping as we worked, when Jean Greene, a girl in our English class, asked Brenda Sue when Steve and Audrey had stopped dating. Both Charlene, who had gone to the football games with Joe Gillett, and I paused, waiting for Brenda Sue's response.

Brenda Sue shrugged. "Oh, they stopped going out in October. I don't think he's interested in anyone now."

My heart leaped for joy.

Charlene smiled and tossed her hair over her shoulder.

Tossing her hair was a sign she felt confident Steve would turn to her. But if I, or anyone else, thought he would ask Charlene or me out, we were mistaken.

At school, Steve was friendly to both Charlene and me but seemed perfectly happy going to school functions without a date. He gave his sister a ride to school activities and often picked me up.

Charlene continued to charm Joe, and he was always willing to be her companion. Brenda Sue and I had yet to be asked to a school event.

<hr />

FIVE DAYS BEFORE Christmas, Mom received a letter from Mr. Clayton in St. Paul. He'd sold one of her consignment paintings and felt the possibility of another sale within a few months existed.

"Perfect timing," she said. "We should get the check soon. He'll try to get it in the mail next week."

"I saw an ad for an estate sale near Three Rivers and thought we might drive over to have a look." Dad stood at the breakfast table. "We might find a few good quality items."

After breakfast, we headed northwest to the estate of Jeb Johnson. In the ad, a piano was listed for sale and Dad wanted Mom to look at it.

We drove past small family farms and larger plantations. The land, cleared to the road, was barren of its summer crop. Straggly, leafless trees lined sections of ditches. The life we'd seen in June lay asleep, resting, before again bursting forth with growth next spring.

I was daydreaming about Steve—I did that a lot lately—when the car unexpectedly stopped, throwing me against the back of Mom's seat.

"You okay, Trudy?" Mom turned and asked.

I got back onto my seat. "Yes."

"I should have been paying more attention," Dad said, scolding himself. "They surprised me."

Three deer crossed in front of the car. The larger deer stopped and turned, huge dark eyes reflected our images. Once the two smaller deer cleared the roadway and entered the trees, with four long jumps, the larger deer quickly followed and disappeared.

A few miles farther, a handwritten sign announcing the sale and an arrow pointing to a gravel drive were nailed to a tree. Dad turned into the drive and joined the line of parked cars.

"Can we go into town next?" I'd brought the Christmas money Mom had given me and wanted to shop. And, I wanted to see the town of Three Rivers. Charlene and Brenda Sue talked about a shop there they liked.

Dad's eyes grinned at me through the rearview mirror. "I figured you women might want to check out that little town."

Mom straightened her hat and picked up her purse. "I hope the piano is in good condition and has been tuned often." She opened the door, got out, and pulled the seatback forward for me to climb out.

The house was similar in style to Mr. Dalton's. It had been built in the mid-1800s with small square windows bordered by wide shutters and a large porch that held tall columns supporting a slanted roofline.

We stepped inside, and Mom was instantly drawn to the piano—an upright with tapered legs, square edges, and a simple, uncluttered appearance. As she ran her hand over the shiny wood, a short, stocky man with black, curly hair limped over and introduced himself as Charles, Mr. Johnson's nephew.

"The piano is very nice," Mom said.

"It's in excellent condition. The felts and hammers havin' all been replaced a few years back," Charles assured her.

"Did Mr. Johnson play?"

Charles shook his head. "No. My Great-Aunt Claire played. She kept the piano in top shape, but she's been gone for over a year now."

"Are you selling the estate, as well?" Dad asked as he glanced around the room.

The man nodded. "No one wants to run it anymore. And none of our family lives in the area except me. The war took its toll. Some of the farmers with foresight switched to a crop needed to feed the population, so they were exempt from service."

I left the three adults by the piano, ventured into the library filled with books piled on long wooden tables, and found a stack of classics. I debated whether I should buy one for Steve. I liked him and considered him a friend, like Eddie. Well, not exactly like Eddie. I liked Steve in a different way. Moving to the window, I counted my money. The books were a bargain, and I chose Dickens's *A Tale of Two Cities*. I could always keep it for myself, I rationalized.

Before we left, Mom took Charles's phone number and said she'd call about the piano within a few days.

We drove west into Three Rivers and ate lunch at Annabell's Café. After eating, Mom and I left Dad at the table with the *Jackson News* and headed for the shops.

At Pearl's Clothing and Gifts, I bought Christmas presents. I got Dad a brass pencil holder and a glass paperweight with a fishing scene inside for his desk, then chose a set of dark combs with rows of cultured pearls along the top edge for Mom. In the cosmetics section, I selected nail polish and hand cream for Brenda Sue and Charlene and a hand cream for Mom.

After I paid for my gifts, I went to meet Mom in the men's section.

"Are you ready to go?" Mom asked, holding up two shirts.

I nodded. "Is that what you're getting Dad?"

"Yes. I think he could wear them to work." She folded the shirts over her forearm. "I think I'll buy sweaters for Ellie Mae and her niece," Mom said.

I walked with her to women's clothing.

Later, as we started to leave the store, we spotted Miss Baker.

"Hello, Minnie. Are you doing your Christmas shopping?" Mom walked down the aisle toward her.

Miss Baker's mouth widened into a smile. "Hello, Edvina." She tossed a skirt over her arm. "And Trudy." Her eyes shot to the door behind us. "Actually, I'm picking up a few items for the Christmas pageant." She held up a skirt by the waist. "I saw these and couldn't resist." The black skirt was like the one she was wearing, but she was dressed differently than usual. The rose pin was missing and her blouse collar was unbuttoned. She reached up and self-consciously touched her hair. A wide blue ribbon was tied around the bun. And Good Lord! Her cheeks were rosy! She was wearing rouge!

"Do you need a ride back?" Mom asked.

Miss Baker didn't drive. She rode the school bus to school and caught the county bus into Willow Bay to do her weekly shopping.

Again, her eyes flashed to the door. "Thank you for the offer, Edvina, but a friend gave me a ride today."

"Good," Mom said. "We need to get back to Karl. When he runs out of news to read, he'll get tired of waiting."

"Bye." I gave a quick wave.

"See you next week, Minnie." Mom hurried out the door.

Dad was still reading the newspaper when we got back to the cafe but stood when he saw us. "Ready to go?"

"Yes," we said in unison.

As we walked to the car, the mild winter weather reminded me of Texas and our Christmases there.

A block from the café, I saw Chief Castle's car parked down the street from Pearl's Clothing and Gifts.

So did Mom.

She turned to me and smiled.

Chapter 29

A new year had begun.

I opened my eyes and scooted lower under the covers feeling warm and comfortable. Light danced around the edge of the window shade casting shadows on the wall. Spring of 1949 was not far off.

I thought of the past year and the small house on the alley in Minnesota. I could almost see Mom standing in front of the sink staring out the window as if her eyes were searching for anything that might threaten or take away our freedom.

And Dad, sitting at the scarred green Formica and aluminum kitchen table writing letters of application for local schools and districts from a list provided by a former colleague.

The wounds and pain of our internment so fresh in our consciousness, we displayed an unnatural awareness of our environment.

I lay revisiting the memories that had been shoved into a box like an unattractive sweater knitted by a great-aunt that must be kept, even if hidden away, to be pulled out and worn when she visited.

Now, in a different part of the country, we lived in a

home again and were creating a new life. Dad was pleased to be teaching, and he'd happily bought the used piano for Mom's Christmas gift. Mom was busy making plans to offer music lessons. Miss Baker, Chief Castle, Mr. Dalton, and Miss Gracie came often for Sunday dinners. At other times, we ate at Miss Gracie's or Miss Baker's homes. The six adults talked, argued, and laughed like they were longtime friends.

Mom had been right about a romance blossoming between Miss Baker and Chief Castle. After a Sunday dinner in early January, they'd announced plans for a spring wedding.

ONE SATURDAY AFTERNOON, Mom and Dad went to call on Miss Gracie.

I sat alone on the riverbank with Dad's fishing pole in my hand. This morning, Eddie's book had fallen off the single wall-shelf above my desk, drawing Eddie into my thoughts.

We had not heard from him or his family since they left Texas. In a phone call, Matt told Dad that he'd written several letters to our government and to authorities in Germany searching for news, and the replies were the same. Many were unaccounted for in the bombed cities, and the Gutschmidt name had been added to the list of the missing.

Ruth's son, Frederick, also kept in touch with Dad, and wrote that the American families who had left for Germany hadn't been allowed rail access at the Belgium-German border. Since Eddie's father had been from Wiesbaden, they would have had to make their way to the town on their own.

I wondered where they were and what Eddie's life was

like. Deep down, I knew he was alive, otherwise, he would have come to say goodbye like Granddad and Ruth.

High school was everything I'd hoped it would be. Still, often, Eddie filled my thoughts, and I pressed Dad to call Matt or Frederick for information about him.

I felt a tug on the line, and was hauled back to the present. Standing, I reeled in a clump of weeds and mud. I wasn't much of a fisherman but learned from Dad that sitting on the bank of the flowing river contemplating life's troubles was good for the soul. Day after day last month, I'd sat here reflecting on Steve. At times, he seemed to like me, giving me that special smile that made my stomach feel weird or letting his hand touch mine. He'd given me a book for Christmas, too, and had seemed overjoyed with the one I gave him. But he had yet to ask me out. I hadn't realized boys were so complicated.

I knew I wouldn't catch a fish. I hadn't caught one yet. Calling it quits, I made my way to the trail for home. Insects swarmed on this mild afternoon. Walking was difficult while holding the long pole and slapping at insects. I walked slowly, remembering to follow Dad's advice to watch out for snakes as the weather warmed.

When I got near the house, I heard music. I quietly walked up the steps and left Dad's fishing pole on the stoop. Entering the living room from the kitchen, I spotted Ellie Mae at the piano.

Her lean, brown forearms paralleled the floor and her long, slender fingers flew back and forth over the keyboard—the notes were loud and strong, and her face glowed.

Puzzled, I stood silent, watching, and listening.

After minutes passed, she stopped playing, swung around, and then jumped to her feet. "I's sorry. Yourse Mama said comes by for a loaf of raisin bread." Head down, she hurried from the room.

I followed her into the kitchen thinking I could never play the piano that well. "Where'd you learn to play?"

She shrugged and picked up the loaf of bread Mom had left on the table. "I's needs to get on home."

⁓

I DIDN'T SEE Ellie Mae again until Monday after school. She and Mom were in the kitchen making a berry kuchen. I joined them long enough to get a glass of milk and a slice of banana bread before going to my room to do homework.

I had just finished an assignment when I heard Dad's car pull up to the side of the house. I met him at the door. "Hi, Dad."

He removed his hat and dropped it onto a chair. "Did you have a good day, Trudy?"

I nodded.

He took a deep breath. "Is your mother baking?" He placed his briefcase on the floor next to the chair.

"Yes, sur," Ellie Mae said as she entered the room—a wide smile spread across her face. "We's knows kuchen be yourse favorite."

I thought of a surprise for both Dad and Mom. "Mom," I called. "Could you come in here?"

"What is it, Trudy?" Mom appeared in the doorway in the process of removing her apron.

"Ellie Mae has something to show you." I smiled and nodded to Ellie Mae. "Go ahead, play for them. They'll love it."

Ellie Mae lowered her head and gazed at her bare feet. "No, ma'am."

"Ellie Mae, trust me. They'll be happy to hear you play."

"It's okay," Mom encouraged, then looked at me curiously lifting her brows.

Ellie Mae shuffled cautiously to the piano, held her hands above the keyboard, and took a deep breath. Music filled the room. Again, the notes were clear and strong, the tempo perfect. The music flowed from her entire body, and no one could doubt she had a gift.

Mom's face held a look of amazement and admiration. She walked closer to the piano. A smile brightened her face when Ellie Mae glanced up.

The music stopped. Ellie Mae jumped to her feet, her hands clasped in front of her, and her head down.

"That was wonderful," Mom praised. "Absolutely wonderful. Why didn't you tell us you could play?"

Ellie Mae shrugged.

"Edvina's right. That was remarkable." Dad moved next to Mom.

"She's really good, isn't she?" I asked.

"Excellent," Mom said. "You're good enough to play professionally."

Ellie Mae shook her head. "Professionally?"

Her voice was full of doubt, but I agreed with Mom and was happy Ellie Mae had such talent.

Chapter 30

My life continued as before, and the following week, I had a day off from school. The temperature rose to the mid-sixties, but gray clouds blocked the sun as I walked into town. A chilly breeze blew through my hair, and I buttoned my sweater around me.

Brenda Sue, Charlene, and I were meeting at the soda fountain. Steve was working today. Even though he hadn't asked me out, I knew he liked me, but rationalized he was holding back since he was Brenda Sue's brother and she was my best friend.

As I got to Main Street, I saw Ellie Mae coming out of Mabel's General Store. Mom had sent her earlier with a list. She failed to see me, so I changed directions to intercept her to let her know Mom had taken a loaf of bread she'd baked this morning to Mr. Dalton. I quickened my steps, and when I reached the corner of the fabric store, Ellie Mae moved into the shadows of the alley, taking a shortcut to avoid walking along Main Street. I hurried to catch her.

The alley came into view. Ellie Mae was being harassed by a group of high school boys. Joe was the one I recognized first.

I jerked back behind the building and then slowly leaned forward.

One of the five boys knocked the box Ellie Mae carried from her hands.

"You stupid negra!" Joe yelled. "Watch where you're going."

The other boys laughed.

I didn't know all the names, only Joe and Paul, but I would not forget the looks of disdain on their faces. I wanted to scream at them, but instead, stayed silent.

Ellie Mae remained calm. Her face held no sign of panic. Her brown skin glowed in the narrow ray of sunlight pushing its way through the gray clouds.

Joe turned to the others, shoved back his hair with his left hand, and grinned.

He was showing off for his friends.

At that moment, I'd never hated anyone more.

Ellie Mae squatted to pick up our groceries.

That's when I spotted the broken eggs on the ground. I couldn't breathe. I reached for the wall of the building, memories whirled around in my head, a wooden toy top spinning faster and faster, making me dizzy. I was caught in random images from my past, pushing me toward a place that threatened to release the memories from my closed box and shatter the thin wall of denial I had built to live in. I was back inside the barbed wire—the library book in my hand and my feet frozen to the floor of the hallway. Lise's terrified face was as clear in my head as Ellie Mae's.

A moment later, Mom and I were staring at the eggs she'd dropped on the floor that awful November morning, the morning after my first kiss. The morning I woke happy and excited to tackle the world. The morning I thought life would be perfect and instead, learned the world had not changed. We had not escaped hatred.

I leaned forward again, strong, and going to Ellie Mae's defense. My mind screamed for me to help her, but I could not move. The stench of urine, vomit, and rotten food flooded my senses. Discarded cigarettes littered the dirt alleyway.

With the grace of an older woman, Ellie Mae sat calmly on her heels next to several empty, discarded pop bottles, the broken eggs in front of her. The other items had been put back into the box.

"Well, pick up your eggs, you cow!" a hard voice shouted. Then a roar of laughter.

I couldn't tell which of the five boys spoke. Fear from my past and fear of the future paralyzed me. What could I do? I alone couldn't change the situation.

Ellie Mae lifted her head, defeat and resignation written on her face, a look I'd seen before, the look worn by the women and men in the camp.

I was frantic. I was nauseous. I wanted her to yell, to scream, to fight back, but she could do nothing.

She turned toward Joe.

I recognized those awful words came from his mouth.

The rock tumbled in my stomach and my chest tightened, squeezing the air from my lungs. I rushed away, ran into the park, and sat on the first bench I came to. Tears streamed down my face—first, a light rain, then a torrent. I knew I would not act. I was a proven coward. The fear returned, and I didn't know if it was for Ellie Mae, myself, or both of us.

My body shook. I wrapped my arms across my chest, not

wanting to think of what I'd seen. I was sick with disappointment. How could I be unable to help?

I sat there, ashamed of myself for giving in to fear and weakness. I was also frustrated with Ellie Mae for not standing up for herself. Hate, fear, and anger, so familiar to me, surged inside. This time, some of the anger was aimed inward. Not standing up to those bullies, running away instead, was a terrible thing to do. I thought of how I'd felt when Maggie walked away from me after Dad's arrest. She'd been younger and was following her father's orders, a father she was frightened of. I had done worse, and only I was to blame. A braver person, a Paladin, would have helped Ellie Mae. After all, she and I were . . . what? Friends? Were we friends? Tulah told me we were not. Did Tulah know I was not brave enough?

My stomach quivered and tears blurred my vision. My nose dripped onto my hands. Suddenly, my body lunged forward. I vomited. Eggs from my breakfast landed on my shoes, a yellow ooze from the monster growing inside me. More ooze sprang out and landed on the grass in front of my feet, and a third time, until I was too weak to move. I sat there, head down, and watched the flies attack the yellow gunk. I closed my eyes. Minutes later, I removed my sweater and wiped my mouth and nose, then stood and headed for the park restrooms. Inside, I threw my shoes into the rusted sink and washed them under the trickle of cold water that dribbled from the faucet. I threw the sweater into the garbage, never wanting to see it again.

As I left, the WHITES ONLY sign over the fountain caught my eye. Next to it was the broken one marked COLORED. I kicked at the WHITES ONLY fountain. Again and again, I kicked, my wet shoe slipping from the porcelain. I didn't know what I wanted, maybe to have it dangle from the wall, as unusable as the other fountain. Unable to cause any damage, I attacked the sign with my fingers. I tore and scratched at the sign, but the nails in the wooden board did not loosen.

I was hopeless. I couldn't even remove a sign, let alone stand up for people I cared about. I took a ragged breath and glanced around, grateful no one else was here. I straightened my clothes, and, in wet shoes, I went across the street, pretending nothing had happened.

⸎

BRENDA SUE AND Charlene relaxed on stools at the counter, ice-cream-soda glasses in front of them.

Steve leaned forward on his elbows. He grinned when I entered.

Brenda Sue swiveled on her stool. One look and she jumped to her feet and came to meet me. "Are you all right?"

Charlene turned. "You're late."

"I'm sorry. I helped Mom this morning and got a late start," I lied.

"I thought your mom had a colored girl working for her," Charlene challenged.

Steve placed a chocolate shake on the counter. "Here you go."

Charlene glanced from Steve to me and back to Steve. Frowning, she hopped off her stool.

"Thanks." I sucked hard on the straw, the cold, sweet

chocolate soothing my throat and washing the horrible taste from my mouth. I couldn't stop drinking, and soon, I heard the slurp from the bottom of the glass.

"You all right, Trudy?" Brenda Sue leaned close.

Behind me, the bell above the door jingled. I swiveled around as Joe sauntered in, wearing a wide, arrogant smile, like he'd scored a touchdown.

The chocolate in my stomach became bitter and burned my throat as it spurted from my mouth onto the counter and dripped from my chin.

"Eww!" Charlene leaped farther back and looked down at herself. Running her hand down the front of her dress, she stepped away.

Steve grabbed a towel and shoved it into my hands.

"What's wrong?" Brenda Sue's hand was on my back. "Was it the soda? Ice cream?"

I wiped my face on the towel and shook my head. "Sorry, I'm not feeling well. I should go." I had no words to describe what had happened, and when I closed my eyes, the Paladins I aspired to join rode farther away.

"Let me drive you. Brenda Sue can cover the fountain," Steve said, placing his hand on my arm.

"No. I want to walk. The fresh air will help me feel better."

Charlene stood next to Joe when I left.

A perfect match, I thought, and rushed away.

Chapter 31

For more than a week, gray skies brought spring drizzle to match my gloomy mood. Guilt weighed on me. I was heartsick. My carefully constructed façade was crumbling. At night, unable to sleep, I stared out my window. I talked to Granddad and studied the heavens but found no relief. To lift the intense burden, I invented reasons I hadn't acted. None were valid.

I shifted the blame to Ellie Mae. If she had not gone into that narrow alley, after all, she'd lived here her whole life, she should have known better; if she'd gone to the store earlier in the day when Mom first wrote the list; or if she had spent a few more minutes inside the store this wouldn't have happened.

If, if, if.

I didn't believe any of them. At times, I felt her eyes on me and worried she could read my mind.

Mom allowed Ellie Mae to practice the piano for an hour each morning after Dad and I left for school. If that routine had been interrupted and she was practicing when I was around, she'd stop and turn to me when I entered the room. I'd smile, assuring her everything was fine, and go through the day wearing a mask.

The shame continued to eat at me. Each day, I wished she would finish her chores and leave. I no longer wanted to be around her. She reminded me of what I was: A person who'd looked the other way. A person who had failed to confront a group of narrow-minded boys.

By Saturday morning, the rain had stopped and the sun was out.

Mom asked me to help Ellie Mae plant the daffodil bulbs Miss Walker had given her the day before.

We squatted and worked in silence.

I tried to think of something to say, to reassure her nothing had changed between us. I was edgy and tired. Not having Ellie Mae in my life would be easier. Each time that thought surfaced, I felt badly and reminded myself to appreciate her thoughtfulness. My life had become too complicated, and I wasn't sure what to do.

"Youse still likes school?" Ellie Mae asked.

Her effort to continue whatever relationship we'd established earlier made me feel worse.

I studied the bulbs, pretending the onion look-alikes fascinated me. "Yes, I do." I lifted my head and looked into her dark eyes. Old eyes for a teenager. "You would, too."

She nodded slightly.

"How's Hattie?"

She smiled. Those old eyes sparkled. "Shes likes school, too. She does her homework every night, likes you."

"That's good."

"I's tells her hows much youse read and hows much youse learnin'." She scooted forward to dig another hole.

"Does she like to read?"

Ellie Mae halted, her hand hovering above the ground. "Shes don't have any books. The teachers don't let hers bring books home cause she's so young yet."

My breath caught. I couldn't envision a childhood without books. When I was young, books were my companions. They kept me company and took me to different worlds, worlds I could not have imagined. I wanted those worlds for Hattie and began mentally preparing what I would say to the first-grade teacher when I asked to borrow used books.

Mom appeared in the doorway. "Trudy, would you take this jam over to Jackson?" She placed the jar on the veranda and went back inside.

"Sure, Mom." I called not certain she could hear me.

I got to my feet, and at that instant, Joe and Paul drove by. They waved.

As much as I disliked them, I waved back. I knew what they were, but they were popular, so I kept silent. Several times this spring they'd parked at the end of the road and walked down to the river to fish. I assumed that was their plan today.

Ellie Mae looked up. "I's walk with you."

"No!" I said harsher than I'd intended. "You finish planting." My voice calmer, I smiled and made an attempt to be friendly by telling her I'd find a book for Hattie. But it was too late. She'd sensed the change in me, and from the dejected look on her face, she believed she'd done something to make me unhappy. My guilt became heavier.

I grabbed the jam and stomped away. I could no longer pretend everything was okay. I lingered at Mr. Dalton's as long as I deemed appropriate, pretending I was captivated by his collection of swords, asking questions I had no interest in and only half listening to his answers.

Since it was Saturday, Ellie Mae was gone when I got home.

"Trudy, what's wrong?" Dad asked from one of the two rockers placed at the corner of the veranda to get maximum sun during these cool spring days.

I strolled over and took the chair next to him. "I don't know."

"You were downright rude. That's not like you. You and she have always gotten along."

I nodded. If I tried to speak, tears would come. We sat in silence.

Dad's chair squeaked as he rocked back and forth.

What's wrong, what's wrong? played over and over in my head. Dad expected me to explain, and I didn't have the words. I wished Granddad was here, and I could crawl onto his lap and tell him how I felt. He'd understand. "You don't understand, Dad," I cried. "You don't seem concerned that Ellie Mae is black." My voice got louder. "Nobody walks anywhere with a black person."

"Oh, Trudy." Dad's voice was soft. "We shouldn't let others' actions define *ours*. Or what's right." He rose to his feet. "She's a good girl, Trudy." He turned and went inside.

I was heartbroken, my spirits dimmed. Dad was right, but he didn't understand the situation—my double lives. I had to do something, so I stayed in the rocker and devised a plan. I would arrange a school activity or a visit to Brenda Sue's on Saturday mornings. I would avoid Ellie Mae and ease my guilt.

I became worried that if any of our neighbors found out

Mom was teaching Ellie Mae music and allowing her to practice, Mom would be shunned. All of us would be shunned, or worse. In a book Steve loaned me, homes of white folks here in Mississippi had been burned for befriending a black family. Didn't Mom realize what she was risking? Look what happened after the math books had been given to the county school.

For the first time I could remember, I was disappointed in my parents. They didn't care what was at risk for me. How could they expect me to go through the rejection I'd suffered in Somerville? I convinced myself my parents had changed into people I did not know and were naïve of the ways of Willow Bay.

A week later, friction still existed between my parents and me. They'd noticed the change in my behavior toward Ellie Mae.

As usual, Mom sided with Dad.

"Each action is a choice. And remember, Trudy, your life is built on those choices."

I ignored her and went ahead with my plan. I volunteered as a student tutor in Miss Baker's class, joined after-school track, and spent a lot of time with Brenda Sue. Since she also joined the track team, a practice run was a ready excuse to spend Saturday mornings at her house. But I ignored Steve these days. I was too confused with my own life to care about him.

I rarely saw Ellie Mae and meals with my parents were downright agony. They never lectured or criticized. Their voices were calm, too calm, but the worst part was the regret and disappointment in their eyes when they looked at me.

In the evenings, once my homework was done, I hid in my room—reading or listening to a music station from New Orleans on the radio I'd gotten for Christmas. I began to enjoy jazz and learned to recognize songs Ellie Mae played. Loneliness returned, the deep loneliness I'd experienced in Somerville, and I wished for a friend to talk with, but who in Willow Bay would understand?

On a rainy, windy spring evening, I was at my desk having completed a history paper on the Louisiana Purchase. In 1803, US representatives in Paris agreed to purchase land stretching from the Mississippi River to the Rocky Mountains and from the Gulf of Mexico to Canada. This land included parts of Texas.

I had not spoken to anyone about our years in Texas. No one. I pulled secrets from my box, examined them, and then picked up my pencil and wrote to Eddie. I wrote of our time together in Texas. I wrote of my return to Somerville to find our home sold. I wrote of Duluth and Willow Bay. I wiped the tears from my face, blew my nose, and continued. I told him of my life here, my double lives. I wrote pages and soon felt Eddie there in the room with me. I wrote until the lid on my box of secrets closed easily. I wrote until I fell asleep, my head atop the words only Eddie would understand.

I continued to write Eddie every night, pouring out my guilt and private thoughts. Words streamed, secrets flowed, a chain in motion, until the lead in my pencils no longer marked the paper. Then I slipped the pages into a drawer safely beneath my socks, wishing I knew what Eddie was doing.

Chapter 32

J'd run five miles and was limping up the drive to our house when a faded blue, white-topped Buick with a missing hubcap and broken rear window pulled up alongside and continued to the back of the house.

Ellie Mae ran out and opened the passenger door. She glanced my way, then stood with the door open behind her. A smile crossed her face. "Miss Trudy," she said formally. "This is my boyfriend, Owen Barker." She stuck her head inside the car.

A moment later, the driver's door opened and a large, good-looking black man stepped out. He stood over six feet with broad shoulders and a thick neck.

I stared. His short hair curled tight around his head.

His large eyes roamed brazenly over me as if measuring me for a costume. He smiled. An infectious, cocky grin.

Ellie Mae walked around and took his hand. "Owen and I is seein' each other. He's been takin' me to the Blue Tavern. I's been playin' the piano there."

Ellie Mae had a life outside our home? I realized we were her employer but was that all my family meant to her? She had become such a big part of our lives. "Hello, Owen."

He bent slightly at the waist. "Howdy, ma'am. Ellie plays mighty good. They's likes it a lot."

I was disturbed Owen used her first name only. And everybody in Willow Bay knew of the Blue Tavern—a honky-tonk about twenty-five miles south on the river. A place no person I knew would even think of visiting. We'd heard drunken brawls broke out there on weekends, and a month after we moved here, a man was stabbed to death one night in a fight over a dog. People in Willow Bay simply shook their heads when they spoke of that place. "The Blue Tavern? Do you like to play there?" I asked.

She gazed adoringly at Owen. "They's pays me to play. Put change money into a jar for me, don't they's, Owen?"

He slipped his tree-trunk arm around Ellie Mae's waist. "We's big plans, right, Ellie?"

I stepped closer. I was liking Owen less and less. He was too charming and obliging. "What kind of plans?" I demanded, suddenly feeling protective of Ellie Mae.

"Well." He gave me one of his cocky grins and pulled Ellie Mae close. "We's may end up in a club all the ways up in Jackson."

"Do you play?" I squatted to tie a shoe-lace dragging on the ground. His large hand hanging at his side could easily play an instrument.

"Naw. I's sing, and Ellie's the best player I's ever performed with."

"He's good." Ellie Mae came to his defense. "He knows all of Ellington's and Gillespie's songs. He sounds an awful lot likes Charlie Parker."

Pleased by Ellie Mae's praise, Owen straightened and opened the car door. "We's should git goin'."

Ellie Mae scooted into the front seat from the driver's side. "Bye." She waved as they backed down the drive.

Ellie Mae was playing at the Blue Tavern. I couldn't wait to tell Mom and Dad. They would be as upset as I was to think of her in that dangerous place.

⌒∽

"WE HAVE NO right to interfere in her life," Dad said. "We don't know what kind of person Owen is, but if he's who Ellie Mae wants to date, she can make the choice. She's nineteen."

"But, Dad, he takes her to the Blue Tavern. And he's a lot older than Ellie Mae. I didn't like him." My voice became louder.

"Trudy, it's not our business." Dad shook his head.

I wanted Mom to be upset about Owen. Instead, she basically repeated what Dad said. "Ellie Mae lives her own life. Whatever she does is not our concern."

"Don't you think you should warn her to be careful? Mom, he's much older than she is," I said, describing Owen again. "And Ellie Mae is too trusting."

"Trudy, what's gotten into you? Ellie Mae will make her own decisions." Dad picked up the newspaper and went out onto the veranda.

Mom went to the piano.

I followed.

"Mom, Ellie Mae isn't much older than me," I pleaded as I moved closer. "Owen is no good! He's going to get her in trouble," I shouted, shocking myself as much as Mom. I had no idea where those words came from.

Mom stopped playing and looked at me. "And how do you know that, young lady?"

"He looked at me funny." I didn't know how to describe the uneasiness I'd felt when Owen's eyes roamed over me.

Mom nodded. "Well, you're a very pretty girl, and boys will notice."

"But Mom . . ."

"Lord, Trudy. What's wrong with you lately?" Her fingers glided over the keys, playing *The Viennese Waltz.*

"Mom! Don't you care about Ellie Mae at all?" I cried, ran to my room, and slammed the door. "What has gotten into you, Trudy?" That was all my parents said when I wanted to talk to them. Nothing had "gotten into me," I thought bitterly. They were the problem. They were happy with their lives here and had stopped seeing the world as it is.

I turned on my radio and threw myself down on the bed, shoes and all. What *was* wrong with me lately? I worked hard to fit in and be like the other students at Willow Bay High. Every time I thought I was making progress, I got knocked off-center.

I rose and went to my desk, pulled memories from my box again, and wrote to Eddie. These were good memories. Memories of us riding the bus to Ashland to meet Mom for lunch. Memories of reading to Ruth, and memories of playing match—recalling how swiftly his hands dealt the cards. "Oh, Eddie, I don't know what to do," I said aloud. I needed someone *real* to talk to. I wished I could call Steve. Tears trickled down my cheeks into my mouth. Suddenly, I thought of someone who might understand, who could advise me. I jumped to my feet.

I felt lighter, and Miss Walker's colorful flower garden lifted my spirits as I headed along the road. A butterfly, yellow and black, fluttered around a pink petunia. I'd seen similar butterflies in Duluth where the spring temperatures were much cooler.

"Life has a way of adjusting to its environment," Mr. Porter, our science teacher, said last week. I thought of how Mom and Dad had changed in our short time here.

Tulah opened the door after the first knock.

"Hi, Miss Tulah."

"Miss Trudy. Come in," she sang. "I's a git Miss Gracie."

That's when I noticed a slip of paper in her hand. I thought I saw Ellie Mae's name on it before she slid it into her apron pocket.

"She's finished hers lunch."

Having second thoughts now, I was nervous. Should I tell Miss Gracie about Ellie Mae and Owen? She'd probably ask what my parents said about the situation.

"Trudy, come in. I do so enjoy a visit from my neighbors." Miss Gracie wore a long black skirt and dark green blouse. Pearls adorned her neck and hung from her ears, and her hair was pulled back, leaving her strong features exposed.

I glanced down at my wrinkly shorts and running shoes.

"How are Edvina and Karl?"

"They're fine. Thank you for asking, ma'am." I quickly decided not to speak to Miss Gracie about how I felt. She thought highly of Mom and Dad. She'd told me so.

My throat was dry from the walk.

As if reading my mind, Miss Gracie asked, "Would you

like something to drink? I see you still have on your runnin' clothes."

I wiped my hands on my shorts.

"Have a seat and tell me how school is going." Miss Gracie took her seat in the regal chair, a queen ready to listen to her subject. Sunlight hit the top of her chair presenting a halo effect. My eyes flew to the portrait of her great-grandfather and a strong family resemblance was clearly visible.

Tulah came in carrying a tray with a glass of water and several oatmeal cookies. "School's fine, ma'am."

Miss Gracie nodded. "Your mother said you've adjusted very well to high school. Good grades. Tell me, do you like school here?" She placed one hand over the other.

"Mostly." At the moment, I felt I didn't belong anywhere in the state of Mississippi.

She lifted an eyebrow. Waiting.

I emptied the glass and placed it back on the tray. "Actually, I dropped in to borrow a book on the Civil War for a history report."

Her eyes widened.

I knew she doubted that was the real reason I'd arrived so unexpectedly at her door. Nonetheless, she was happy to loan me a book.

Not until I was leaving did I find myself alone again with Tulah. "Miss Tulah, do you know Owen Barker?"

She paused and studied me, then slid her hand into the pocket of her apron. "Yes'um, I's do. He's as poison as a sidewinder. Don't youse go and have nothin' to do with him, you hear?"

◦๑๏

I DIDN'T HAVE to worry long about Owen Barker.

Three weeks later, Ellie Mae said she was leaving town with Malcolm Stanley. Malcolm was Tulah's grandson's friend, and he lived in Jackson. He'd heard Ellie Mae play one night at the Blue Tavern and offered her a job in his dad's place, The Jazz Lounge. She would be playing in a real jazz club and could make a lot of money, she told us.

"Put a jar on top of the piano, and in Jackson, customers will stuff it with dollar bills," she said.

A week after that, Ellie Mae said her goodbyes. With the green dress Mom made for her and the shoes I'd bought with the money I'd saved from my allowance, she walked down the road and onto the path through the woods for the last time. Her life would be different, and so would ours.

I was sad to see Ellie Mae leave. She was a part of my life here. But I was also relieved. I hoped to send my guilt along with her. Since I wouldn't be reminded daily of my failure to act, I wouldn't have to face the cowardly person inside. I could make-believe everything was okay, bury the scene deep inside my box with the other secrets, and pretend it never happened.

◦๑๏

A MONTH PASSED, then two, and then three. We did not hear from Ellie Mae, and when I asked Tulah about her, she'd smiled and said, "They's fine. Everybodies likes hers playin'."

Under pressure from Mr. Dalton to give employment to another young woman, Mom created excuses. Soon she would start to look for domestic help, she told him over and over. Mom missed Ellie Mae. So did Dad and I.

MISS BAKER AND Chief Castle chose June 25 as their wedding date, and everyone in Willow Bay seemed excited to see the two of them together. Their wedding plans were talked about by almost everyone at church, and many of the parishioners offered to help—put together a bouquet arrangement, decorate the church, or furnish a dish for the reception.

The chief dropped by regularly to sit on the veranda with Dad, and the two of them chatted for hours, drinking coffee and eating whatever pastry Mom had baked that morning.

Often, Mr. Dalton walked over to join them.

Last Halloween's incident had been forgotten.

And the months had passed quickly.

Miss Baker was the faculty member in charge of the upcoming spring dance, the last big party before summer break.

Charlene was Joe's date, having turned down Larry.

Each morning, Brenda Sue and I heard of other classmates who had been invited. However, she and I waited, longing to be asked. The rumor was Eugene wanted to ask Brenda Sue, but he was too shy.

One afternoon, Brenda Sue and I made a list of ways to put her in his path. She bumped into him in the hallway the next day, and the two walked to their lockers together, got their sack lunches, and went out to sit under the large oak at the back of the school skipping their fourth-period classes. Brenda Sue was invited to the dance.

For the next three days, my life was one of pure embarrassment. Every girl who wanted a date seemed to have one, except me. Then, Friday morning when I was at my locker—five lockers down from Charlene's—Joe joined Charlene in waiting for the bell to walk her to her first class. Moments later, Paul swaggered over and stood next to Charlene.

"It's not fair," Paul said to her.

"What's not fair?" She asked, tossing her head, her silky hair swinging over her shoulder.

He leaned in and spoke loudly. "Joe's got the prettiest girl in school."

Charlene made a production of handing Joe her books, one at a time, her shoulders back and her face glowing with the compliment. Then she whirled around to me and announced, "Paul, why don't you ask Trudy? I don't think she has a date yet."

Everyone at their lockers turned in my direction.

I was humiliated and torn between crawling into my locker and closing the door or throwing my thick history book at Charlene. As I contemplated which to do, I felt a hand on my shoulder.

"Sorry, Paul. Trudy has a date for the dance," Steve said. He took the history book from my hand and shoved it back into my locker. "You don't have history until after lunch," he said, his breath on my neck.

Excitement danced up my spine. I shivered.

Charlene hurried over to us. "That's great, Trudy," she

said, batting her long lashes. "I didn't know he'd already asked you."

"He . . ." I couldn't think.

Steve's gaze narrowed. "The gossip isn't always accurate, as we both know, right?"

Charlene blushed and looked away.

Joe and Paul strolled over. "We could go together," Joe said.

The bell rang.

"We'll talk later." Steve and I walked away hand in hand.

"I wanted to ask you earlier but wasn't sure if your dad would let you date. Brenda Sue assured me last night asking you would be all right. She said you had to decide soon if you were goin' with Butch."

"Butch?"

Steve's cheeks reddened. "Yeah. I know he likes you."

Butch Williams was a nice boy in my math class who had a girlfriend. He and I compared methods and answers often and had worked together on a project. I was sure he thought of me only as a friend. Still, I could have kissed Brenda Sue.

♾

AFTER SCHOOL THAT day, I had another surprise waiting. We'd received a letter from Frederick who now worked as a clerk for the Department of State. The Gutschmidts were in the American sector of West Berlin. They had applied to return to the States, and Frederick felt confident their application would be approved.

"So, for now, we simply wait," Mom said with tears in her eyes.

Mom and I were overjoyed with the news, and when Dad arrived home, he found us at the kitchen table laughing and crying. During dinner, we talked about ways to help the Gutschmidts, and Dad decided to call Frederick the next day to ask what could be done.

⌒∽⌒

THAT EVENING AS Mom and I were washing supper dishes, the phone rang. Mom answered. "Trudy." She handed the phone to me. "Brenda Sue."

Believing Brenda Sue wanted to talk about the dance, I moved as far away from Mom as the cord would stretch.

"I'm madder than a hornet."

Brenda Sue's voice was loud in my ear.

"What happened?"

"Didn't you hear? Shirley Price, the valedictorian this year, will not be allowed to graduate. After all the work she's done."

"Why?" I grasped the receiver tighter.

"She's pregnant. Charlene told me after school today." Brenda Sue's voice was now a whisper.

"Pregnant." I was stunned even though I hardly knew Shirley. "Does she have a boyfriend?"

"That's the thing. No one knows. Charlene said he was a senior, too."

"She hasn't said who the father is?" I heard a crash and figured Brenda Sue was doing two things at once. "Will she get her diploma?"

"I don't know if they've told her for sure or not."

"Brenda Sue," Betty called in the background.

"I have to wash the dishes. Steve told me you're going to the dance with him. I knew he liked you." Her voice lowered. "Do you like him?"

"Brenda Sue!" Betty shouted.

"Mom's mad. Let's talk later. I'm dying to know what you think of him."

After the kitchen was clean, I found Dad in his favorite rocker on the veranda. "Dad, can I ask you a question?" I pulled the other rocker closer to him.

He closed the book in his hands and placed it on the small round table between our chairs. "Sure, Trudy."

I chose my words carefully. "Will you keep this private?"

His head snapped around. "From your mother?"

I shook my head. "No, not Mom, but from everyone else." Frowning, he nodded.

"Say a senior learns she's pregnant, and she has all her class credits, can she get her diploma?"

"Are you speaking of Shirley Price?"

I scooted forward on my chair, surprised Dad knew about Shirley. "You know?"

"Yes. And to answer your question, her teachers are recommending she receive her diploma even though she won't be allowed to participate in the ceremony."

"What about the boy?"

"I don't think she's named him."

"But if she did, would he be allowed to participate?" My voice was full of anger.

"Probably. I know where you're going with this, Trudy, and I cannot honestly say what would happen to him. Shirley is eighteen." Dad lifted his arm in a wave.

I followed the path of his gaze. Mr. Dalton and Lady Belle were walking our direction. I stood to leave.

"Trudy, don't feed rumors."

"Yes, sir."

I went to my room and wrote Eddie regarding another wrong. A wrong even sweet Brenda Sue recognized and openly acknowledged.

My list of injustices was growing.

Chapter 33

The spring dance was just days away, and I sat day-dreaming while listening to the radio warn of hurricane winds from the gulf marching north, yanking buildings from their foundations and sending them splintering and flying through space. Sheets of rain began drumming on the roof, a harsh, deep-toned sound, and the house shook. Suddenly, the power went out, plunging me into a thick cloud of gray. I jumped up to get the flashlight Mom kept on the top shelf of the broom closet.

Earlier in the day, the forecast had the hurricane hitting farther east over Mobile and Pensacola, the strong winds missing Willow Bay. Now, the storm had hit west of its predicted landfall.

Believing we would have only moderate winds, Mom and Dad went out to see Betty and Dave. Betty had not been feeling well, and Mom wanted to visit her before Dad went back to work on Monday.

The wind gained momentum and the house began to rock back and forth like a giant pulling it from its foundation. Even though it was mid-afternoon, I sat at the kitchen table with a glass of milk, a ham sandwich, and a flashlight. The round light draped the table displaying it in a yellow cocoon.

Without warning, the wind rattled and pounded the door, jarring it, trying to pry it from its hinges.

Startled, I picked up the flashlight and ran to the door. For some reason, I thought I could grab the doorknob, holding the door in place until this latest gust calmed. As I gripped the knob, I realized someone on the outside was turning it. It wiggled, first left then right. The house shook so violently I was afraid it would fly north. My heart hammered in my chest. Then I heard a voice. A tiny voice. I opened the door shocked to find Hattie Benson's large eyes looking up at me. Water dripped from her hair down her face. She wiped her eyes with a forearm. "It's Ellie Mae. Come."

"Hattie, how did you get here?" I looked around for someone else.

"It's Ellie Mae. Come," she repeated, waving her hand.

"Ellie Mae's home?" I yelled over howling wind.

She nodded. "She's visitin'."

"But, Hattie . . ." I turned back to the kitchen and my half-eaten sandwich on the table.

"Hurry," she said.

I reached for my rain jacket on the hook by the door, pulling it on as I followed Hattie off the stoop. She wore a short dress and her Christmas sweater, no shoes. Barely aware, I still held the flashlight. I took Hattie's hand, letting her lead. We followed the narrow beam of light as we leaned into the wind and made our way through wet weeds, puddles, and running streams, my shoes wet and squishy.

Strong gusts blew against us, stopping our forward movement.

Hattie quickly squatted behind a rock. I squatted next to her. We waited until the gusts moved eastward before we stood and continued along the makeshift trail.

Trees became monsters waving their arms back and forth to keep us at a distance and slinging water directly at us. I kept my head bent, and yet, water blew into my face.

Logs jammed a narrow channel in the river damming the water behind them. As we turned to head upriver, I picked up Hattie and placed her on my hip.

She wiped the wet hair from her face and stared at me. Her large, round eyes reminding me of Ellie Mae's.

The water rose above my ankles and scared, I stumbled, nearly falling. I tried to increase my pace, but the wind and water raging against my legs made walking difficult.

"Where?" I yelled. Water covered the district, and I grasped for the first time why the area was called Lowland.

Hattie pointed, and we sloshed forward. The small shacks built high off the ground came into view. Ellie Mae lived at the entrance to the community, closer to the woods. I forced myself to ignore the tarpaper structures and hurry directly to Ellie Mae. I stood Hattie on the porch and rushed up the steps to follow her inside.

Ellie Mae, drenched in sweat, lay on her side, her knees drawn up, and a hand on her protruding stomach. Blood crept down her legs. She looked large on the small bed tucked into the corner.

Miss Washington stood in the kitchen next to a small table situated in the opposite corner of the room. "She's hot. I'ds been holdin' a wet cloth to her head."

"We need to get her to the clinic." I'd heard of a Latimer

County Clinic where blacks went for medical care. Otherwise, I didn't know where they went if they needed surgery or had a more serious disease.

Miss Washington shook her head.

Hattie wrapped her arms around her grandma's leg.

No one moved. Water dripped from the ceiling into a lard can placed next to the small, wooden table.

"What?" I asked.

"No doctor's thar now."

"No doctor?" I screamed to be heard.

Ellie Mae's body twisted. She let out a loud moan.

Time stopped. The plunk, plunk, plunk of water dripping into the can was like a drum setting a tempo. The air in the room became stifling. I couldn't breathe. My heart throbbed loudly in my chest and blood rushed to my head. Face after face from my past slid swiftly before me, a slide-show malfunctioning, repeating, and speeding out of control—Granddad's hazel eyes reassuring me, Maggie's questioning, Eddie's and Ruth's, followed by Joyce's, Brenda Sue's, Charlene's, and Steve's. All eyes fixed on me. *Who are you, Trudy Herman?* they seemed be asking. I shivered. This was a question I'd been unable to answer.

I closed my eyes. *The Paladins were returning.*

I straightened. "Stay here. I'll be back." I spoke aloud to the room.

I fought against the pelting rain and howling wind, half running, half walking through the rising water as I headed back to town. "Oh, Granddad," I said into the wind. "Another storm's coming."

Eventually, I stumbled up the steps to Miss Gracie's door.

Tulah answered immediately. "Lordy-be child, what's you doin' out in this storm?" She stuck her head out into the wind. "Youse alone?"

I nodded and stepped inside, a puddle formed at my feet. "Sorry," I said. "I need to see Miss Gracie."

"Miss Gracie's in hers parlor."

"Please tell her I'm here."

Tulah walked down the sparkly hallway.

I wiped away tears with the back of my hand.

"Trudy?" Miss Gracie came toward me, her brows crinkled. "What's wrong?"

"Miss Gracie, I need to borrow your car. Please. I don't have time to explain." Only now did the thought I could not legally drive occur. But Dad had sat beside me while I drove through our neighborhood and pulled into our driveway.

She nodded to Tulah and the black servant wiped her hands over her white apron, took a key from a silver dish, and handed it to me.

Then, surprisingly, Tulah's large hand wrapped around my forearm.

I looked up.

She nodded.

Without another word, I ran to the door.

The dirt road to Lowland was off Roberts Road northwest of town. I drove slowly and haltingly in the center of the highway, reasoning no one else would be out in these gales. When I reached the turnoff, a ditch cut access to the shacks beyond. I stopped the car, got out, and waded into the fast-running water. My ankles were covered, but not much else. Reassured I could make it across, I got back into the car and with hands rigid on the steering wheel, drove through.

Faces watched from windows as I drove down the road to Ellie Mae's. When I got to the shack, Miss Washington came out waving the gray cloth.

"She's worse!" she yelled as I climbed the steps, the wind and rain slapping at us.

I found Ellie Mae leaning over a bucket vomiting, a bare leg hanging over the side of the narrow bed. Blood dripped nearly to her ankle. She slowly raised her head when I entered.

"Ellie Mae, let's get help." I grabbed her shoulders and pulled her forward. "Come on," I said.

Hattie stood by the wooden table, sucking on her thumb watching us, her large eyes full of fear and questions.

Miss Washington, still holding the gray rag, leaned over the bed. "Stand up there, girl."

With Miss Washington on one side and me on the other, we got Ellie Mae down the steps and into the back seat of Miss Gracie's car. Grinding the gears, I was unable to get the car in reverse. I drove in a rutted circle around the house and got back on the dirt road, which had transformed into a washboard. Not sinking into a rut as water flowed over the road in the lower areas was difficult, and a back tire got trapped in a pothole. The car strained to get free until I stomped on the accelerator.

On the way to the main road, people appeared on porches to stare as I drove by.

The Willow Bay Hospital—built at the turn of the century, everyone proudly stated, which meant it was old and outdated—stood on the southeast edge of town. The storm was moving northeast, and I told myself if we were lucky, the rain and wind wouldn't be as strong there. The hospital would probably have power.

The windshield wipers pushed the water back and forth without ever clearing a spot. Ignoring everything else, I squinted and leaned forward, the headlights illuminating not much more than the small flashlight I'd thrown on the seat next to me.

My hands gripped the steering wheel as the winds blew against the car, moving it in a zigzag pattern. I blinked then began crying with relief when the tall brick structure came into view. Pulling up to the entrance, I stopped the car and yelled, "I'll be right back."

A woman with short salt-and-pepper hair and glasses sat behind a desk in the lobby.

"I need help," I said, waving a hand toward the entrance.

Her eyes quickly scanned the length of my body. She jumped to her feet. "What's wrong?"

"She's in the car. And she's pregnant. She's bleeding. She's sick." The explanations tumbled from my mouth.

The woman pushed back her chair and ran around the desk to join me. "Where is she?"

"Here." I hurried to the door, the woman right on my heels.

I opened the car door, and Ellie Mae let out a groan. "Here," I said again as I reached in for her.

The woman stepped back and raised her hands. She looked at Ellie Mae. Disgust painted her face as her eyes hardened. "We don't take them here," she said, turning and walking away.

"But . . ." I ran after her leaving the car door open and Ellie Mae leaning against the back of the seat in front of her. "She needs help."

Standing taller with her hands on her hips, she rotated her round body and glared at me. "They have their own place."

"That place has no doctor. She needs a doctor. Please," I pleaded. "She's in pain."

"Look here now. This is not a county hospital. We don't take colored people here."

"But, I'll pay."

Without responding, she spun around quickly and went inside, back to her desk.

We were forgotten.

I rushed inside after her. "Someone could help."

"Not here." The woman bent to pick up a chart, dismissing me.

"Is there a doctor here?" I asked, my voice loud. "I'll pay." I repeated.

She refused to answer, to even acknowledge me. She stood there with a folder in her hand, the same kind of folders stacked on Mr. Ridge's desk in Texas. The folders that held our lives, our future.

The lid flew off my hidden box, and the hurt and bitterness growing inside me for years stormed out. Our home, our friends, our personal possessions in Somerville gone. Two years hidden away without liberty and the loss of Eddie and Ruth. Secrets no one would understand. And here again, I'd met the face of hatred, of absurdity, of indifference to suffering, and the eyes of condescension.

I was filled with anger, and with shaky hands, I reached for the glass beaker on the corner of the desk, crashed it against the wooden edge, picked up a large piece of broken glass, and ran it down the inside of my arm. Red spotted my jacket, the desk, the floor, but I felt no pain. "I need a doctor."

The woman looked up and shook her head. Her lips were a thin line. She picked up the phone and asked for a doctor.

Seconds later, a tall man in a white coat with sleepy eyes and a bushy mustache walked in.

He had a kind face, and I prayed he'd help us.

"Yes?" he asked the woman.

Without speaking, she nodded toward me.

Blood ran down my arm to my fingers and dropped onto the brown flooring.

The doctor walked closer. "What happened?"

I set off for the door. "I have a sick woman in the car. She needs help."

The woman behind the desk pushed back her glasses. "Doctor, she's Colored."

The doctor took a step and then turned. "Get my bag," he ordered the woman, "and a couple of blankets."

"We don't take *those* people here." The woman declared before rushing off.

The doctor followed me out.

We found Ellie Mae as I'd left her, leaning against the back of the front seat.

"Let's scoot her back and make her comfortable." The doctor reached into the car to guide Ellie Mae into a reclining position.

Ellie Mae lay on the sheet from her bed, her long feet and legs hanging out the door. The woman appeared and quickly handed the doctor his bag and two blankets and left.

The doctor leaned farther into the car. "Get that arm taken care of. I'll see to her." He motioned to Ellie Mae.

Exhausted, I slowly walked inside holding my arm.

Without a word, the woman left the desk and exited through another doorway.

A nurse came to the doorway and waved for me to follow her. "Come in here," she said with a kind smile.

With my arm bandaged, I returned to the car. Ellie Mae was asleep, covered by a blanket.

"That's all I could do," the doctor said, his white coat red with blood. "She's lost some blood, but they'll be all right." He removed his red stained gloves and pulled the blanket over Ellie Mae's chest. "Get her home and in bed. She needs rest." He closed the door then placed his hand on my shoulder. "You did the right thing, young lady."

⌒⋑⋐

I DROVE ELLIE Mae home and helped her mother get her back into bed. Miss Washington was there to care for her daughter.

My arm began to ache as I set out to return Miss Gracie's car. Fear and fury formed in my throat, and I thought I would be sick. The car weaved across the roadway. The winds had diminished, the rain slowed, and shadows glistened on the wet pavement. But these were not the black shadows that had followed us. These shadows were different—gray, sprinkled with light.

The hatred, apathy, and discrimination I'd witnessed flooded my mind. Ellie Mae was not free. She had never been free. She was confined inside an invisible barbed-wire fence and could have died there.

I entered town to find debris-covered streets. I slowed and stopped the car by the park where we'd celebrated our Independence Day, America's freedom. A broken limb hung at a grotesque angle from the tree Dad and I had sat beneath to enjoy the fireworks, and smaller branches strewn the grass. The black garbage can that stood by the restrooms lay on its side, the contents surrounding it. Across the street, the light on the front of the courthouse above the eagle and carved declaration of equality was dark. Leaning my head and arms on the steering wheel, my trembling body rocked with sobs. I felt a familiar hand on my shoulder. "Oh, Granddad," I cried. "I did what was right."

I'd changed. These tears were not for past hurts and losses or for impending consequences of my actions. For once, my anger and tears were not for me, but for Ellie Mae and the justice she was denied.

Acknowledgments

Thank you to the individuals who broadened awareness of this aspect of American history by writing your personal stories, (German American Internee Coalition - www.gaic.info), and to Marcella Pendergrass for your words of wisdom.

Also thank you Sandy and Nancy for reading and listening to several versions of this manuscript and offering advice and to the members of my writing groups for your encouragement.

To my family, for your patience and support, thank you.

Topics and Questions for Discussion

1. What events in your life inspired you to become the person you are?

2. Did you have an elderly relative or friend that made a difference in your life as a child?

3. Did you know German-Americans were interned during WWII?

4. Did Ruth remind you of Granddad Weber?

5. How did you feel about repatriation? Would you have chosen to repatriate?

6. How did you feel about Trudy and Ellie Mae's relationship? Was it a friendship?

7. What did you think of Steve's warning to Trudy?

8. Why do you think Hattie came to Trudy for help?

9. What could Trudy have done differently to get medical help for Ellie Mae?

10. Are you a Paladin? Describe yourself.

About the Author

B. E. BECK is an educator and writer. She taught at the University of Minnesota, Duluth, before moving to the Seattle College District. She and her husband live in the Seattle area. Her work has appeared in journals and anthologies.

SELECTED TITLES FROM SHE WRITES PRESS

She Writes Press is an independent publishing company
founded to serve women writers everywhere.
Visit us at www.shewritespress.com.

The Sweetness by Sande Boritz Berger. $16.95, 978-1-63152-907-8.
A compelling and powerful story of two girls—cousins living on
separate continents—whose strikingly different lives are forever
changed when the Nazis invade Vilna, Lithuania.

All the Light There Was by Nancy Kricorian. $16.95, 978-1-63152-
905-4. A lyrical, finely wrought tale of loyalty, love, and the many
faces of resistance, told from the perspective of an Armenian girl
living in Paris during the Nazi occupation of the 1940s.

An Address in Amsterdam by Mary Dingee Fillmore. $16.95, 978-1-
63152-133-1. After facing relentless danger and escalating raids for
18 months, Rachel Klein—a well-behaved young Jewish woman
who transformed herself into a courier for the underground when
the Nazis invaded her country—persuades her parents to hide with
her in a dank basement, where much is revealed.

Tasa's Song by Linda Kass. $16.95, 978-1-63152-064-8. From a
peaceful village in eastern Poland to a partitioned post-war Vienna,
from a promising childhood to a year living underground, *Tasa's
Song* celebrates the bonds of love, the power of memory, the solace
of music, and the enduring strength of the human spirit.

South of Everything by Audrey Taylor Gonzalez. $16.95, 978-1-
63152-949-8. A powerful parable about the changing South after
World War II, told through the eyes of young white woman whose
friendship with her parents' black servant, Old Thomas, initiates
her into a world of magic and spiritual richness.

In a Silent Way by Mary Jo Hetzel. $16.95, 978-1-63152-135-5.
When Jeanna Kendall—a young white teacher at a progressive ur-
ban school—becomes involved with a community activist group, she
finds herself grappling with issues of racism, sexism, and oppres-
sion of various shades in both her professional and personal life.